F 5044

LIBRARY

JULIA RIED

LIVING BOOKS®
Tyndale House Publishers, Inc.
Wheaton, Illinois

Living Books is a registered trademark of Tyndale House
Publishers, Inc.

ISBN 0-8423-3182-4

Printed in the United States of America

01	00	99	98	97	96	95
7	6	5	4	3	2	1

CONTENTS

WELCOME

by Grace Livingston Hill

As long ago as I can remember, there was always a radiant being who was next to my mother and father in my heart and who seemed to me to be a combination of fairy godmother, heroine, and saint. I thought her the most beautiful, wise, and wonderful person in my world, outside of my home. I treasured her smiles, copied her ways, and listened breathlessly to all she had to say, sitting at her feet worshipfully whenever she was near; ready to run any errand for her, no matter how far.

I measured other people by her principles and opinions and always felt that her word was final. I am afraid I even corrected my beloved parents sometimes when they failed to state some principle or opinion as she had done.

When she came on a visit, the house seemed glorified because of her presence; while she remained, life was one long holiday; when she went away, it seemed as if a blight had fallen.

She was young, gracious, and very good to be with.

This radiant creature was known to me by the name of Auntie Belle, though my mother and my grandmother called her Isabella! Just like that! Even sharply sometimes when they disagreed with her: "Isabella!" I wondered that they dared.

Later I found that others had still other names for her. To the congregation of which her husband was pastor she was known as Mrs. Alden. And there was another world in which she moved and had her being when she went away from us from time to time; or when at certain hours in the day she shut herself within a room that was sacredly known as a "study," and wrote for a long time while we all tried to keep still; and in this other world of hers, she was known as Pansy. It was a world that loved and honored her, a world that gave her homage and wrote her letters by the hundreds each week.

As I grew older and learned to read, I devoured her stories chapter by chapter. Even sometimes page by page as they came hot from the typewriter; occasionally stealing in for an instant when she left the study to snatch the latest page and see what had happened next; or to accost her as her morning's work was done with: "Oh, have you finished another chapter?"

Often the whole family would crowd around when the word went around that the last chapter of something was finished and going to be read aloud. And now we listened, breathless, as she read and made her characters live before us.

The letters that poured in at every mail were overwhelming. Asking for her autograph and her photograph; begging for pieces of her best dress to sew into patchwork; begging for advice on how to become a great author; begging for advice on every possible subject. And she answered them all!

Sometimes I look back upon her long and busy life and marvel what she has accomplished. She was a marvelous housekeeper, knowing every dainty detail of her home to perfection. And a marvelous pastor's wife! The real old-fashioned kind, who made calls with her husband, knew every member intimately, cared for the sick, gathered the young people into her home, and loved them all as if they had been her brothers and sisters. She was beloved, almost adored, by all the members. And she was a tender, vigilant, wonderful mother, such a mother as few are privileged to have, giving without stint of her time, her strength, her love, and her companionship. She was a speaker and teacher, too.

All these things she did, and *yet wrote books!* Stories out of real life that struck home and showed us to ourselves as God saw us; and sent us to our knees to talk with him.

And so, in her name I greet you all, and commend this story to you.

Grace Livingston Hill

(This is a condensed version of the foreword Mrs. Hill wrote for her aunt's final book, *An Interrupted Night.*)

FOREWORD

"I believe in fiction; I feel every day more sure that pure, wholesome stories have their place in God's work."

Those were the words of Isabella Macdonald Alden, beloved aunt of Grace Livingston Hill, in 1898. By the time those words were printed in Alden's column in *The Christian Endeavor World,* a weekly publication for young people, she had published more than one hundred stories. At the end of her career, more than two hundred works, including novels and collections of stories, were listed under Isabella's name.

Born in Rochester, New York, November 3, 1841, to Isaac and Myra Spafford Macdonald, Isabella was surrounded by literary people. Her maternal grandfather, Horatio Gates Spafford, was an author and inventor. Her uncle, Horatio Gates Spafford Jr. wrote the hymn "It Is Well with My Soul." Another uncle, Duncan, printed a weekly newspaper in Johnstown, New York.

Two of Isabella's sisters, Marcia and Julia, contributed to the *Pansy,* a weekly children's paper that Isabella edited and published from 1874 to 1896. Isabella and Marcia also collaborated on several books.

Isabella's niece, Grace, with encouragement from her "Auntie Belle," became one of America's best-selling inspirational romance novelists. And Isabella's only son, Raymond Macdonald Alden, was an author, professor, and Shakespearian scholar. He composed his widely known Christmas story *Why the Chimes Rang* while a senior in college.

From this literary family have flowed many wondrous and helpful words. As one reader wrote to Isabella, "If I should undertake to tell in detail the good your writings have done me and those I have known, I'd have to write a book instead of a letter. I believe that, probably, under God, you have been the means of helping more people to a higher plane of living than any other person of whom I have known."

Throughout her life, Isabella wrote with the singular purpose of winning souls for Jesus Christ. She saw her stories as the best means she had of helping people know him. Her faith and belief in fiction as a vehicle for truth was strong. In her column for *The Christian Endeavor World,* she encouraged busy readers to "read a little fiction occasionally, even though, or rather, perhaps *because,* you have a busy life. A good story helps to lift one out of a rut, uplifts, quickens thought, stimulates to action, helps one to understand the lives of others."

Julia Ried, which was published two years after the popular *Ester Ried,* does just that—it is a story that uplifts, motivates to action, and helps one understand others. Julia, Ester's youngest sister, tells in her own words the story of moving, at sixteen, from her home to a manufacturing town to earn a living. As she relates the influences upon her by certain people and chronicles the struggles she encounters, she gives readers a fresh view of the providence and power of God in everyday life.

Like many of Isabella Macdonald Alden's stories, *Julia Ried* was drawn from the author's personal experiences. And like her other stories, it still has a place in God's work today.

1

FINDING MY SPHERE

I AM Julia Ried. All the people who were acquainted with my sister Ester will, perhaps, have some memory of me. There have been many changes in our family since Ester went to heaven. When Sadie was twenty she was married to Dr. Van Anden, and they went to live in New Haven.

Soon after that our mother's health failed, so that she was unable to keep boarders any longer, and Dr. Van Anden opened his heart and his home and took Mother and Minie in. He wanted to take me, too; but his heart is larger than his home, and the latter was quite full enough without me: especially with my brother Alfred being a clerk in a dry-goods store there and boarding with them. Indeed, the whole family just transplanted themselves one day to New Haven, this one branch excepted.

Before that time, however, I came here. "Here" is a manufacturing town on the railroad, ten miles from our old home. One day I sat in my room, resting my elbows on the window seat and my head in my hands, and thought hard. I was sixteen. I had no money with which to continue my education. I could not live on my brother-in-law. I would not live on Uncle Ralph. I must support myself. How? I could teach a common district school—that is, I knew I could listen to recitations in spelling and geography and the like; but I also knew that I did not like the idea. The thought of the great bare schoolroom with bruised seats, and dilapidated books piled on the desks, and a troop of naughty children dropping slates and throwing paper balls, and eating apples slyly, and making faces at me behind their books, while the July sun streamed in at us all from every uncurtained window, was utterly distasteful to me. I had no heart for the work. When I was ten years old I attended a district school. I had a teacher to whom we were all distasteful. *She* had no heart for the work. She was very cross to us. We did not like her in the least. I decided that I would not teach school! What next? There were very few avenues open—very few ways in which to turn. I had to think very hard.

Sewing! I laughed a little, even in my perplexity. If there was any one thing more than another which was decidedly not my forte, that thing was sewing. I was not naturally of an idle disposition. Give me the proper utensils and I could work—a garden hoe, a broom, a slate and pencil; even a hammer and some nails; all these I could and had used—but a needle and thread! Never those, when it was possible to avoid them.

At my feet lay a newspaper. I picked it up and glanced aimlessly down a column of advertisements. The paper was one that Dr. Douglass had sent me the day before from the manufacturing town where he lived. Among the list of wants was a call for a book-keeper in the paper-box factory of Messrs. Sayles &

Getman. I read that with some animation. This was certainly something that I could do. The paper did not specify of what gender the bookkeeper must be; but the town was only ten miles away, and Dr. Douglass lived there—one friend, anyway; and at least it would do no harm to try.

I looked at my tiny watch (Uncle Ralph's gift on my sixteenth birthday); there would be a train in twenty minutes. I sprang up, hurried myself into my brown alpaca dress, gloves, hat, and the like, and scampered downstairs; opened the sitting-room door to say to Mother, "I am going out for a little while, Mother. I will be back in time to get tea"; and then I started on the first little independent venture in my life. I remember that afternoon so very well. It seems strange to me that every little trifle connected with that venture should stand out so clearly before me tonight.

It was a clear, crisp autumn day. The air had a brisk hint of winter in its touch, and yet a summer glory lingered in the sunshine, and everywhere there fluttered golden and crimson and brown leaves. They were lying in great glowing heaps over Ester's grave as I caught a glimpse of it from the corner; they fluttered all along my path, and sometimes they seemed bright to me, and sometimes sad. I rustled through them, though, in a burning haste to catch that train; and Mr. Stuart swung me on the platform, at last, after the train was in motion—a thing which Mother would not have liked at all, if she had ever known it.

I found my way without difficulty to the box factory. I had been in the town often before and noticed the sign. But how warm and tired and nervous I felt as I pushed open the outer door and entered a room piled high with boxes of all sizes and shapes and colors! How red my cheeks felt, and how horribly one ear burned! There was no one in the large room, so I made my way toward a door in the distance. In that next room sat a man with his feet on the stove in front of him. He arose as he caught a glimpse of me and stood silent and indifferent, awaiting my order.

"Is this Mr. Sayles?" I ventured. He bowed dignifiedly:

"The same."

Then I plunged into business, my left ear burning horribly the while.

"I have called to see if I can secure the situation of bookkeeper. I saw your advertisement."

Before Mr. Sayles answered me, he turned squarely around and gave me the benefit of a front view; it had been a sidewise one before. Then he gave me such a prolonged, thorough, scrutinizing gaze from the brown feather on my hat to the tip of my patent leather shoes that he started the burning in my right ear. Then he spoke:

"We have always employed men for bookkeepers."

I was puzzled how to answer this, if it needed an answer, and he looked at me as though he expected one. I certainly was not a man, and if they always employed men, why, clearly, I would not do. Fortunately it occurred to me to say this aloud; and as I spoke I turned toward the door.

"I am not so certain of that," Mr. Sayles answered meditatively. "Wait a moment, if you please, young lady; because we have always employed gentlemen is no sign, you know, that we always must. What salary would you expect?"

"I suppose I should expect the same salary that you have been in the habit of giving your bookkeeper," I said with considerable dignity. Whereupon he laughed and drummed with his fingers on the table before him and seemed to think.

"Well," he said at last, "I don't know; the idea is an original one to me. Do you know that, as my book-keeper, you would have to be present at all sales, and keep a careful account of the same, and make out bills, and receive payment, and be responsible for considerable sums of money, besides looking after the shop girls, and keeping everything straight in that direction?"

"I could do all that," I said; "at least I think I could. I am sure I would like to try."

"And pay the hands every Saturday night?" he added, eyeing me attentively.

"Certainly," I said, "provided I had money enough to do it with."

"Well," he said again, after another good-humored little laugh, "suppose we talk this matter over in a businesslike way? Take a seat, if you please. What name did you give me, ma'am?"

And the end of our business talk was that I was a regularly engaged clerk when I went out from the front door, and had promised to report myself in two weeks from that date—subject, of course, to my mother's decision; and, in event of that proving unfavorable, I was to let him know on the following day. I went from the factory directly down River Street to Stone Street and climbed two flights of steps and knocked at the door of Dr. Douglass's office.

"Why, my dear child!" he said, rising and coming forward when he saw it was I; "what good fairy sent you hither?"—then, quickly and anxiously, "No one sick at home, I trust?"

"No, Doctor," I said gleefully; "I only represent myself today. I've come out to find a vocation, and I have found it; only I have stepped out of my sphere," and then I told my story. The doctor listened attentively, doubted a little at first, then approved, but decidedly doubted my obtaining my mother's consent. I didn't, I told him; not in the least. Mother could see that I must do something; and this was honorable and not difficult; and Mother was altogether too sensible to think I lowered myself by trying to secure honest work.

"Of course," he answered quickly, "I did not think of such a thing; but you must remember, Julia, that you are very young to be thrown on your own resources, and your mother might very naturally object."

"Very probably she will," I said; "but, you see, objections will not pay my board and furnish me the wherewithal to be clothed in—and bookkeeping *will*. So will you be kind enough to direct me to a possible boarding place?"

"Suppose you leave that matter in my hands. Drop me a line tomorrow in regard to your mother's decision, and I will then undertake to secure a suitable boarding place. Meantime, if you are going home tonight, your movements must be speedy."

I submitted to Dr. Douglass's hurrying and was very glad to leave the rest of the business in his hands. I bustled around the little sitting room at home in a sort of subdued glee. My first independent venture, and its results elated me. I remember I steeped flaxseed instead of tea in our little teapot and tucked up the muffins under the stove to bake, instead of in the oven; but I had a long, late, hard talk with Mother. She was utterly unreconciled. Dear Mother, she seemed to think that her first and greatest duty in life was to toil for and spare her children. Patient, faithful, tender Mother! Tonight, as I recall her sweet, pale, tired face,

I can think of no frown of impatience or anger that ever marred its sweetness. I can think of nothing left undone that she could do to smooth the path in which her children trod. I conquered at last. I knew I should; for what else was there to do?

"To be sure," Mother said, "the doctor is there. It isn't as if you would be quite away from us all. The doctor will see to you. If—"

And then my mother stopped, and drew a little, patient, submissive sigh, and went and sat at the east window, which looked toward the spot where Ester was sleeping. And I knew she meant to say:

"If Ester was only living there now, as she would have been. If—"

Ah me! I was gleeful that night; but it was gone in the morning. I wrote my note to Dr. Douglass in a subdued and businesslike manner and went away afterward in a grave way, realizing that we were packing up and the old home and the old life were going away from me together. I remember thinking, as I braided my hair, that I would wear it in bands across my head no longer—that childish fashion belonged to the little girl Julia, who had played through so many years of life, and with whom this grown-up Miss Ried, who was going away from home to board and earn her living, had nothing in common anymore. What desolate work it *is*, this packing! We had not so very much to pack. Mother sold all the furniture, except the great armchair in which Father died, and Ester's little red rocker, and a few like treasures. House and carpet and furniture, all sold together; and sometimes I think that that was really the hardest part of it. If we could have taken down all the shades, and set the chairs upside down into each other, and tied them up, and piled boxes and trunks and rolls of carpeting and

oilcloth in great heaps everywhere—utterly disman-
tled and disorganized everything, you know—it seems
to me as if it could have been easier; but instead, it was
just turning the key on every dear home thing, as if
we were going out for only a walk or a little visit, and
yet knowing and realizing that we would never, never
come home to it all again. Mother had to go first. I
was glad of that. I am glad of it tonight. I could not
have had her lock those doors and take her last look
alone. As it was, I stood on the doorstep, while brother
Alfred, who had come for her, tucked her into the
carriage and looked taller and more manly while he
did it. I looked as if I might be going back into the
house to hurry dinner and have it all ready for them
when they returned from their ride. Some strangers
who passed by just then doubtless thought so. And yet
we knew, we three, that the last dinner in that house
that would ever be enjoyed by us had been prepared
and eaten, and the dishes were all sold and packed and
gone away.

"Take good care of yourself, for my sake, Daughter," Mother said once more as they drove away. Dear
Mother! It almost broke her heart to go away and
leave me standing there alone, and Minie cried outright, and bitterly; and Alfred pushed his hat over to
shade his eyes and would not look around at me at all.
But I answered gaily:

"Oh, I'm all right; the doctor will take good care
of me."

Then I ran in and shut the door; and I went out,
away out to the back kitchen, and sat down on one
end of the old wash bench, and I am glad Mother
never knew how hard I cried. It was hard, harder than
I had dreamed. There was nobody to stop crying for
now; nobody to care; and I just let all the tears that

had choked me, and fought at me, and been conquered by me, all the last two weeks, pour forth.

I was supposed to be going to Mrs. Griswold's to dinner. Vesta was married and was at home on a visit, she and her husband. He was a wealthy man from Washington. I knew he had brought Vesta's mother a fur cloak, and she was going back to Washington with them, to spend the winter. Vesta and I used to play together, and now *my* mother was gone. I did not go to Mrs. Griswold's to dinner. I did not have any dinner. It took all my time between the eleven and the three o'clock trains to shed my tears and then to bathe my eyes from time to time, in hope that they would not look as though the tears had been shed. Finally I gave myself just time to lock the doors hurriedly, not stopping to peep into the family sitting room, and rushing quickly by Alfred's chamber door. I turned the last key while the whistle was blowing for the train; gave the entire bunch to Mr. Stuart's boy, who stood in the store door as I passed, and said cheeringly: "You will be late."

And so at last, in haste and excitement, I turned away from my old home and began my career in the world. But a few days before I had received a brief note from Dr. Douglass. I took it out on the cars and reread it:

"*Dear Sister Julia,*—I have secured you a boarding place. Will meet the 3:50 train on Friday. Yours, Douglass."

Meager enough information, this, concerning my new home, but all that I possessed. A wretched, drizzly rain was falling when the engine whistled into the station at Newton. I remember I felt glad of it. Nothing had seemed so seasonable, so in keeping with events, during that day as did the steady drip, drip of that dismal rain. I wondered what the doctor would say first; whether he would fall to pitying me—say, "poor child," in that compassionate tone of his. If he did, I felt certain I should cry again—and that I felt too tired and wretched to do. What he did say was: "Have you rubbers on?" And all the way as the carriage rolled down the streets he said only the merest commonplaces to me, such, for instance, as: "That is Grace Church, that first building at the right"; or, "Our Mission Sabbath school is located in this vicinity."

I wondered then if he knew how little I cared whether Grace Church was located on the bank or in the river. To all his remarks I made no answer, until finally he said:

"Ah, here we are at home."

Then I roused in great surprise.

"Why, do *you* board here?" I said.

"I certainly do," he answered, smiling. "So you see, I shall have a fair opportunity to exercise my office of guardian-in-chief."

The house, too, was a surprise to me. It was large and handsome. Grand almost, only that it was in too exquisite taste to be called exactly grand. Why the people living in it should keep boarders was a mystery to me.

I made my wonderment known to Dr. Douglass and asked for a reason, while we waited in the gem of a sitting room for the entrance of somebody. He turned toward me with an amused shrug of the shoulders and answered:

"Wait one month, won't you, Julia, and then answer that same question for me."

"What is the lady's name, Doctor? You did not mention it in your lengthy and communicative letter."

"The name is Tyndall," he answered briefly.

I may as well say, just here, that it was watching Mrs. Tyndall and listening to her that led me first to desire to write this book. And because I saw and heard much of her, and saw to what uses she put her tongue, and saw the contrast between her tongue and the tongues of some other people, and the results of all this, I resolved to write it out for you all.

And just then the door swung noiselessly and gracefully open, and Mrs. Tyndall entered.

2

+—⋈—+

A PUZZLEMENT

SHE came forward with that inimitable air of grace and ease which I afterward discovered always characterized all her movements. She was a slight, delicately formed lady with fair hair and bright eyes—a lady who wore pale blue dresses and looked well in them. Dr. Douglass introduced me briskly:

"Here is a very weary, very damp young lady, whom I commend to your tender mercies, Mrs. Tyndall. Miss Ried."

And Mrs. Tyndall laughed a low, silvery little laugh; she herself shook the raindrops from my hat, sent the doctor into the hall with my cloak and rubbers, and had me buried in the depths of a crimson chair with a sort of at-home atmosphere floating around me, before I had time to realize that I was in a strange land, and alone.

"Now cuddle yourself up there, and put your feet on the register and be comfortable, while I give some directions concerning your trunks," she said brightly as she floated from the room.

"Doctor," I said the moment the door had

closed, "why have you never told me how lovely she was?"

The doctor's smile seemed rather grave, but he only answered:

"Do you like her?"

"Like her!" I said with the enthusiasm of sixteen. "Why, I think she is perfectly lovely."

Ere we had time for comparing our views the lady was back and chatted volubly a hundred bright, airy nothings, addressing herself principally to the doctor, bidding me be quiet as a mouse and rest a great deal; which thing I at least appeared to do until supper was announced.

The dining room was a perfect fascination. I had never been in a room quite like it. I thought of Ester's description of Uncle Ralph's home in New York and felt the similarity. It was not so much the grandeur that impressed me—though everything was certainly grand enough in my eyes—as the exquisite fitness of things, the blending of colors and shades, the matching of everything without seeming to be matched; indeed, just as things match in the woods on a perfect day, when the sunlight shimmers in between the leaves.

The carpet was thick, and soft, and green, with sprays of autumn leaves strewn here and there, as if a soft wind had fluttered them down and soft feet had pressed them smooth before they had time to wither. The walls were hung with paper of that particularly creamy tint that gives one the fancy that there is a golden sunset outside, and that somehow the rays have managed to gild every side of the room at once.

There was a bay window, and plants in it—an oleander, very large, like a tree, and a bird hovering over it; and the bird chirped and twittered gently and tenderly as we passed by. Two or three different varieties of geranium were in bloom, and as the leaves shivered when I brushed my dress against them, they breathed their fragrance all about the room.

Old English ivies came out from behind pictures and wound around the frames, and trailed over mantles, and crept around doorposts, apparently following the bent of their own wild, sweet fancies; and one spray actually reached down and lay among the green mosses and brown and yellow leaves of the carpet, stopping first, though, to twine itself around a little table and lay one of its great green leaves on a plate where mosses and ferns had seemed to fling themselves together, having red berries nestled lovingly among the green, and now and then a gray old lichen standing sentinel.

There was furniture in the room, of course—chairs, and tables, and sofas, and silver and china on the dining table—but these all seemed to have retired quietly into the background; necessary articles, indeed, doing their duty gracefully and well, but by no means pushing themselves forward to be looked at and admired. I have been in many rooms since—grand rooms where much money had been expended on their furnishings—and they seemed to me elegant warehouses, where elegant upholstery and exquisite carving had been gathered together; the chairs and sofas seemed to me to stand out pompously, saying: "Admire us; are we not elegant beyond description?" Into the chairs and sofas of Mrs. Tyndall's home one sank luxuriously and murmured inwardly: "How delightful all this is"; not the furniture, you know—not the carpets—not the money so lavishly exhibited by proxy—but "it"; that indescribable, blended whole, which mountains of money can never gather and arrange.

At the table I first met Mr. Tyndall, a tall, handsome man, with exceeding suavity of manner—one of those men who are continually given to complimenting, not coarsely, nor even obnoxiously, except as you find yourself wishing that he would forget himself and yourself for little whiles at a time and talk about something else. One thing I remember which impressed me strangely—the instant, well-bred clatter which Mrs. Tyndall began among the cups and saucers, together with an immediate flow of talk, and the slightly bowed head of Dr. Douglass as he shaded his eyes with his hands and offered his silent thanks; a movement which no one seemed to notice or respect in the least. For myself, I found no chance to follow his example; and I am not sure that I should have done so in any way. I felt confused, not at home. My life in my mother's house had been a very secluded one, and this was really the very first time I had ever sat down to partake of food where no blessing was asked.

I remember I felt sad to think that Mr. and Mrs. Tyndall were not Christians, and also I thought it strange that they did not ask Dr. Douglass to perform so simple and proper a duty publicly. Stranger still that they did not respect his silent offering.

The doctor donned his coat and hat immediately after tea, came to me to know if I had any commissions for him; then saying that he had several calls to make, but would try to get in early, took his departure.

"Will you rest here in this easy chair and have a cozy little time with me, or would you like to go directly to your room?" Mrs. Tyndall queried in her kindly tone as the door closed on the doctor and her husband.

The sitting room was as bright and perfect in its way as the dining room had been. I dreaded the thought of my own room and its silence and loneliness. I shrank from the feeling of desolation that was trying to creep over me and accepted the easy chair and Mrs. Tyndall's company. She brought a bit of bright-colored fancywork and curled herself among the cushions of another easy chair and then began her busy little tongue:

"Dr. Douglass is a very dear friend of your family, I think he said?"

This inquiringly, and I assented.

"I suppose you are very fond of him, then, as is every mortal who comes in contact with him."

"Is he so very popular?" I asked, feeling extremely gratified; for Dr. Douglass seemed almost as much a part of our family as my brother Alfred did.

"Oh, very, I think myself that he has but one fault, and that is—don't you think him the least bit in the world fanatical? Did you notice him this evening at the table? That does amuse me so; such an utterly unnecessary parade of goodness: not that he does it for parade. I don't think that of him for a moment, but all people are not entirely charitable, you know; and then I am always just a little bit sorry on Mr. Tyndall's account. He isn't a Christian, I am sorry to say, and such unimportant little trifles do have such an influence over some people. I really think we cannot be too careful of our own influence. Don't you think so?"

To say that I was amazed by this kind of talk will hardly express my state of mind. Certainly, I thought people ought to be careful of their influence; but what possible influence for evil could there be in a man's bowing his head in silent acknowledgment of his mercies? Here had I been reflecting a little on the same subject, only to be filled with shame that I, a professed Christian, had eaten my bread like a heathen. But it seems there were two sides to the question.

"Yes," I said hesitatingly, "I think we ought—but then—I—don't you think it is proper for a man to ask a blessing on his food?"

"Well, my dear, that depends, like everything else in this world, on circumstances; for instance, where the man is (if he is) at the head of his own table, of course it is eminently proper; but if, on the contrary, he is only a visitor or a boarder, and the head of the house is not a Christian, why then the influence may be very unfortunate. Now, in this case, of course it does Dr. Douglass no particular good. He can remember his mercies, if he finds any at our table, in his private room to his heart's content, and run no risk of prejudicing others. Besides, a prayer, you know, does not need to be accompanied with bowed head or closed eyes. It can be utterly unseen or unknown to men, and quite as acceptable. So where is the use in exposing oneself to ridicule? Mr. Tyndall cannot be persuaded to look on such things in any other light than as a pretty little scene gotten up for effect. He says it is equivalent to saying: I am holier than thou. And while he has too high a respect for the doctor to think so of him, yet the provoking man persists in saying that a little religion sets well on a professional man, because it is so unusual. So you see, it just exposes the whole thing to ridicule; and while I have the very highest opinion of the doctor and his motives, I cannot help feeling sorry that he will not think of his influence a little, just on Mr. Tyndall's account, you know. It is natural that I should feel anxious about him. But how I am running on, about your dear friend, too. How do I know but that you will tell him every word I have said? Only I *do* know that a young lady whom Dr. Douglass calls his friend could never be guilty of anything of the kind."

I was very much astonished. Evidently, there was a side to this subject on which I had not thought at all—a danger of injuring people by our consistent lives as well as by inconsistent ones. I wondered that I had never heard this view advanced before. I felt sorry for Mrs. Tyndall that she should have so peculiar a husband as to be injured by what seemed to me so simple a thing. But there had been weight in her words, I thought; and I supposed I need not add to her evident anxiety by my own thoughtless adherence to custom in this matter. It certainly was very true that one need not cover one's eyes in order to be thankful for one's daily bread.

I was rather sorry for that closing sentence of Mrs. Tyndall's, for I was very eager to disclose my new ideas to Dr. Douglass and had not until that moment imagined an impropriety in it; but the moment I heard that sweet voice say, "could never be *guilty* of anything of the kind," with a strong emphasis on the word *"guilty,"* I straightaway grew shocked at my own wickedness and resolved not to open my lips to the doctor.

"Of course not," I said aloud and promptly, in answer to her last sentence; and Mrs. Tyndall laughed, a low, sweet ripple (her laugh was the softest, clearest, and most musical one that I ever heard), and answered:

"My dear, I hadn't any idea that you would do such a thing. I know you ever so much better than that already."

"Do you attend the same church that Dr. Douglass does?" was my next query.

"Oh yes; and our seat is directly opposite his, and it is directly behind the pastor's pew, for which latter fact I am very sorry. Our minister's wife is a good soul as has ever lived; but she has absolutely no more taste in dress than a post has. Her mixture of colors is terrific. Mr. Tyndall declares it will give him the lockjaw yet. And her children are such forlorn little frights; it is too ridiculous. I positively think it is a sin for a woman to be so regardless of appearances. There is no excuse for it; and Mrs. Mulford injures her husband's usefulness by that very thing. I really feel sorry for you, Miss Ried. I know your taste in dress is exquisite. There is no surer way of indicating that fact than by suitable traveling attire; and to think of you having to sit behind Mrs. Mulford, in her green bonnet, is terrific. She is the last person in the world who should wear anything green; and so, of course, she has appeared in a green velvet hat for the last three winters."

I wonder if there was ever a girl of sixteen, possessed of sufficient brain, not to be gratified over a delicate, gracefully worded compliment about her taste in dress? I am not sure that it is a desirable quantity of brain to possess. I am to this day a believer in sincere compliments, and decidedly a believer in exercising taste in the matter of dress; and yet I know tonight, perfectly well, that it would have been better, for both Mrs. Mulford and myself, if Mrs. Tyndall had not said on that November night a single word of what I have been telling you. Well, I didn't know it then, and I laughed at her description, and flushed a little over the personal part, and glanced down at my dress and wondered if it could be true. I was simply enough dressed. Nothing could be quieter than my plain brown alpaca. It fitted nicely; but that was a matter of course with me. Nothing that my dear

mother's hand had cut and made ever fitted other than
nicely. The shade of brown was exquisite, reminding
one of autumn leaves (Sadie had selected the dress for
me), and the knot of ribbon which finished the plain
linen collar at my throat was just that peculiar tint of
blue which matches so wonderfully with rich browns.
I had a fastidious eye for colors. I rather prided myself
on it; so I was the more ready to laugh over Mrs.
Mulford's green bonnet.

"What of her husband?" I asked presently. "He
doesn't wear a green bonnet, at least. Do you like
him?"

"No, thank fortune, he cannot distract me in that
way; but there are various ways of doing the same
thing. Do I like him? Oh, certainly, and his wife too. I
would not be guilty of disliking our clergyman and
his wife. But he is somewhat peculiar. He has extremely odd ways. In the pulpit he makes the most
comical use of his handkerchief. If he would only
forget to bring it just once it would be a great relief.
I am sure he must need a great many sets in the course
of a year. I think he ties knots in them; at least he twists
and untwists them a great many times during service.
Then he has a curious little twitch in his mouth that
is really very mirth-provoking. Just pass me that book
at your left, please. I can read just like him, and I'll
favor you with a specimen, lest you should be taken
unawares next Sabbath and your nerves not prove
equal to the occasion."

The book I gave her was an elegantly bound copy
of their church hymnbook, and the page at which she
chanced to open contained that glorious old hymn—

When I survey the wondrous cross
On which the Prince of Glory died,

My richest gain I count but loss,
And pour contempt on all my pride.

It had been my father's, it was my mother's favorite.
Many a time I heard her dear voice, low and tender,
tremble through the touching words. Until this time
I never had heard them without feeling something
very akin to tears struggling in my heart. But that
evening, as Mrs. Tyndall's lips sweetly syllabled the
words, the small mouth twitched and twisted in so
ludicrous a way that before she had finished the first
verse I was convulsed with laughter. The amusement
proved to be too fascinating to be resisted, and Mrs.
Tyndall and I giggled, and choked, and frolicked
through the four matchless verses of that matchless
hymn. Her face resumed instant gravity when the last
line was read and she said kindly:

"I am very sorry that Dr. Mulford has allowed
himself to contract such a ridiculous habit. I have
given you a specimen, not, of course, for the purpose
of ridiculing him, but simply to show you how nearly
impossible it is, for young people especially, to maintain their gravity. I don't think he has an idea how bad
it can be, or he would certainly try to correct it. Isn't
it sad to think what trifling things will mar the
usefulness of ministers? I sometimes wish they could
overhear all the funny remarks that are made about
them, so that they might learn a greater carefulness."

"Is he a fine preacher?" I asked, grown grave too,
and not a little ashamed of my outburst of mirth.

"Yes—and no—that is, he writes well and is quite
an orator, but his sermons are apt to be all in one
strain, the style which Mr. Tyndall calls being personally preached at. He says Dr. Mulford never seems to
think that the sheep need special attention, for he is

constantly pitching into the goats. He will talk in that absurd way," she added with the sweetest and lightest of laughs. "Of course I cannot but be grieved at his utter indifference. I am fearful that he is becoming more and more unconcerned. Dr. Mulford's unfortunate habit of lashing all who are not Christians, his really uncharitable way of speaking, is having a very unfortunate effect on Mr. Tyndall. Still, the doctor is a good man and means to do just right; these are only errors in judgment, you know. I fancy that he must have been preaching to a very different class of people before he came here; and either repeats his old sermons, or else he has grown into that old-fashioned style and cannot overcome it."

"Do you attend Sabbath school?" I asked with a slight hesitation. Someway I fancied a sort of incongruity between the elegant little lady in front of me and Sabbath school work; but she answered promptly and brightly:

"Oh yes. I have a class, a very pleasant one. Senator Dowling's daughter is in it, and Judge Coleman's two daughters, and several other young girls of that stamp. I have only one trial, a girl who has recently been placed in the class. She is the daughter of a widow, a dressmaker, who has lately moved here. The girl is a good, respectable creature, but it is the most inconsiderate thing to place her in my class. Of course it isn't possible for her to feel at home there; she has no associates, and it is unpleasant for her and disagreeable for the girls and positively painful for me. I spoke to Dr. Mulford about it. He is not the superintendent, but I had a good opportunity, and I thought I would let him know how matters stood; but men never understand such things, especially ministers. Dr. Mulford bestowed a withering look on me and said: 'We must remember that the girl has an immortal soul that needeth caring for as much as any in my class.' Don't you dislike that style of talk? It sounds wonderfully like cant to me, and I *do* think if there is any one thing that a Christian ought to try to avoid it is cant."

I answered very few of Mrs. Tyndall's questions that evening—indeed she did not wait for any answers; her talk flowed smoothly and musically on without pause or hindrance, which was fortunate for me, as in truth I should have found it very difficult to answer her, for I was beginning to realize that I was not quite sure what I thought about anything. She expressed so many new and startling ideas, all in so sweet and gentle a spirit, and seemed so thoroughly imbued with a desire to be watchful over her influence, careful not to do injury to the cause of Christ, that I was well-nigh bewildered, and contented myself with asking questions. My next was in regard to Dr. Douglass's class. That he had one I had learned from himself.

"His singular tastes, or whims, or whatever one ought to name them, are very prominent in Sabbath school," Mrs. Tyndall said, speaking of the doctor. "There was a very important class of young ladies, some of the very first young ladies in our church; some, too, whom we had been at infinite pains to get to identify themselves with the school, and we wanted Dr. Douglass to take the class; the ladies expressed their willingness to receive him as a teacher, and don't you think he declined the class! Would not desert his post, so he said. You must know he has a pet class, a half-dozen or more of wild girls, whom he has picked up from goodness knows where. Shop girls, I believe somebody said they were; but they are not connected with our church in any way, and I think myself that their proper place is in the mission school. Well, he refused to give up those girls for this important class. I really felt provoked with him and told him so."

"What did he say?" I asked, wondering secretly how she ever found courage to interfere with Dr. Douglass's plans. She answered carelessly:

"Oh, the old story about those girls having no religious training outside the Sabbath school and his hoping to gain an influence over them. All very true and proper, of course; but then the very fact that they are so ignorant only proves that a teacher could readily have been found competent to teach them, while it is really very difficult to secure a suitable teacher for the Bible class of which I spoke. We had a great deal of trouble and only half succeeded. Mrs. Mulford took the class, but I don't think she is very popular, and some of the ladies are just a little offended to think that Dr. Douglass declined the class. I do think the doctor is too good a man to allow himself to be governed by whims at the expense of his usefulness. Mr. Tyndall says that Dr. Douglass is—" And just at that point the arrival of Dr. Douglass himself checked my companion's volubility.

3

THE SOCIAL QUESTION

WE were alone for a few minutes after that. Callers took Mrs. Tyndall to the parlor, and the doctor drew his chair nearer to mine with a look of genuine pleasure beaming on his face.

"Do you know, Julia," he commenced at once, "there is one reason why I am particularly glad of the position you have assumed? There are some girls with whom you will come in contact for whom I am specially anxious. They are in my class in Sabbath school; gay, wild girls, who have had few advantages, religiously at least, and most of them few enough of any sort. I think there is no influence, save that of absolute indifference, brought to bear upon them now; at the shop, I mean. So do you see why I am glad of your position? It will be a responsible one, Julia. I want you to use it carefully and prayerfully."

Instead of answering him at once, I fell to thinking of Mrs. Tyndall's description—"Girls whom he has picked up from goodness knows where. *Shop* girls, I believe somebody said they were," with a strongly marked emphasis on the word "shop." I remembered what injury Dr. Douglass had done by refusing the other class. I reflected that he was evidently considered a fanatic by at least some of the people in Newton, and for the first time in my life I questioned the wisdom of the doctor's proceedings. Added to this was a feeling of vague irritation that he should seem to class me so promptly with the shop girls. There was a difference, I argued, between a bookkeeper and a girl who dabbled in the paste all day. While underneath it all lay a sense of shame that I was really so shallow-brained as to care for this distinction, and a vague sense of wonderment as to whence it had sprung; for I had fancied myself above it. All these feelings combined gave point and sharpness to my tone and words when I finally answered my waiting friend:

"I will use my influence as well as I can, of course, when I am with the girls; but I suppose I can hardly be expected to find associates among the shop girls."

The slightest possible elevation of the doctor's eyebrows showed me that I was giving him a new phase of my character. But he answered me gravely:

"It is a Christian influence of which I am in search; and that, if true and pure, will be exerted wherever there are souls to call it forth and an opportunity offered, and it will matter very little what work the bodies of those souls happen to be engaged in."

I was familiar with these and like sentiments expressed by Dr. Douglass and had been wont to admire them; but on this particular evening of which I write they sounded to me decidedly fanatical.

The doctor at once changed the subject by asking me if I had passed a pleasant evening. I assured him that I had and grew animated in my admiration of Mrs. Tyndall; and again I noticed that grave, almost sad look come into his face, and he replied thoughtfully:

"I fancied you would not particularly admire her."

"Well," I said testily, "is that the reason why you exerted yourself to secure board for me here, because you thought I would at once take a dislike to the lady of the house and so find my abiding place extremely pleasant and desirable?"

The doctor brought his eyes back from vacancy and fixed them on me with a little good-humored laugh.

"I beg your pardon and hers," he said brightly. "I didn't mean that. I only meant to say that I imagined you a remarkably penetrative young lady. It is an honor to you that you are not. I am sure I don't like suspicious people; but come, Julia, you and I must not quarrel; we are brother and sister, you know."

But, although I hadn't the slightest idea what was the trouble with me, I could not get back into a pleasant humor.

"No, we are not," I answered sharply. "That is nonsense. How do I know but that you are going to be married next week—in which case we would be only strangers to each other."

I have never forgotten the look of pain which swept over Dr. Douglass's face as I made this allusion to his sorrowful past, nor the absolute pallor which settled upon it as he answered me in a low, grave voice after a few minutes of silence:

"Julia, I will not remind you that my wife is in the grave—that you already know; neither will I say to you that I shall never marry, because all such expressions seem to me foolish and uncalled for; but perhaps it would be as well to say to you that nothing is further from my present plans and intentions than marriage, before I add that if I were to be married tomorrow I do not see how that would alter the fact that I have always tried to be to you the friend that Ester loved to think I would be, and that I have a most earnest desire to continue to be your friend and helper in every possible way."

I have always been glad that for a moment at least, I came back to myself and said frankly:

"I don't know what possessed me to speak such rude and nonsensical words to you, Doctor. I hope you will forgive me."

He smiled and bowed in his old frank way and said:

"Now let me speak at once of a matter which I have in my mind. How about the books, Julia?"

Then, indeed, he touched upon a sore subject. I had most earnestly desired a thorough education, and great had been the battle to be fought ere plain common sense won the victory. I answered the question meekly enough:

"The books are at the bottom of my trunk, and likely to remain there. It is bread and shoes now instead of books."

"Why not devote your evenings to them? Two of your evenings will be occupied; at least I hope they will. Thursday is the church prayer-meeting evening, and on Saturday is our young people's meeting, and I have greatly counted on your presence and assistance there. But that arrangement leaves you four; and in the line of teacher I think you could manage; at least I used to earn the bread and shoes that you speak of in that way during my vacations of study."

"Do you mean that you will help me?" I said with brightening eyes and thought that was the best thing he could ever do for me. So before I went to my room that evening, a course of study had been planned and all but commenced. I was very excited and glad over it and moved around my gem of a room not at all with the sense of desolation that I expected to have. On the whole my prospects seemed very pleasant. I rather dreaded the morrow's ordeal; but after all, I told myself, there could be nothing so very hard about that, and the evenings should atone for the days; how I *would* study. Then certainly nothing could be more charming than this home into which I had been cordially received, and no person could be more delightful than Mrs. Tyndall. At thought of her my mind went wandering over our evening's talk, and one little uneasy feeling possessed me. I recalled the fact that of every person whom she had mentioned that evening she had said something—should I call it uncharitable? Oh, no, certainly that sweet low voice could not have said other than kindly words; besides, she had seemed so anxious not to impress me unfavorably. She had spoken repeatedly of the goodness of Dr. Mulford and his wife, and then I laughed again at the memory of the comic faces and said, "What a queer man he must be"; and it certainly was foolish of Mrs. Mulford to offend tasteful people in such a simple and easily regulated manner as a choice of colors; and Mrs. Tyndall spoke very kindly of them both, and how interested she was in her Sabbath school class. Who was that girl, I wondered? Who was that one discordant element? Of course Mrs. Tyndall was not to blame if her class did not assimilate. Perhaps this one was a shop girl and would be better in Dr. Douglass's class. I winced a little at the thought of those shop girls with whom I must mingle, more or less. Shop girls had gone two steps down the social ladder since morning. Why? I couldn't possibly tell. Was it that particular tone which Mrs. Tyndall's voice had taken when she spoke the words? And there struggled together in my mind the two thoughts—to be faithful to the girls of Dr. Douglass's class, to use my influence in the right direction, and to let Mrs. Tyndall know that I belonged to a different class of beings and had been accustomed to different society; and while I was trying to decide whether or not Mrs. Tyndall was right and Dr. Douglass a most decidedly fanatical man, I fell asleep.

Just as I was moving to my desk the next morning, after a somewhat lengthy explanatory conversation with Mr. Gatman, Mr. Sayles called to me—"A word with you, if you please, Miss Ried"—and I went to him, in the little square room where the box stove was, whose object seemed to be to serve as a footstool for the two aged gentlemen.

"I am afraid you will have not very pleasant persons to deal with, for a few days at least," he began, nodding his head toward the workroom by way of explanation. "The fact is, there is a sort of blind insurrection in there; the girls are disposed to resent this infringement on what they consider their rights; you see, they have been used to having a gentleman to torment, and they managed to plague the life nearly out of the last one we had. What I wish to say is that perhaps you will do well not to notice any little annoyances or trifling rudenesses more than you can help, and the thing will probably come all right in a few days. You see, they are in something of a predicament themselves; they have no complaint to make to us, because they don't want us to know that they rebel, so that they have no resort but to revenge themselves upon you. Oh, there will be nothing serious, only a little nonsense perhaps; they are a gay set, but good workers; their places would be rather difficult to fill, and one trouble is, they know it."

This talk did not serve to increase my composure.

It seemed to me to mean, "You will have trouble enough, but don't complain to us." I only bowed in response and went at once to the workroom. My seat was at the further end of the room, near a window. I traversed the length of the room, conscious that ten pairs of eyes were leveled at me, and my ears gave me evidence of ill-suppressed giggles. On my chair was a huge pan of paste, in which I had nearly seated myself before I noticed it, and the merriment increased. I had it in my heart to peremptorily order somebody to take the thing away, but, on reflecting that I knew none of them, and that my order was quite likely to be disregarded, I had the good sense to wait on myself. I dumped the sticky pan hard on the floor, with, perhaps, an unnecessarily hard thud, helped myself uninvited to an apron which hung near me, and used it to wipe off the daubs of paste that had dripped from the pan, then took my seat and my account book. I have reason to think that my first composed and independent reception of their courtesies was a success, for, although the whole bevy of them continued in the highest state of frolic and laughter during the day, I was, despite Mr. Sayles's awful warning, left in comparative peace. In the course of the morning, having put my account book into something like working order, I had leisure to observe the girls; and despite the fact that they were every one of them shop girls, I found myself actually admiring them. What a bright, pretty company they were! Every one of them had a good, intelligent face, and several of them were extremely pretty. The most of them had rather dashing manners, a sort of recklessness about their movements, unpleasant to see, and at first unaccountable to me; but I came in time to this decision, which I never had occasion to change, that whatever of recklessness or indifference to public opinion was noticeable in them was due, in a marked degree, to the public itself, to the air of superiority which that public constantly assumes toward them; not because they are interested, for Frank Hooper, a shop girl, was better educated than General Park's daughter Anna, who ignored Frank's existence when she met her on the street; not because they were girls of disreputable character, for I never met a purer, sweeter girl than Ruth Walker, the fair-haired young creature who worked down at the lower end of our shop; but simply and solely, so far at least as I can discover, because they are shop girls, and so belong, of necessity, to the lower rank of beings; this, at least, was the demoralizing process brought to bear upon the girls in our shop, and it had its results. Now I, in my busy, secluded life, had known very little about the daily companionship of girls of my own age. In school I had been a hard student, and of late years had only gone thither for recitations, and hurried home betimes to help my dear, overburdened mother. So, among the things about this new life of mine that had seemed pleasant to me was this one of having friends among the girls, and I honestly think that no idea of being infinitely superior to them all had entered my brain until that first evening spent in Mrs. Tyndall's sitting room.

What had called it forth? I did not realize then. I do now.

4

THE SUBSEXTON

THAT morning, before coming to the shop, a most unpleasant thing had occurred. As we moved away from the breakfast table Mrs. Tyndall observed pleasantly:

"It is fortunate for you that Mr. Tyndall is obliged to breakfast at a barbarously early hour. You will never have cause to be a tardy schoolgirl."

I turned an embarrassed and, I think, a flushed face toward Dr. Douglass, who came at once to my rescue.

"Are you laboring under the impression that Miss Ried still ranks among the schoolgirls?" he asked, and added in a quiet, matter-of-course way: "I supposed I had mentioned the fact that she is bookkeeper for Messrs. Sayles & Getman—an equally pressing necessity for early hours, you will observe; and therefore Miss Ried has reason to congratulate herself on her boarding place."

Did I see, or did I imagine, the slightest possible shrug of Mrs. Tyndall's shoulders, the slightest possible curl of her pretty lips, ere she spoke her next sentence in her usual and beautifully modulated tones?

"I beg your pardon, Miss Ried, for classing you among the juveniles. Dr. Douglass, manlike, told me nothing whatever about you, except that you were a particular friend of his, and quite young. I imagined the rest, or took it up as a matter of course."

Thus smoothly and gracefully did she receive the news. Not a word, you see, of astonishment or disapproval, spoken or implied. And yet, for the first time, I felt an utter distaste for my new sphere, and had Messrs. Sayles & Getman been just then offering me the coveted position, I should have peremptorily declined it. I remember I somewhat abruptly expressed my feelings to the doctor, on our way up to town, and that he gave me very little comfort.

"Was Mrs. Tyndall annoyed, do you suppose, to learn that I belonged to a shop instead of a schoolroom?" I asked him; at which he smiled somewhat curiously, but answered quietly enough:

"I think very likely she was. You, of course, expect to meet that class of people occasionally. Had I not believed you to be superior to them, I should have tried to dissuade you from accepting this position."

"But why should people act like simpletons? What is there dishonorable in an attempt to earn one's living?" I said this sharply and impatiently, speaking as I felt, and the doctor laughed.

"You have asked a question now which it is impossible to answer. I know no more why people should act like simpletons than you do. All I know is that many of them act just that way."

"But Christian people, Doctor—why should they have to stand aloof from those who have to work for their bread?"

And at this question he was very grave and answered me with a gentle sadness:

"There are some very un-Christlike Christians in this world, Julia. Don't *you* be one of them."

Yet in spite of all this, or rather because of some of it, I sat in my high chair and wrote names and figures with a somewhat clouded brow. Life was not what it had looked to be, only last week even. I seemed to have had a glimpse of degrees and grades of society of which I had not dreamed; and I seemed to myself to be in neither one grade nor the other, but balancing miserably between. Where did I get my glimpse? What did I know that morning that I had not known the morning before—say? It was impossible to tell. "Did Mrs. Tyndall curl her lip, or didn't she?" That was all I knew about it.

Mr. Sayles came in presently and gave me some instructions: the book was in a tangle, and I was beginning to understand what I must do to right it; I worked away industriously. Between times I watched the girls. There was a leading spirit—Frank, they called her. Frank Hooper I found her name to be in course of time. I studied her, to know what there was about her that made her a leader.

Her distinguishing feature was plainness—of attire I mean, not of face; that was . . . Well, if she had not been a shop girl it would have been called beautiful; but her plain linen collar was pinned with a common black-headed pin. All the others wore fancy collars and rather dashing-looking bows, except little Ruth down in the further corner—she had a narrow white frill in her dress. Altogether she seemed to have studied plainness as carefully as most of them had studied their bits of decorations. Even her hair was brushed back from her forehead straight and smooth, and bound into a fierce knot at the back. I wondered if she knew how this distinguished her from the rest, in their frippery, out-of-place adornments. I did not discover why she led them, or even how; but that she did, in a measure at least, was plain. They appealed to her a dozen times an hour, and when disputes arose, as they did endlessly about nothings, there was a general cry of: "Let's leave it to Hooper."

Presently I was summoned to the salesroom and, pencil and book in hand, took the rapidly given orders and made out bills of sale. It was pleasant enough work, and I began to enter into the spirit of it. As I was returning to the desk to make duplicates of my bills, Mr. Sayles recalled me.

"I want to introduce you to my son, Miss Ried," he said in a friendly tone. "You will excuse my calling you back. I don't like to introduce you in the other room. Of course I can't do it with the girls, and some of them are high-flyers and can't see the difference." Then he turned and made the introductions.

Mr. Sayles was a well-dressed, gentlemanly young man, with a handsome face and manners which could easily be made fascinating.

"That's all nonsense, Father," he said good-humoredly. "I would as lief be introduced to all of them as not. I know them all, anyway."

"Yes, yes, Jerome, I know. You are one of the free-and-easy sort. But all men are not made after your pattern. Some, now, would consider it a downright insult to be introduced to shop girls. And I want Miss Ried here to understand that whenever I don't introduce her in the shop, it's because of them, not her."

I did not tarry to talk with my new acquaintance, but returned to my seat and my bills, speculating, meantime, over these new truths. There was a well-recognized distinction, then. I was not a shop girl, but an introducible person. But wherefore? I occupied the same room. I worked hard all day as they did. Was it because of the pasty aprons and the sticky fingers, and were grades in society formed with paste? It was a bewildering question. I puzzled over it until I found that I had credited the firm of Harter & Coles with seven hundred and fifty-nine shop girls instead of boxes. Then I took a fresh start and resolutely gave myself to business.

Mr. Sayles, Jr., sauntered in presently, bowed right and left, and answered the merry greetings showered at him on all sides with equal merriment. He certainly needed no introductions here. Only one of the girls seemed oblivious of his presence. Frank Hooper sent her boxes flying around her wheel with marvelous rapidity and neither turned her head nor spoke. Even little Ruth nodded, and smiled, and blushed, and turned back to her work, while Frank worked on unceasingly. Mr. Sayles had a most uproarious time with two of the wildest girls in the room, teased poor little Ruth into a burning blush all over her fair face, and stirred up the various elements in the room in a masterly way before he halted for just one moment at Frank's stand. Not a dozen words passed between them, but they were low and dignified. Then Mr. Sayles nodded and shouted: "Good-bye all," lifted his hat with a respectful bow to me, and departed.

"Hooper," one of the girls said, when the clamor of tongues that succeeded the gentleman's departure had somewhat subsided, "are you going to the meeting tonight?"

"No, I am going in another direction."

"Not to the concert?"

"Yes, to the concert."

Then arose a tumult, clapping of hands, cries of "Good, good!" and "That's jolly in Jerome!" interspersed with mimic groans and sighs over their less happy lot, in the midst of which a voice louder than the others cried:

"Oh, Hooper! what will Dr. Douglass say to you?"

Then Frank's eyes flashed, and she answered with haughty dignity:

"Dr. Douglass is not my keeper."

"He thinks he is anyhow. I just wonder what he will say. I say it's a shame, Hooper, when he considers you caught, to slip away in this fashion."

I reported so much of the conversation as pertained to the meeting and the concert to Dr. Douglass. The other part, not understanding as yet, I preferred to be silent about. He listened with a troubled face, gave a start of surprise or annoyance, or both combined, and said abruptly:

"I am very sorry to hear this. I think that man—you must help me, Julia, to counteract—he is— Oh, well; never mind. Some other time I'll explain."

I don't need any explanation, I said to myself with a wise nod of my head. *You don't like that man a bit. I wonder why.*

"Did you meet young Mr. Sayles?" Mrs. Tyndall asked me at the tea table. "That gentleman is quite a favorite with me; indeed, he is a general favorite, isn't he, Doctor?"

And the doctor answered, with as near an approach to rudeness as I ever saw in him:

"I do not know."

As I made ready to accompany the doctor to the young people's meeting, I wondered if they two—Dr. Douglass and Mrs. Tyndall—ever agreed in anything. Also, when they differed, which was right.

The evening was glowing with moonlight, and as

we slipped along the pavement, Dr. Douglass remarked cheerily:

"I think we shall have a large attendance this evening. Such glorious moonlight will woo the young people out."

Matters looked most uninviting to me when we reached the building where the meeting was held. It was far away from the church—a room used for a select school during the day, chosen because of its being more central as well as easier to warm than the long church. Chapel or prayer room they had none. The fire had died down in the ugly-looking stove, and there were various reminders of the children who had peopled the room during the day.

The doctor, however, went briskly to work, putting bits of sticks together and coaxing into a blaze the dying embers. Then he lighted the lamps—gas had not found its way into this schoolroom. One or two of the lamps required trimming, and the doctor's scissors did duty. Then, from some out-of-the-way pocket he produced a handkerchief, and with a roguish side glance at me, proceeded to dusting the lamps, remarking as he did so:

"This is not the handkerchief that I use when I am in personal need of that article."

Gathering energy from his example, I finally set to work, picking bits of paper and apple core from the floor, and adding them to the crackling fire; then I tidied up the schoolmistress's desk—and most sadly was it in need of such attention. I remember I said to the doctor:

"If I were a schoolteacher, I should put my desk in something like order before I left it at night."

And he replied:

"I have discovered that it isn't possible for me to

decide what I will do or say, under given circumstances, until I have been several times through said circumstances."

"I don't believe that," I answered promptly. "I know exactly what *I* should do under a great many circumstances."

Nevertheless, I pondered over his answer considerably, and have thought of it with a smile and a sigh many a time since then.

While we were still at work there came in a gentleman. His face attracted me at once. I remember I thought I had never seen a more noble one. Yet it wore a pale and weary look, as if the man were overburdened with care or work, or both. I thought him a brother physician, because Dr. Douglass called him "Doctor." He came forward to our end of the room and spoke cheerily:

"Ah, Doctor, hard at work, making ready for your flock? I wish I could be with you in these meetings. I believe they would do my soul good. What cheer?"

"A very pleasant meeting last week, and a very hopeful spirit. Tonight I someway feel that the meeting will be a precious one. Can't you remain, Doctor?"

"Wish I could; but old Auntie Frisby sent for me, and I must try to carry a crumb of comfort to her and look in on Father Durfee on my way back. Gather all the sunshine you can from the meeting, and bottle it up for me."

At this point Dr. Douglass turned toward me as he said:

"Why, I beg pardon, Julia. Let me introduce you to Miss Ried, Dr. Mulford. She is a member of our household at Mrs. Tyndall's."

"Ah," said Dr. Mulford quickly as he held out his

hand for a cordial greeting, "a member, also, of the household of faith, I trust?"

I do not think I answered him. I was struck dumb with astonishment. I had a mental picture of Dr. Mulford so utterly unlike this living one. Mine I had manufactured out of the fragments which Mrs. Tyndall had given me. How was it possible, I wondered, for that pale, pure face ever to look comical in the pulpit?

"He is a glorious man," Dr. Douglass said enthusiastically as the door closed after his pastor. "A hard worker, an earnest preacher, and a faithful pastor. I wish there were more men like him in the world. Well, now we are ready for our people. But, first, you may distribute the books, if you will."

He unlocked a small desk in one corner and produced therefrom a quantity of tiny books, neatly bound, which I distributed according to his directions, placing one on each desk. Then he announced himself as entirely ready, and in exact time.

"Are you the sexton always?" I asked as I took the seat indicated to me; "or is this evening an exception?"

"This evening is the rule, and there is an occasional exception; however, I do not mind it in the least. Let us sing the hymn on the twenty-fourth page, Julia."

5

◆━━❧≡❧━━◆

ETERNITY'S WORK

AND immediately he began to sing. He had a noble voice, full and round. I always enjoyed hearing him sing. There were six verses of the hymn, and he sang them all, I joining in. Then, almost without pause or break, he sang the words on the following page, to another tune. I never hear the words of that precious hymn without a sweet and solemn memory of that evening meeting stealing through my heart.

Meantime the room was filling up rapidly. Young boys and girls, some with skates strung over their shoulders, as if they had just dropped in on their way from their evening frolic, some with bundles or mail matter, which they quietly deposited; nearly all of them had the air of people who had stopped on their way to or from work or play to rest awhile. I noticed, among the girls, four or five familiar faces, little Ruth Walker's among the rest. For them all Dr. Douglass had a smile and a bow; but still sang on; and the newcomers seemed to find their own places in the little book by instinct, or more probably by familiarity, and joined in the music, until presently the house was filled with song. A moment's break at the close of one hymn, and then they sang, in more subdued voices, one verse of that wonderful old hymn:

> *"Lord, we approach the mercy-seat,*
> *Where thou dost answer prayer.*
> *There humbly we fall before thy feet,*
> *For none can perish there."*

Then, in an instant, all heads were bowed on the desks, and solemn silence filled the room. The doctor's voice broke in upon the peculiar stillness with words of prayer that I never forgot. They were:

"Holy Spirit, come now and fill our hearts. Help us to pray. We are poor and needy. Show us what to do tonight. Dear Jesus, wash us from sin; make us pure in thy Father's sight; help us to bear our crosses, thinking always of the one thou didst bear for us. May we love thee more than any other, and fear thee more than all earth combined, and trust thee with a never-failing strength. Amen."

Then, immediately, as if it were a portion of the prayer, they sang:

> *"Jesus lead me, Jesus guide me,*
> *In the way I ought to go."*

Then Dr. Douglass repeated one verse: "Lo, we have left all, and followed thee." He repeated it, I said. I *should* have said that they repeated it. I think nearly every voice in the room took up the sentence with him on the second word. Then he said:

"Will anyone prove whether that is necessary?"

One of the boys answered him promptly:

"Love not the world, neither the things that are in the world."

"Charlie," said Dr. Douglass, "I am in the world; must you not love me?"

And Charlie's answer was low, but clear:

"Not more than Christ, sir."

"Anyone else?" said the doctor; and this time it was the voice of a young girl that responded:

"Be not conformed to this world: but be ye transformed by the renewing of your mind."

Then followed, in quick succession, other verses, such as: "Set your affection on things above, not on things on the earth." "If any man love the world, the love of the Father is not in him"; and "This I say, therefore, and testify in the Lord, that ye henceforth walk not as other Gentiles walk, in the vanity of their mind."

"Fred," said Dr. Douglass, "what should you conclude from all these repeated and careful warnings about the world?"

"That there is danger of its getting hold of us, sir."

"Yes, great danger. The Bible does not waste words. Well, have we to carry on this struggle between the world and our hearts all alone? How is it, Harry?"

"No, sir. 'In the world ye shall have tribulation: but be of good cheer. I have overcome the world.'"

The doctor smiled and bowed, and at once commenced singing:

"He leadeth me, O blessed thought!"

One verse, then immediately he said:

"To return now to our verse for this evening. Will, have you found anything that you had to leave this week, in order to follow the Master?"

The young man addressed answered in tones full of suppressed feeling:

"Yes, sir, I had to leave a dear friend. He would not go my way, and I could not go his."

"Are you praying for him, brother?"

"Yes, sir."

"We will help you. Charlie, will you pray for this dear brother's friend, that he may come with us?"

All heads were bowed; and I never heard a shorter, simpler, more earnest prayer. I could not help remembering the words:

"O Jesus, we want this friend to come our way. We know that thou dost want him more than we do, because thou didst die for him. Follow him, dear Savior; don't let him think he is happy until he finds thee. Help us never to stop praying for him until he is safe in the fold. Amen."

And Dr. Douglass's voice added:

"Nor even then. Dear Lord, may we never cease to pray for him, until he and we get home to the everlasting rest. Are there others who have found something to leave?"

A young girl answered him:

"I have left a place where I have been in the habit of going, because I found that I couldn't follow Jesus there."

"Thank God," said the doctor earnestly. "Let us all think carefully of that, dear friends; let us all pray about it. Do we go to any place where we cannot follow Jesus? Fred, will you offer a word of prayer for us all?"

And then came another of those wonderfully simple prayers:

"Blessed Jesus, show us how to follow thee. Help us to search our hearts, to see if we are following. Help us to be careful not to go where thou dost not lead. Amen."

"Notice one thought in that prayer," said the doctor: "Help us search our hearts to see if we are *following*—that is a very important prayer. Let us be careful that we do not try to *lead* instead of follow. Go on, friends."

My little Ruth spoke next:

"I have been trying to leave my troubles," she said simply.

"Ah," said the doctor, "that is very important. Oftentimes we build up great walls of trouble, so high that we cannot look over them and see Jesus on the other side, lifting them to bear for us. Be careful of that."

Then he broke into singing:

> *"His goodness stands approved,*
> *Unchanged from day to day*
> *I'll drop my burdens at his feet,*
> *And bear a song away."*

The talk went on, after that, rapidly and simply—not at all as if it were a meeting in the general understanding of that word, but as if these people had met together to help and be helped. Many things were mentioned that it had been discovered must be left in order to follow Christ.

"How many," asked Dr. Douglass at last, "how many can say that verse, making the language their own: 'Lo, we have left all and followed thee'? Will all who feel that they have done this raise their hands?"

Not a hand was raised.

"Ah," he said gently, "we have none of us left all, it

seems. We are following but afar off. Well, will someone tell me who it was who said these words?"

A prompt voice answered him:

"Peter."

"Yes; and, Harry, do you think Peter was mistaken
in his heart, or not?"

"I think he was, sir," answered the young man who
had been addressed as Harry.

"Sadly so," said the doctor. "You remember that it
was after this bold declaration that Peter, loudly and
repeatedly, denied all knowledge of the man for whom
he thought he had left all. We must be very careful then
in searching into these hearts of ours. Even after we
think that all is left, we are liable to find, as poor Peter
did, that we have not left our pride, our fear of the
world, our vanity—something will still be clinging and
hiding the footsteps of our Lord from us. Now I should
like to know how many have been led by our verse
during this past week to leave something for Christ."

More than a dozen hands were raised, Dr. Douglass's among the number.

"This is very encouraging," he said. "So many of us
trying to follow the Lord, so many of us being helped
on the way. I myself have been greatly helped this
week. I found one thing to leave of which I had not
dreamed before. Will one of you lead us in a prayer of
thanksgiving that Christ is leading us to follow more
closely and carefully?"

There was an instant response to this request, and
the prayer was brief and very simple, like the others.
Then they sang:

> *"Come, said Jesus' sacred voice,*
> *Come and make my paths your choice."*

One verse, and immediately the doctor said in a very tender voice:

"Is there one who will come tonight? We want to pray for one, knowing that he or she has left all to follow Jesus. We mean by that, one who has resolved to try to leave all. Have we such a one among us?"

A young man who had sat with bowed head during the latter part of the evening now suddenly sat erect and raised his hand.

The doctor instantly began to pray. "O Master," he said, "we thank thee for this. Thou art present calling thy disciples. We cannot doubt it. We pray for this dear brother. Help him to give himself to thee, to roll the burden of his sins, and doubts, and fears, and hesitations, all upon thee and step boldly forward."

The spirit of prayer seemed then to come over the little meeting. There followed in quick succession four young voices, and they could not have taken five minutes of the time, so short were their petitions, yet so wonderfully to the point. It was to me a very strange meeting. I do not remember that I had ever before been so thrilled. There was such an air of simple earnestness and directness on the part of all who took part, except the four girls from our shop, who had sat silent and apparently unimpressed. The only look of interest I could detect upon their faces seemed that excited by curiosity when I, led on by the earnest voices all around me, and feeling as if I should disown my Master by silence, said simply, "I am trying to follow him, too"; curiosity, and I fancied a flash of surprise, but of that I was not certain, passed over their countenances. I remember being greatly surprised when the doctor, looking at his watch, announced that there were but two minutes left of the hour; for although in looking back I could realize that a great deal had been said and sung, yet I had all the time the feeling that the meeting had not yet been formally opened, but that this was a sort of preliminary little social talk. There was at this point a little box passed around by one of the boys, into which many dropped slips of paper. Then the doctor said:

"I have changed our verse for next week since I came into the meeting. The development of this subject, and particularly one verse which has been recited, has suggested to me a thought, for which I want a part of that verse to serve as a foundation. 'Be of good cheer, I have overcome the world.' No, on second thought we will take the entire verse; we need it. 'In the world ye shall have tribulation: but be of good cheer; I have overcome the world.' And these are the thoughts: Ye *shall* have tribulation. Notice the language—not ye *may* have, but ye shall—that is, it is to be expected. The world and Christ are not on friendly terms—they do not accord in feeling; therefore when you and the world are in unison, when matters are gliding along smoothly and gracefully, nothing to disquiet you, have a care; then is the time for special watchfulness. But Christ says, 'Be of good cheer'; this is not a cause for discouragement, because, says Christ, 'I have overcome the world,' and this is the special thought. If Christ has overcome the world, and we have left all to follow him, we must *not* let this same world overcome us. Sing,

"Lord, dismiss us with thy blessing."

It was some little time after the meeting closed before we were fairly started homeward. Nearly everyone present lingered for a clasp of the hand and a word or two with Dr. Douglass. Especially with the young man who had asked prayer for himself did the doctor stop to talk. The moonlight was clear and solemn when we went out into it, and I felt more solemnized than I had ever done in my life. The doctor was very happy over the meeting.

"It was a precious hour," he said. "Didn't you think so, Julia? The prayers of those young men do my very soul good; and that boy who asked us to pray for him. Oh, I cannot tell you how we have been following after him. Why, Satan seemed determined to have him. Every possible temptation that can be conceived of almost seemed to start out before him. I don't know when I have watched such a struggle before; but our Leader is stronger than Satan. I realized that so fully tonight. Why, Julia, for that young man to lift up his hand tonight, and thereby indicate his determination to come with us, required more courage than it would to fight in a dozen battles with sword and bayonet. Those girls from the shop, they were his great trial. I think he would rather have faced an armed battery than evince any interest before them; there is such an utter want of sympathy, you see, and such a disposition to ridicule the step which he has taken. I could see it in their eyes, and the poor fellow is very susceptible to that weapon, especially when it is in the hands of *one* of the girls, Caroline Brighton. She is the most dangerous character among them. I hardly know what to think of her; she troubles me. You know which one she is? Well, do you know, I depend very much on your influence over her? Try to get her under your influence as soon as you can, Julia. And there is Frank Hooper, another decided character, about whom I want to tell you as soon as I can. But meantime I must leave you here; I have four professional calls yet tonight."

6

THE OTHER SIDE OF THE QUESTION

I HAD intended to go directly to my room, but the wide, hospitable hall was brightly lighted, and the folding doors were thrown open, giving a glimpse of the parlor and Mrs. Tyndall all alone in one of the great easy chairs with her inevitable bit of bright-colored fancywork lying idly in her lap.

"I was just wishing for your arrival," she said winningly. "Mr. Tyndall is late this evening, and I am the most social of mortals. I don't like being alone."

As she spoke she wheeled forward, with a touch of her hand, another of the easy chairs, and into it I sank.

"You poor victim!" she said, eyeing me compassionately, "it is really inconsiderate in Dr. Douglass to smuggle you away with him to that little den of a schoolroom. I believe I shall have to tell him so. I hope you were interested!"

"I certainly was," I answered with spirit, for the tone of her voice jarred on the mood which I had brought in with me. "I never find a prayer meeting other than interesting. I trust I never shall."

"Is it so?" she said with a little touch of wonderment in her tone. "I confess I should not agree with you. I think there are, or at least should be, prayer meetings (like sermons or books) adapted to various intellects and capabilities, and what might be eminently suited to the class for which it was calculated might not be particularly edifying to me."

"It is a new idea to me," I said, "that there are different intellectual gauges for prayer meetings. I thought they, at least, were in favor of equality of race."

"Yes," she answered quietly; "it seems to be a fact not taken into consideration by many people; and herein, I think, lies the main cause of so many failures to do good to certain classes of people. We try, in this one matter of religion, to lift people up above their intellectual capabilities, or else drag them below it; and of the two, I really think the latter the more disastrous."

Tonight, sitting here in my room, looking back upon this conversation, I can take in at a glance all the ridiculous sophistry embodied in Mrs. Tyndall's words; but then I could not do it. I know that they sounded not right; that they were unlike Dr. Douglass, unlike my mother, unlike Dr. Mulford's face: and yet they seemed plausible. I answered nothing, and Mrs. Tyndall continued:

"It is rather a singular meeting, I have been told. Kate, my upstairs girl, is a regular attendant, much to my inconvenience, I must say. However, of course, I am willing to sacrifice my own personal convenience if the girl is really going to get any good. She sometimes waxes quite eloquent over the meetings, and I hear her giving the cook some strange reports of the proceedings. They all talk—girls and all—so she says. Of course I don't more than half credit Kate's reports.

I have too high an opinion of Dr. Douglass's good sense to believe all that she says. But you, poor little victim, I have been feeling sorry for you all the evening. Dr. Douglass's class attend quite regularly, I am told; and they, as I told you, are shop girls, or something of that sort; then two of Mr. Tyndall's office boys are always there; and an admirer of Kate's who works at the printing office; and all of the boys from the mill; and, dear me, I don't know who else. Quite a conglomeration, you perceive; but what could have possessed Dr. Douglass to mix you in with that class of people I cannot imagine."

A confusion of motives prompted my reply. I did not like to hear Dr. Douglass blamed. I certainly did not like the idea of being "mixed" with people not proper for me to mix with. I had greatly enjoyed the meeting; but in view of Mrs. Tyndall's evident belief in my superiority over the others whom I had met, I didn't like to own it; and yet I was half angry with Mrs. Tyndall for jarring upon the lofty impulses with which I had entered the room not ten minutes before. Governed by all these feelings combined, I answered coldly:

"These people all have souls, I presume, notwithstanding the fact that they are office boys and upstairs girls. I fancy that Dr. Douglass takes that fact into consideration."

Mrs. Tyndall arched her eyebrows and sent her gleaming crochet needle several times through the meshes of her work before she answered me, prefacing her words by a light laugh.

"Let us hope they have, my dear, though some of them certainly act as though souls were the very last articles they imagined themselves possessing. However, that is only one reason more why they are in need of instruction; and I really hope you do not misinterpret my words. I'm sure I think the meeting an excellent thing, one which, if rightly managed, may be considered a great blessing to these poor creatures. No one can possibly admire Dr. Douglass's devotion to them more than I do; though at the same time I cannot see how he can possibly spare the time that he gives to them from his profession, and that, of course, he would never neglect. Oh, I assure you, I am a staunch admirer of Dr. Douglass. What I am scolding him for is the unnecessary martyrdom to which he has subjected you; that certainly is quite unnecessary—his own sacrifice is amply sufficient. Now, my dear, I see that you are going to assure me that there wasn't the least bit of martyrdom about it; that you never thought of such a thing. I can see it in your bright eyes, and besides, I know how you young enthusiasts talk. Now, you must let me give you a bit of advice, just as an older sister would, my dear. As Christians grow older they come to realize that there is a commonsense side to this question. We may talk about equality and sigh for it, and remind each other that all people have souls; and yet, in spite of it all, equality does not exist, and never will as long as people are made with different-sized brains. Now just look at the thing. Here is my Kate, as good-hearted a creature as ever lived, and undoubtedly she has a soul, and you and I wish her well; but do you really believe that either of us would particularly enjoy it if I should invite her in to spend the evening with us? Go farther than that. Do you imagine she would enjoy it herself? Shouldn't we succeed in making three very uncomfortable people, all for the sake of a quixotic idea? And that is precisely what enthusiasts are doing the world over, only they don't bring their ideas down to everyday life so people can realize their ridiculousness. I assure you there is nothing like a little practical common sense to show people the folly of their flights into Utopia."

She uttered this last sentence with a triumphant little nod of her shapely head and in a tone that plainly said: "There, I have given you an unanswerable argument."

Oh, that I, Julia Ried, could have been gifted just then and there with a little of that vaunted common sense so that I might have shown to her the ridiculous flight that she had been taking, and all because Dr. Douglass had invited me to a prayer meeting. Instead of which I was suddenly plunged into a bewildering maze. This awful social question loomed up before me mountain high, met me like a stern fate at every turn, was even connected, it seemed, with a quiet little prayer meeting, though how or why my brain refused to show me. Uppermost among my thoughts was a comical vision of Kate, Mrs. Tyndall's red-cheeked, giggling, upstairs girl, sitting bolt upright in one of Mrs. Tyndall's crimson chairs, her large red hands engaged in her favorite occupation, that of knitting coarse blue yarn socks for numerous brothers at home, and vainly trying to sustain her part in the conversation. Herein, I believe, lay much of the wonderful power which Mrs. Tyndall exerted over those who came under her influence: the art of painting with skillful touches a picture that might or might not have anything to do with the question at issue, but with a point to it so ludicrous or grotesque that it would seem to have everything to do with the argument, and which would loom up for you to laugh over or flush over so soon as ever you tried to seriously weigh the question. Mrs. Tyndall turned deftly to another phase of the subject.

"Now, Miss Ried, I really must confess to a little vulgar curiosity on one point. I have not liked to question Kate, because I never descend to talking over matters with my girls; but do the girls really have anything to say in these meetings?"

"They certainly do," I said shortly, feeling vexed at myself and at her, and hardly understanding my reason for the feeling.

"What, right out during the meeting, in plain English!"

I laughed a little. "Why, Mrs. Tyndall, they are all Americans, I think. You do not suppose they are gifted with tongues for the occasion, do you?"

She laughed also, her low musical laugh as she said: "Now, you naughty sprite, I believe you are hoaxing me. Won't you tell me honestly?"

"I have answered you with perfect honesty; there were nearly a dozen who spoke this evening, I should think."

I will not attempt to describe Mrs. Tyndall's face as she asked her next question, "My dear Miss Ried, do *you* ever take part in these meetings?"

"I often have," I answered, a little triumphant defiance in my voice.

"But you did not tonight, I am sure?" anxiety and suspense in her voice.

"I am sure I did, Mrs. Tyndall. Why not? I assure you it is not more than I have done many times before."

Mrs. Tyndall dropped her glowing worsted in her lap and clasped her small, fair hands, with a mixture of surprise and dismay. "This is really too bad in Dr. Douglass," she said at last. "I am astonished at him. I do not see how he could have thought it right."

I answered her in a cold, hard tone: "I beg, Mrs. Tyndall, that you will not consider Dr. Douglass to be at fault for every movement that I make. It is entirely on my own responsibility that I took part in the meeting this evening; and I have done nothing but what I have heard my own mother, and my sister who is in heaven, do many times."

Mrs. Tyndall returned to her worsteds, and her voice was as sweet as a bell when she answered:

"My dear child, forgive the pet name, but you are so young and sweet and innocent. Don't fancy that I am blaming you. Your home has been in a quiet little village, and since you have been educated in that manner, nothing was more natural than for you to continue your old custom tonight; but you must let me be just a little provoked with Dr. Douglass; he really *should* have informed you of the views which the society of Newton take of such matters. Dr. Douglass knows perfectly well that *here* it is considered in a high degree immodest and unladylike, and it was certainly unkind in him not to tell you so. You, of course, are not in the least to blame."

I think my cheeks vied with the worsted in color as I responded:

"Will you be kind enough to inform me why Newton should use such terms concerning so simple a matter as speaking a half-dozen words in a quiet little prayer meeting?"

Mrs. Tyndall shrugged her beautiful shoulders.

"My dear little Puritan," she said lightly, "what a task you have set before me! I don't pretend to understand all the reasons. There are many people, you know, who consider it morally wrong and quote St. Paul with energy. Of course all such ideas are nonsensical, have been exploded, indeed. I personally have always believed that people's consciences would guide them aright in this as in other matters. My conscience, I am happy to say, has never obliged me to speak in a meeting. I don't think it ever will; but I certainly think that there is one important objection always to be considered. Public opinion is decidedly against hearing our voices in religious meetings, and I, for one, feel that my influence is far too precious to be thrown away. Oh, my dear, if you could hear the many laughable things that I have heard about this matter, you would never open your lips again in religious meetings."

"Whether I consider it right or wrong?" I asked.

"Oh, but you would feel it to be wrong, or at the very least inexpedient—that is a Bible word, you know, my dear. I think the influence it has on the unconverted is most unfortunate—they invariably ridicule it."

"I never heard anyone do so," I said stiffly.

"Ah, but my dear innocent child! you must constantly consider the difference in places. Newton is peculiar in many respects, I will admit. There are, perhaps, more educated persons here than generally congregate in places of its size—people of wealth and culture, you know—who have had every advantage of society, and that class of people, you will find, feel very strongly on this subject. My dear, I really must tell you of my experience in listening to people of my own sex in mixed assemblies—"

At this point Mr. Tyndall sauntered in and dropped into an easy chair beside his wife.

"What is the subject under discussion, my dear?" he asked briskly. "Anything that masculinity can appreciate, or must I retire?"

"Decidedly you can appreciate it. Oh, Mr. Tyndall,

I must tell you. Dr. Douglass has beguiled this little Puritan into making a speech to his boys and girls tonight."

Several feelings struggled within me for the mastery, among which were indignation and embarrassment, and while I was struggling for calmness, Mr. Tyndall responded by a low, quick whistle—then laughed and said good-humoredly: "I beg your pardon, ladies—nothing else would express my state of mind. Dr. Douglass is a shrewd man, wise in his generation. I would almost sit an hour in that dreadful schoolroom myself for the pleasure of hearing your voice, Miss Ried. So that is the spell which is brought to bear upon my office boys; I have often wondered."

"I was just about to tell Miss Ried of our experience with Miss Hillyard. Do you remember Miss Hillyard, Mr. Tyndall?"

"I am inclined to think I do. Let us have the story, by all means. I am in a state of mind to appreciate it."

"She was a little wizened-up woman, Miss Ried, with just the very squeakiest voice that you can imagine, and she invariably had a cold in her head. Well, she was a solitary female who used to honor us with her experience at prayer meeting. Mr. Tyndall and I sat directly behind her and had a fair view. She always addressed her remarks to the ceiling. She used to roll her eyes in this manner." And Mrs. Tyndall clasped her hands and, fixing her gaze on the wall overhead, rolled her beautiful eyes until nothing but white was visible, and drew a prolonged sigh—an indescribable sound, produced by a long drawn-out letter *a* suddenly dropped into space.

"Give us the speech, Fanny," said her husband, laughing immoderately.

"Oh, the speech was nothing, the same words

nearly, but the manner was unique. This was the opening sentence: My dear brethren—ah—ha— (a *very* long-drawn breath between these two words) and sisters. I feel—ah—ha—that I must give voice to my heart tonight. I feel ah—that (and here she invariably had recourse to her handkerchief), I feel that the spiritual part of this meeting depends upon the sisters; I feel to lament my cold state; I feel that we must wake up and do our duty."

I have always from a child been ridiculously susceptible to ludicrous impressions; and on this evening, although my cheeks were burning with indignation over the language in which Mrs. Tyndall had been indulging, although I felt the utter fallacy of her arguments, yet, at this picture, rolling eyes, nasal tone, long-drawn breaths, and finally voice changing into a whine, with sobs and chokings, and frequent applications of the handkerchief, I joined hopelessly in the laugh. Mr. Tyndall enjoyed the exhibition immensely, and went away laughing to attend to a business call. His wife's face became grave almost instantly, and she drew a little sigh and spoke in a saddened tone:

"I have not exaggerated the picture in the least, Miss Ried. Mr. Tyndall used to accompany me to prayer meeting quite frequently in those days, and that is exactly the sort of martyrdom he was called upon to endure, and I am sure you cannot wonder that he has entirely given up the habit of attending prayer meeting."

My brain was in a whirl when I went to my room that evening. I do not know that I was more easily led than other girls of my age. I did not entirely believe Mrs. Tyndall. I saw through many of her sophistries, but at the same time there were many that I did not see through; and everything about her had a sort of fascination to me. I felt myself insensibly slipping away from my moorings. I sat down, Bible in hand, and tried to read, but it is safe to say that I read only what Mrs. Tyndall had been saying, and laughed a little over her picture of Miss Hillyard, even while I had sense enough to realize that with such home comments as Mr. Tyndall heard, it was not strange that he lost faith in prayer meetings.

One thing I did that evening for which I am glad. I copied and retained a copy of every word that I could remember about that young people's meeting, to which copy I am indebted for the account of it that I have written tonight.

7

A TROUBLED SUNDAY

I HAD a serious time dressing for church the next morning. It was the first time I ever remember to have had very earnest thoughts about the matter of dress. I had been, perhaps, fortunate in that respect, having very little variety in my wardrobe to choose from, and very little time to spend in choosing. I think the first thing that led me astray on this particular morning was the absence of family worship. I had always been accustomed to it in my home for many years, with Dr. Van Anden to lead us; and after he and Dr. Douglass both went away we had met in my mother's room—Mother, Alfred, and I—and Alfred had been the leader. On this morning I lingered downstairs after breakfast, missing this morning service as only those can who have been accustomed to it all their lives and find themselves suddenly adrift in the world without it. I lingered, talking with Mrs. Tyndall, not in a particularly Sabbath strain, until Dr. Douglass, passing through the hall, warned me about the lateness of the hour. This, too, was a surprise. I had been used to long Sabbath mornings in my mother's home. I went upstairs and began that business of dressing at once.

My hair was refractory at first, or I was overparticular, and the first bell rang before it was in order. Then I donned my brown alpaca dress and felt satisfied with it until I suddenly remembered that I had worn it for a traveling dress! True, I had only traveled ten miles; but what of that: Had not Mrs. Tyndall complimented me on the taste and propriety of my *traveling* attire? I hurried it back to the clothespress with a nervous feeling that I had a reputation for good taste to sustain, and selected next my one silk dress—plain black, made neatly and simply, but undeniably my very best dress. It had been a gift from Sadie, Dr. Van Anden, and dear brother Alfred, the latter having saved his pocket money for months to add to what Sadie called the "Julia Silk Dress Fund." I looked exceedingly well in it, I told myself as I enjoyed the luxury of a full-length survey of myself. Next I added real lace collars and cuffs—Cousin Abbie's gifts when Sadie was married; but I finally returned them to their box, feeling someway that I looked unlike myself and church, and selected a plain linen band and cuffs; even with them I had trouble. I tried a pink bow before I remembered that the bird's wing in my gray felt hat was as blue as the sky. I discarded that and tried a blue one; but it was so different a blue from the wing on my hat that I, remembering the green velvet bonnet that was to sit before us and Mrs. Tyndall's horror, hastily took it off and clasped my collar with a plain gold pin. Meantime, the bell tolled and tolled, and the more I hurried, the more exasperatingly it seemed to toll. My Bible lay unopened on the table, and I had no time for a word of prayer that morning; at least I told myself so, choosing to ignore the time spent in the parlor after breakfast.

I had never been to church on Sabbath morning without first having at least the form of private prayer. I kneeled down hastily and tried to collect my thoughts; but I remember that while I knelt I unclasped the pin that fastened my watch chain and drew the chain outside of my cloak. It was a handsome chain, and I did not want it hidden. Then Dr. Douglass knocked at my door and called out that it was quite late, and there was a long walk to take. I sprang up hastily, ran to the glass, and, I am thankful to be able to say, changed my mind about the chain and hid it under my cloak, donned my grey hat, drew on my grey gloves that exactly matched the hat, and, on the whole, felt satisfied with my appearance.

The church was larger and handsomer than any I had ever attended, and the grand organ rolled its music through the house as we went down the aisle. It thrilled and solemnized me. I began to realize that it was the Sabbath day, and that we had come to worship the King in his beauty. There was no green bonnet in the seat in front of us, but there were three neatly dressed little girls and a manly boy. I found myself taking particular note of their dress and thinking that I saw no very marked indications of uncultivated taste after all. I liked their faces—they looked bright and fresh. I could not help thinking that they must have a good mother. The voluntary from the choir and organ was very impressive, and my heart seemed solemnized for worship when Dr. Mulford arose. At first I did not notice the peculiar quiver to his lips of which Mrs. Tyndall had spoken, nor did I take in the sense of what hymn he was reading until I caught a glance of Mrs. Tyndall's eyes. There was that in the glance which seemed to carry me to her back parlor and cause me to see and hear again the ludicrous description that she had given me of Dr. Mulford's reading. It was then I noticed that the hymn was the same—

"When I survey the wondrous cross."

I began to give close attention to Dr. Mulford, and noticed presently a nervous quiver of the lip, like a twitching of the nerve. Even then it did not impress me as being particularly ludicrous; and more because I felt that Mrs. Tyndall expected me to, than for any necessity therefor, I smiled. But presently, as I allowed my thoughts to rest upon her description, there suddenly burst over me a vivid scene of her extremely comical appearance, and I laughed outright.

Mrs. Tyndall by this time was perfectly grave, with eyes bent on her book. I felt frightened to think that I had laughed in church. I wondered if it had really been aloud, so the people could hear me. Then a sort of hysterical feeling came over me—that feeling which no mortal who has not been guilty of laughing, and continuing to laugh, in exactly the wrong place, need attempt to understand. I tried in vain to regain my dignity. I thought of every serious thing I had ever heard. I tried to imagine what my mother would think if she knew her daughter were guilty of such unbecoming behavior. I thought of all the little Mulfords in front of me, and of the example that I was setting them; and it was all no sort of use. I laughed again, not aloud, but that distressing inward laughter that shakes one's body to a jelly; that shakes the seat and the footstool, on which are other feet than yours; a kind of laughter that no one within twenty feet of you can be ignorant of. In vain I choked, and pretended to cough, and drew my face into very uncommon lengths of severe gravity, only to burst forth again into uncontrollable shakings and gigglings. My one comfort in looking back on my folly is that there was not a bit of mirth about the laugh; it just originated from silly schoolgirl lack of self-control. No, not originated. I could have avoided the very first inclination to laugh had not Mrs. Tyndall's face seemed to expect it, and I been anxious to please her. Very suddenly, at last, was I sobered, not by resolution, nor by contrition, but by indignation. Dr. Douglass, sitting beside me, bent forward and gravely whispered:

"Shall I give you an opportunity to pass out?"

A vision of Mr. Tyndall and Dr. Douglass politely rising, and myself brushing past them and marching down the aisle, my face as red as the carpet on which I trod, burst suddenly upon me. I wonder that I did not laugh again at that; but it instantly sobered me. I raised my flushed and indignant face and, turning quite away from the doctor, gave undivided and grave attention to Dr. Mulford. He was just announcing his text. I opened my little Bible as was my wont, and marked and dated the text. I have just taken that Bible and found the words: "What will ye? Shall I come unto you with a rod, or in love?"

I had no difficulty remaining grave and dignified during the rest of the service, partly through shame and anger, and partly because of my interest in the sermon that followed. It must have been a forcible one, for there are certain portions of it that I remember vividly today.

I remained for the Sabbath school service and had a seat in Mrs. Tyndall's class. She introduced me to several young misses in rustling silks and many flounces. My little Ruth was the only one that I had seen before. I nodded and smiled at her, and was shocked to find that I was the only one who in any way recognized her, save Mrs. Tyndall, who gave her a cold bow. I felt little Ruth was decidedly out of her element and was sorry for her. I looked over to Dr. Douglass's class. Frank Hooper was there, and several others, Ruth's companions. If I had not been very angry at the doctor, I should have motioned him to me and proposed an immediate change, thereby relieving Ruth and her teacher. But what I was pleased to call his insufferable impertinence could not so soon be overlooked. I remember very little about the lesson. I failed to become interested; but after the question-book forms were gone through with, and Bibles closed, I remember an animated discussion that ensued concerning the getting up of tableaux for a certain festival, which was to be held at Christmas-time. Mrs. Tyndall gave minute descriptions of the style of dress needed to personate certain characters, and I suddenly became an object of importance, because I had not only seen, but participated in one of the tableaux mentioned and could give accurate information as to whether the young lady who personated religion should dress in white or black. Miss Florence Hervey, the most supercilious young lady of all that supercilious clique, and who had evidently been almost inclined to ignore me, seemed suddenly to decide on patronage instead, and asked innumerable questions, even whispering them at intervals during the closing prayer, and said as we were passing out:

"I shall call on you, Miss Ried. My engagements are so many that I call on very few strangers; but I shall make you an exception."

Then she turned and addressed her teacher:

"Mrs. Tyndall, I really think it is insufferable having that Walker girl in our class. What makes you endure it?"

Lycia Symonds responded:

"Nonsense, Flo. What do you care? I'm sure she is as quiet as a little brown kitten. I think it's refreshing to look at her meek face."

And Mrs. Tyndall, with her sweetest smile and gentle voice, added:

"You know we must not be respecters of persons in Sabbath school, my dear Florence."

"Oh, now, Mrs. Tyndall, that's all very well for you to say, of course; but it is useless to expect the same amount of perfection in us; we never expect to attain to your standard, and she makes us positively uncomfortable."

I looked steadily at Miss Florence, but could not determine whether or not this sentence savored of sarcasm. If Mrs. Tyndall thought so, she did not make it visible, but answered thoughtfully:

"To be sure, the poor girl seems rather out of her element. My dear, do you think the doctor would take her?"

Before I could respond the doctor joined us and, with a grave bow to the young ladies, addressed their teacher:

"Mrs. Tyndall, my girls say you have one of their friends in your class, Miss Walker. Is she properly classified?"

Mrs. Tyndall laughed.

"Ask Miss Hervey," she said playfully. And Miss Hervey, nothing daunted, responded promptly:

"Indeed, Dr. Douglass, she is my thorn in the flesh. She looks so entirely as if she had come out of the ark that my mind is continually carried back to antediluvian times, to the great disadvantage of Moses and the Egyptians, about whom, you know, we are studying at present."

Dr. Douglass's face relaxed not one muscle, and with a grave bow, he merely said:

"Mrs. Tyndall, I will speak to the superintendent about her," and left us.

Miss Hervey's thoughts were thus turned into another channel.

"How can you possibly exist with that man sitting at your table? Haven't you contracted the dyspepsia lately? I would quite as soon sit opposite my grandfather's monument."

"Florence, you are a sad child," Mrs. Tyndall answered with a slight laugh. "The doctor is worth a dozen ordinary gentlemen. Ask Miss Ried if it is not so." Then to me, "Come, my dear, shall we go?"

Her last remark had instantly fixed a battery of eyes on me, and I know the wonder had been started as to what Miss Ried knew of Dr. Douglass. I learned long afterwards that this was Mrs. Tyndall's quiet, ladylike way of gossiping. The doctor had disappeared, but joined us just as we reached the piazza and detained me with a question as Mrs. Tyndall passed in.

"Julia, do you go to mission school with me this afternoon?"

I turned a haughtily indignant face toward him and spoke loftily:

"Is that the only apology which you have to offer for your rudeness to me this morning?"

He looked simply surprised and spoke in his usual tone:

"I have no apology of any sort to offer, Julia, for I certainly was not aware of an occasion. I saw you utterly unable to control yourself, and the wisest thing to do seemed to me to leave the church until you regained self-command."

His composure angered me more than before, and I answered sharply:

"You may look elsewhere for mission-school help. I have no desire to accompany you."

To this he made no sort of reply, only held open the door for me to pass in.

While he awaited in the back parlor the summons to dinner, the doorbell rang, and presently there sauntered in young Mr. Sayles—sauntered is the only word which seemed to me to apply to Mr. Sayles's movements; his whole manner had an air of good-natured languor.

"Will you give me some dinner?" he asked as he dropped indolently into a chair. "Boardinghouse fare seemed to me insufferable today, to say nothing of boardinghouse society."

"Then you are still boarding away from home?" queried Mrs. Tyndall.

Mr. Sayles shrugged his shoulders, then laughed lazily and said:

"Yes, Madam Sayles and I agree much better apart."

"Poor fellow," Mrs. Tyndall said with a sympathetic sigh, and immediately we were summoned to dinner. Dr. Douglass, who came from his room at the bell call, greeted the visitor with a grave bow. The talk flowed on very pleasantly, but not in the least Sabbath-like. The doctor maintained an air of quiet dignity, joining in the conversation only when directly addressed. As Mr. Tyndall passed the dessert to his guest he said:

"Sayles, you scapegrace, where were you today? I didn't see you in church."

"Probably not, as I wasn't there. I worshiped in a more primitive form."

"Where and how?"

Mr. Sayles glanced from Dr. Douglass to Mrs. Tyndall and myself with a good-humored laugh.

"Do you want to disgrace me before this goodly number of orthodox people?" he asked, speaking lightly. "Well, if you are really anxious to know, I went toward the rising instead of the setting sun—more reasonable, you know, in the morning."

Mrs. Tyndall looked shocked.

"You went to the Cathedral, you wicked man," she exclaimed in reproving tones.

"Well, I can't agree with you, Mrs. Tyndall. I don't feel wicked in the least. On the contrary, I don't know when I have been so devotionally inclined as I was this morning. The music was glorious. I thought of you, Mrs. Tyndall; you would have enjoyed the chanting. How is it, Doctor? Isn't it right for one to follow the bent of his nature in choosing his place of worship?"

"One may safely follow his conscience, I think, in this as in other matters, provided he has carefully educated that conscience to the best of his knowledge and ability."

The doctor's voice was courteous but grave toned, and Mr. Sayles responded as usual with a laugh; then he added:

"And provided he has one, you ought to have said. I have never become quite sure on that point as yet. But come now, Tyndall, what did you gain by attending church this morning? Give an account of your impressions."

8

A CHRISTIAN DUTY

"MY impressions," said Mr. Tyndall, "are very vivid, at least. What was the text, Fanny?"

Mrs. Tyndall could not tell, and so long had it been gone from my mind that I could do no better; but the doctor, being appealed to, repeated it slowly and solemnly:

"What will ye? Shall I come unto you with a rod, or in love?"

"Exactly," continued Mr. Tyndall. "Now, if Dr. Mulford had that matter in his own hands, I don't believe he would stop to inquire as to our choice in the matter. He would take the rod and make use of it right and left. The way he did give it to us, Sayles! You ought to have been there. You would have discovered that you had a conscience. That man would have made a good pugilist. I think it is as good as a play, the manner in which he tears around that pulpit. I wonder at you absenting yourself, Sayles. It answers the place of a theater to me."

"Mr. Tyndall!" His wife's voice had a note of reproof in it, but she smothered a laugh as she spoke.

Mr. Sayles looked triumphant.

"There!" he said; "we have positive proof of your devotional feelings. Now, I'll leave it to the doctor if I didn't, evidently, get more good out of my morning than that?"

The doctor's voice was dignified, even to hauteur, as he answered:

"I presume, Mr. Sayles, neither building is responsible for the spirit in which a man enters it."

"But other things being equal, you would say that in an orthodox church a man might expect to receive good?"

"I repeat that I think that must depend very largely upon the spirit of the man."

"Miss Ried," said Mr. Tyndall abruptly, "what was the matter with your spirit and mine this morning? I observed that yours impressed your risibles in a way in which I would have been delighted to join."

"Hush!" Mrs. Tyndall said gently, while I colored to the very roots of my hair; "that was not the poor child's fault in the least. People cannot surely be surprised that Dr. Mulford's peculiar facial infirmity excites laughter when one sees it for the first time. I have been for these three years endeavoring to become accustomed to it, and I am far from being perfected in my endeavor."

The doctor fixed a pair of very sharp eyes on Mrs. Tyndall as he asked:

"To what infirmity do you refer, may I ask? I have never observed any."

The lady first opened her blue eyes very wide, in token of her astonishment, then drew her face into such a ridiculous exaggeration of Dr. Mulford's that her husband and guest roared with laughter. The doctor's answer was dignified, haughty, utter silence;

and almost immediately he excused himself and left the room.

"Is Dr. Douglass's digestion good?" queried Mr. Sayles with a grave face.

Mrs. Tyndall responded laughingly:

"I really can't say. Why?"

"Because, if it isn't, I feel conscience stricken. Such a solemn state as that into which we have put him is said to interfere sadly with dyspeptics."

Mr. Tyndall had regained his gravity and spoke more thoughtfully than I had yet heard him:

"I am afraid we have wounded his feelings. He has sort of a worshipful feeling for Dr. Mulford, I think."

Mr. Sayles glanced up quickly.

"Do you think so?" he asked with an air of real regret. "I should be very sorry. I intended not the slightest disrespect to Dr. Mulford. He is a gentleman, I think. But, Mrs. Tyndall, your face was too ridiculous." Whereupon he laughed again.

Mrs. Tyndall answered him composedly:

"Finish your cream, Mr. Sayles; I'll answer for Dr. Douglass's feelings. He is not so foolish a man as Mr. Tyndall would have you suppose. He knows, as do all the rest of you, that I have unbounded respect and a high regard for Dr. Mulford. But that does not alter the fact that he certainly has a very queer mouth."

The talk flowed on into other channels. About the singing, Mrs. Tyndall asserted that the alto was too heavy, and her husband was as earnestly affirming that it was grand. Mrs. Tyndall seemed to differ, in a graceful, ladylike way, with everybody, on every subject. After we returned to the parlor I gave myself up to uncomfortable thought. The closing of the outer door and the brisk tread of Dr. Douglass as he made his way, alone, to the mission school, did not serve to make my self-communings any pleasanter. I realized that thus far the day had been an unprofitable one. I had faint thoughts of going to my room and endeavoring to atone for my unfortunate beginning. But the parlor was the very perfection of comfort, and the murmur of tongues seemed to soothe the homesick spirit that was in my heart. When I gave attention to them again, Mr. Sayles had returned to the subject that had been under discussion at the dinner table.

"I am really very sorry for the turn that our conversation took and am very much afraid that we hurt the doctor's feelings. I am sure I don't know what would have tempted me to do so. I wonder if it would do to offer an apology?"

"Fanny is the one to apologize, I think, if there is anything of that sort to be done. She shouldn't have been so absurd."

And Mr. Tyndall laughed again at the remembrance, a laugh in which his wife and Mr. Sayles joined; but the latter said immediately:

"I have heard that he is a great admirer and devoted friend of Dr. Mulford; and he must have thought our fun rather severe. Upon my word, I wouldn't have hurt the poor fellow's feelings for the world."

"What a sensitive man you are!" Mrs. Tyndall said, a touch of admiration in her voice. "I wish I were as thoughtful of other people's feelings. I am so given to speaking my mind, without regard to the wisdom of such a proceeding."

"I wish I were as thoughtful before I committed the blunder instead of afterward," laughed Mr. Sayles. "I never discovered that my afterthoughts did any particular good."

"But in this instance, I am sure your regrets are uncalled for. I feel certain that Dr. Douglass is too sensible a man to take offense at a little harmless talk between ourselves. Of course, none of us intend to repeat it. To be sure, the doctor's abrupt departure looks as though his temper wasn't under as good subjection as usual; but his brisk walk in the fresh air will tone him down, and he will see the folly of his ill nature. So, Jerome, don't trouble your head about that for another minute. You have troubles enough of your own, I am sure. I'm not going to let you find anything but pleasure in my house."

And Mrs. Tyndall dismissed the doctor's supposed ill humor with a little laugh and gracefully changed the conversation.

I looked at Mr. Sayles as he lounged in the easy chair, his handsome head bobbing restlessly from corner to corner of the elegant tidy, and wondered what the peculiar trials to which I had heard reference could be. He looked like a man whom trials had never touched. The conversation became animated presently—still about ministers. I noticed, many times since that day, that there are people who think they are having a religious conversation if they talk about clergymen. Dr. Whatley was the name of the reverend gentleman who was being discussed.

"He is really the finest orator in Newton," Mr. Tyndall said. "There is no one here who can compete with him."

"Oh," said Mrs. Tyndall, "I shouldn't think there was. Why, I haven't heard a man in New York City who can surpass him. It is really a perfect feast to hear him preach. Miss Ried, his voice is melody itself, and I have seen many in his audience melted to tears, just by his manner in reading a hymn."

"What about his logic, Mrs. Tyndall?" Mr. Sayles asked with a mischievous twinkle in his eyes.

"Oh, you know he doesn't force his particular views on people. I have heard him often, when I couldn't have determined from the sermon what his religious standpoint was."

Both the gentlemen laughed, and Mr. Tyndall said:

"That is rather hard on him, isn't it, Fanny? When a man has been called to preach for a church, who fully agree with him in his religious views, why shouldn't they have the pleasure of hearing those views presented?"

"Oh, you may laugh," said Mrs. Tyndall emphatically; "but I assure you that is an old-fashioned notion that doesn't obtain among first-class people—the idea that a man must be forever forcing some religious dogma upon his congregation."

"For my part, I like it," Mr. Sayles said sturdily. "I always like to see a man act as though he wasn't ashamed of his belief and thought it a matter of sufficient importance to feel the need of impressing it on other people."

At this point I chimed in.

"So do I," I said, and while I spoke I thought to myself that I liked Mr. Sayles much better than I thought I should. "I like Dr. Mulford for that very reason; he seems in earnest and preaches as though he wanted other people to be."

Mr. Tyndall's tones were complaisance itself.

"That just accords with my view of things," he said. "You good people find the storming of your own consciences a very troublesome business and are happy to delegate it to your clergyman. As for Fanny here, it is getting to be an old story with her, and she begins to think it is an unnecessary proceeding altogether."

Mrs. Tyndall laughed her sweet good-natured silvery laugh and added:

"As for Mr. Tyndall, he never had any conscience to speak of: so his idiosyncracies cannot be accounted for in that way. But I know a delightful way in which to end the discussion: let us take Miss Ried to hear Dr. Whatley this evening, and she will consider herself conquered at once."

"Will she be taken?" queried Mr. Sayles, turning promptly to me; and then followed another discussion. I demurred, faintly enough, it is true; but the others were all clamorous for the plan, and my weak scruples were speedily overruled. Mr. Tyndall suppressed a yawn as he spoke:

"That matter being settled, Sayles, which do you prefer in the meantime—a walk and a smoke with me, or a chat with the ladies?"

Mr. Sayles had the grace to choose the walk and smoke; and I fully intended to go at once to my room, but as the door closed after them, Mrs. Tyndall turned quickly toward me and spoke eagerly:

"Now, isn't it sad, Miss Ried, that of those two gentlemen, Dr. Douglass and Mr. Sayles, the one who makes no pretension to religion should be the one to show such a considerate spirit, and that so good a man as Dr. Douglass should give himself to a burst of ill temper? I was so sorry that he rushed off in the manner that he did this afternoon. I knew that Mr. Sayles's sensitive nature would feel it, and the poor fellow has enough trouble of his own. Besides, how can Mr. Tyndall avoid drawing unfavorable contrasts? I do wish people could realize what an amount of harm they can do by these foolish bursts of passion."

I remained silent and thoughtful. When the doctor left the dinner table I had discovered nothing in his manner but grave and courteous dignity. That he felt hurt I, who knew him so well, could not but believe; but I had even admired the self-controlled face, showing its disapprobation only by its pallor. But viewed in the light of the afternoon's conversation, his manner began to appear decidedly objectionable, and Mr. Sayles's kind-hearted anxiety, lest he had offended, contrasted admirably.

"Yes," I said at last, speaking slowly; "I am sorry the doctor was so sensitive. It isn't like him."

"So absurd in him to grow angry because we laughed at the good old doctor's queer faces—as if anybody could help that! My dear, our good Dr. Douglass tries me occasionally, in regard to his puritan ideas. I verily believe he thinks it wicked for Mr. Sayles to come here on the Sabbath. He doesn't like poor Jerome, anyway, and always treats him with severe gravity; but he adds a tenfold quantity if it happens to be Sunday. Now, shouldn't you suppose he could see that I make it a matter of duty to welcome Mr. Tyndall's friends most heartily at all times; and that I try especially to make the Sabbath a bright happy day to him in his own home? I banish, or try to, all long faces, all sanctimonious airs. I particularly wish to relieve Mr. Tyndall from any of those I-am-holier-than-thou airs—they are always so extremely obnoxious to gentlemen. Isn't it strange that Dr. Douglass doesn't think of any of these little things? And yet I don't know as it is." (With a little sigh and a peculiar sweet drooping of her shapely head.) "I suppose he has always lived in a religious atmosphere. Probably all his friends are Christians, and he doubtless knows nothing about the perpetual anxieties and plannings of one who has so peculiar a nature as my husband's to deal with. I do hope you will help me, Miss Ried. I have needed help."

I was silent and bewildered. I had been compromising with my conscience during that entire afternoon. I had disapproved of Mr. Sayles's Sunday visit and of the style of conversation. I had felt grieved that Mr. Tyndall should be brought under such influence, having heard from Mrs. Tyndall how peculiar he was. I had considered the whole affair peculiarly demoralizing to him. I had been grieved and shocked over Mrs. Tyndall's own frivolous words. Now, was it possible there were two sides to this question? *Were* the doctor's and my own dear mother's ideas on these subjects narrow and puritanic—the result of a straitened system of education? *Was* Mrs. Tyndall conscientious in this matter; and had she taken the right course?

Ah me! it is but little consolation to me tonight that I was sincere in my bewilderments. What right had I, with a Christian mother, and a father and a sister in heaven, and a full knowledge of that old solemn command, "Remember the Sabbath day, to keep it holy," to be bewildered at all? But I was, and it is easy today to see how it all came to pass. Satan desired to have me, and I seemed only too willing to yield myself to his guidance, and began and lived through that Sabbath day without a word to that One stronger than Satan, to the end that he would keep me. What wonder that he stood aside and let that most skillful of all weavers tangle me in his silky-looking web?

Mrs. Tyndall broke the silence suddenly with a total change of subject:

"My dear, why don't you wave your hair and arrange it low on your forehead? It would be very becoming."

"I don't know," I said hesitatingly, a little startled by the sudden transition.

"I wish you would let me arrange it for you," she answered me with enthusiasm. "It is such lovely hair I am sure I could do just what I wanted with it. Do you know you have a very artistic head; and I am a skillful artist in the matter of hair, I assure you. Won't you just come to my room and let me show you what I can do in that line? It will take but a very few moments and would be such an improvement. I quite long to get my fingers in your beautiful hair. It will relieve your head too. I think you said it ached."

It did ache. And as I sat in her low, crimson chair in her dressing room, I told myself *that* was the reason why I let Mrs. Tyndall pull, and twitch, and unmercifully snarl my hair on that Sabbath afternoon. The ringing of the church bells before the operation was concluded recalled me to a sense of Sabbath, and I suddenly wondered if this hairdressing could, by Mrs. Tyndall, be made to seem the right and proper thing to do. In a somewhat blundering fashion I asked her, and she answered:

"There! I have finished; it is perfectly lovely. My dear, won't you please wear a blue velvet knot in your hair tonight? The effect would be so exquisite." Then, bending over, she kissed me gently, caressingly, and added: "My dear little conscientious mouse, don't you know that it is a Christian duty to make ourselves just as pretty as we can?"

And I went to my room and knelt down before my trunk and tumbled it upside down in search of a knot of blue velvet to wear in my hair.

9

A RELIGIOUS CONVERSATION

"FRANK!" I said. "Frank Hooper, won't you wait a moment? I want to speak with you."

And Frank came back and perched herself on a great stack of pasteboard and eyed me gravely while I nervously donned my cloak and hat. I had been in my new sphere not yet six weeks and in some respects was a curiosity to myself. I really at times seemed to myself to be two persons. At my boarding place I was treated by Mrs. Tyndall with unvarying kindness, and indeed with so marked a degree of similarity that her influence over me had become almost unbounded. I was with her constantly during my leisure hours, and she had been giving me delicious and dangerous tastes of the gay world that had heretofore appeared to me only in books. Part of the time I considered myself gloriously happy and singularly fortunate, but there were hours in which I conceived a disgust for myself and formed brilliant plans of an impossible reformation. These times nearly always came upon me in the shop, where the Julia Ried I used to know seemed to lodge, and never by any chance come out from thence to be found at Mrs. Tyndall's. I was more or less familiar with all the girls and had acquired a certain influence over them—not the kind of influence Dr. Douglass had desired me to have, for I rarely spoke with any of them personally on the question of religion; but in a gay, frolicsome sort of way, they all liked me, more or less, and listened with a good-humored toleration to my occasional lectures on propriety. Speaking of Dr. Douglass, my relations with him were rather annoying. I saw very little of him. The evening lessons that had been commenced by me in such glee were so constantly interrupted that they had now only a stray evening—once a week possibly. Mrs. Tyndall entirely disapproved of them, thought I was sufficiently occupied all day, and that at evening my mind needed rest and relaxation, which she was continually finding me in the shape of a rare concert for which Mr. Tyndall had secured tickets, or a lecture of unusual interest, or a little social gathering, or possibly a headache which needed a walk in the fresh air, with me for a companion, to relieve it; and she was so uniformly kind and thoughtful and winning that it became every day more difficult to resist her. Dr. Douglass had ceased to remonstrate, or even to comment; was always ready for me on those rare evenings when I presented myself with my arms full of books, and never questioned me as to my engagements or plans for the coming evenings. But Mother and Sadie wrote constantly of him as if he were my natural protector, and took it so entirely for granted that I deferred to him in all things that sometimes it cheered and sometimes it troubled me. He had ceased all opposition to my plans, and only showed an interest in me by constantly remembering rubbers, and umbrella, and waterproof whenever there came an unexpected change in the weather, or by some such quiet attention to my comfort.

On this particular afternoon of which I write I had been having one of my seasons of reformation, brought upon me by a troubled look in the doctor's eyes as he questioned me closely, when we walked down together, about Frank Hooper's deportment in the shop, and revealed to me incidentally that she had not been to the young people's meeting for a month. It was Saturday, and we were having a sort of half holiday; and although I had engaged to accompany Mrs. Tyndall on a calling tour, I yet resolutely recalled Frank, resolved upon a few minutes' serious conversation with her. So there she sat upon her pile of pasteboard, erect and composed, while I nervously buttoned and unbuttoned my cloak. At last I plunged into the very center of what I wanted to say.

"Frank, why don't you go to prayer meeting anymore?"

The cool gray eyes seemed to be searching me through and through, while Frank composedly swung her heels against the pasteboard. Finally she said:

"How do you know I don't?"

How, indeed? Was that a tacit reproof for my own absence from the meetings, for I had not been there since that first Saturday night that I had spent in Newton. I felt that Frank had me at a disadvantage, but her gray eyes were waiting and must be answered, so I said nervously:

"Dr. Douglass told me so this noon."

Frank's heels were quiet, and a little red spot glowed on either cheek, but her voice was still cool and composed.

"Did Dr. Douglass complain to you of my refractory self and enlist your sympathy and cooperation in my behalf?"

"Now, Frank," I said pleadingly, "don't be ugly. Tell me, please, why you don't go anymore."

Frank laughed and spoke in her old hard tone.

"What's the use? I get no good by it; never did. Satan desires to have me twice as hard the day after I go to meeting as he does the day before; that's Bible, I know so much about the good book. Fact is, I stay away as a matter of principle, because I'm so much less wicked when I don't go."

"Oh, Frank!" I said in great and genuine sorrow, "I wish you wouldn't talk so. I wish you would be serious."

Frank's face had resumed its gravity, but there was a touch of curiosity in her voice as she made her next remark:

"I didn't know you were so interested in the meetings. Why don't you attend them?"

When I look back on that conversation it seems to me now, as it did then, that I would give almost anything if there had been no occasion for asking that question, if I had attended every one of those meetings. The question confused me—my cheeks grew red—I looked down and twisted my cloak buttons. At last I said:

"Frank, I—there are reasons. I have but very little time, and I am differently circumstanced. I—"

She interrupted me. "I know we are," she said with a mocking smile. "Of course your time is very limited. I only work ten hours a day, while you have to work from eight in the morning until five at night. Besides, I board at the Powell Mansion, on Green Street, while you are domiciled at Madam Tyndall's, corner of Harvard and Genesse Streets, and that, of course, makes all the difference in the world, with our ability to go to prayer meeting."

I answered her coldly: "I don't think I deserve such treatment from you, Frank. I have never given you any reason to suppose that I felt superior to you, and you know I don't mean any such thing."

Frank jumped down from the pasteboards and confronted me, erect and dignified:

"*Don't* you mean just exactly that, Miss Ried, only you don't want me to know it? Don't you stay away from the young people's meeting because Mrs. Tyndall has represented to you that it is not quite the thing; that it is well enough for shop girls and office boys, and other scum of creation—but that our set are never found there? That, in short, you would lose caste with the world; that even Mrs. Tyndall couldn't consent to pilot you through its intricate mazes if you lowered yourself to equality with those poor wretches, picked up from nobody knows where? I've heard her talk, Miss Ried. I know just how daintily she sinks herself into the depths of her easy chair when she disposes of her offscourings of the world. I even know in what corner of her elegant room the chair probably stands; my own used to stand just there. My father built that house, and my mother planned it, and I have seen the time when Mrs. Tyndall considered herself honored by an invitation to my father's house; but she passes me on the street now with no knowledge of my existence; her memory is probably defective—she has forgotten me."

I listened to this story in great astonishment. Then the only difference between this girl and myself was that I had always been obliged to turn my dresses, and make over my old hats, and economize in every imaginable way in order to make a very little money meet my needs, while she had known what it was to be the daughter of a man of wealth and position. Strangely enough, the whole matter irritated me, and I spoke suddenly and sharply: "After all, Frank, what is all this harangue about? I asked you a very simple question, which had nothing whatever to do with the subject about which we are talking."

Frank laughed. "Very true," she said carelessly. "I ran off the track; the fact is, I preach a sermon so seldom that I find it difficult to stick to my text. Well, let me see, what was the important question? Why don't I go to the young people's meeting anymore? My dear young friend, after mature deliberation, I have very nearly decided that it is because I *don't*. Now, I'm sure you can't complain that your question has not been answered."

I did not know what to say next. I did not seem to be accomplishing anything. I made another effort. "Frank, have you really no interest in this subject?"

"Which subject? The one on which we stumbled when we ran off the track? Yes, an immense interest. I'm engaged at present in calculating how many sixteenths of inches Mrs. Tyndall's head is elevated above its ordinary poise whenever I meet her; also how much greater elevation the said head will endure before it reaches the clouds and soars altogether from my mundane sight."

I fastened the last button of my cloak with a resolute hand and spoke with dignity:

"I did not ask you to stop in order to hear you talk nonsense about my friend. I am sorry you will not listen to anything serious. Good evening."

Dr. Douglass, walking rapidly, overtook me before I reached the corner; he slackened his pace and said carelessly: "You are early this afternoon, are you not?"

"On the contrary, I am late," I answered, intent upon my desire to have him know that I had been trying to do what I thought my duty. "I have an engagement with Mrs. Tyndall, and I presume she is waiting for me; but I stopped to have a quiet little talk with Frank Hooper and accomplished very little by it, I imagine."

The doctor's face lighted. "Do you mean a religious talk, Julia?" he asked eagerly.

"Yes," I said unhesitatingly. I remember it seemed to me at that time that my conversation with Frank Hooper had been very religious indeed.

"I am very glad." The doctor's words were earnest and hearty. "I have been troubled about her of late. I feared she was hardening. How does she appear to you?"

"Very bitter, indeed; she would not listen to anything I could say, but commenced a very sharp and sarcastic tirade against wealthy people. She evidently feels above her station."

I added this very loftily, as one who looked from an immense height and beheld Frank Hooper miles below me, chafing over her station.

"Against Mrs. Tyndall more particularly?" the doctor asked hesitatingly.

The question angered me.

"Oh yes," I said. "Against her, of course—everyone seems to have a special grudge against her. It must be because people see how far superior she is to them."

"Softly, Julia. The poor girl has special reason for bitterness of heart over the lady in question, and having no Christian principle to sustain her, perhaps it is not to be wondered at that she gives free rein to her feelings."

But I was not to be calmed by the doctor's quiet tones. I spoke more impatiently than before.

"Oh, of course, she has an excellent excuse for her wickedness. It is easy for you to find excuses for everyone but Mrs. Tyndall. I think she must be your embodiment of all that is evil."

His reply was grave and sad.

"Am I, then, so uncharitable, Julia?"

"Yes, you are," I said sharply. "You never omit an opportunity to speak disparagingly of her. I cannot think why you should dislike her so."

At this point old Dr. Holmes waylaid Dr. Douglass, and I went on my way alone, excited and angry, over I hardly knew what. As I expected, Mrs. Tyndall was waiting, and I hurried my toilet as much as was compatible with my lately acquired ideas of the importance of that matter.

Almost the first persons whom we met when I was again on the street were Dr. Douglass and little Ruth Walker, walking uptown and engaged in earnest conversation. Mrs. Tyndall's incredulous stare must have astonished the doctor. She hardly waited for them to pass out of hearing before she spoke.

"Now isn't that the oddest thing for a man in Dr. Douglass's position to do? What *is* the use in his parading the street with that shop girl, making a *companion* of her?"

"She is in his class, you know," I ventured to say. Someway I always had an irritating sense of being forever trying to uphold Dr. Douglass's views to Mrs. Tyndall, and Mrs. Tyndall's views to Dr. Douglass, and never succeeding in either case.

"I know," she said promptly. "And he feels a sort of interest in her, of course; but *is* that any reason why he should treat her as an equal?"

"Why, *isn't* she an equal, in the sense in which he treats her?" I asked stoutly; and she answered with a sort of surprised sweetness:

"My dear child! is this paradise, or is it the earth? Why isn't my Kate our equal? Why didn't we invite her out to make calls with us this afternoon? Why don't I bow to Judge Hervey's chambermaid when I meet her on the street? You see you will get yourself into one interminable tangle if you mix in this subject, and I advise you to keep as clear as possible of the subject and the set."

And at this point, as we turned the corner, to my absolute dismay we came face to face with Frank Hooper! And her low, mischievous bow was not returned!

It was months after that I one day reviewed that "religious conversation" which I imagined myself to hold with Frank Hooper, and I found that the only words I used that could possibly be supposed to be tinged with religion were: "Why don't you go to prayer meeting anymore?" and "Have you really *no* interest in this subject?"

10

CALLS AND COMMENTS

"THAT girl," said Mrs. Tyndall as Frank Hooper disappeared around the corner, "is insufferable to me. She has a very queer history. They were wealthy, but her father made ridiculous speculations and entered into all sorts of wild schemes and finally died bankrupt. The mother was a weak creature, without energy or spirit, and she died within three months of her husband. Then Frank was the only one left, and everybody treated her with marked kindness. I don't know how many homes opened to receive her, my own among the number; but she insolently rejected them all and went to work in this box shop, for very evident reasons: It was plain that she had resolved to ensnare Jerome Sayles, if it were a possible thing. He used to be intimate with the family before their downfall, and the kind-hearted fellow very foolishly continued the acquaintance; and sometimes I am very much afraid, what with the girl's intolerable impudence and his stepmother's malignant interference combined, that the poor boy will get into some wretched entanglement unless you rescue him, my dear."

I winced a good deal over this. There were reasons why I felt peculiarly sensitive. I asked but one question:

"Why does Mrs. Sayles interfere?"

Mrs. Tyndall laughed lightly.

"My dear, she comes from the scum herself and naturally has an affinity for the class. She was a tailoress, or something of that sort, I believe, when she contrived to entrap Mr. Sayles. I never knew that she had any particular fancy for Frank Hooper until she became a shop girl. Well, let us get this call off our list."

And while we waited on Dr. Mulford's steps I tried to cool my glowing cheeks. It had so chanced that I had not yet met Mrs. Mulford. She had been absent from home and then had been ill, and, finally, when she called on me I had not been at home. So my curiosity was great concerning her; for, of course, in this time I had heard much about her. There was quite a delay before our ring was answered, and then we were shown to the back parlor, where a very low coal fire gave us a cold greeting. There were ashes on the stove hearth and a lump of coal on the carpet, on which Mrs. Tyndall's daintily shod foot trod, and she sprang back with a nervous setting of her white teeth, as if the crunching of the coal gave her actual pain. There were two or three newspapers on the floor and a wild array of books and slates and boys' caps on the table; there was a cloak flung carelessly over the arm of the rocking chair, and a half-eaten apple on one of the window seats. Mrs. Tyndall removed a pile of schoolbooks from a chair near the door, drew the chair very close to the gloomy stove, and sank into it with a gesture of comic despair, while she brushed with her embroidered handkerchief a spot of dust from her lavender kid.

"Specimen of ministerial housekeeping, Julia—take warning," she said with an expressive glance around the disorderly room. She had long ceased the formal "Miss Ried" and adopted my Christian name. We must have been waiting at least ten minutes, and Mrs. Tyndall even suggested leaving our cards and going on when the door swung slowly open and Mrs. Mulford entered. A tall, pale woman, with her fair hair combed, straight and plain, behind her ears, and her dress a long, loose wrapper, finished at the throat with a much-wrinkled collar. She looked wan and exhausted—about half asleep, I thought. She apologized briefly for her delay and appearance: "Willie was sick, and she had not left him before that day."

"Is Willie sick again?" was Mrs. Tyndall's exclamation. "My dear Mrs. Mulford, what an unfortunate child he is!"

A weary smile flickered over the mother's pale face as she answered:

"He is a very patient little fellow and bears his frequent illnesses like a martyr."

"But what do you suppose is the reason that his constitution is so delicate? Are you *very* careful about his diet and clothing, Mrs. Mulford?"

"We try to be," was the lady's quiet answer.

"You must pardon the question," Mrs. Tyndall continued in gentle tones. "You mothers of large families, burdened with many cares, must be sorely tempted to neglect or run away from some of your responsibilities occasionally."

This remark called forth not the slightest response, and Mrs. Tyndall was forced to continue the conversation.

"Have you good help, Mrs. Mulford?" and the slightest perceptible glance of her bright eyes over the room said almost as plainly as words: I don't think it possible.

Mrs. Mulford explained that her girl was young and inexperienced, but did quite as well as could be expected; then turned to me with a kind word of greeting. After a little the talk drifted around again to question and answer, until presently Mrs. Tyndall asked:

"What do you hear from your mother, Mrs. Mulford? She is improving, I trust?"

A swift rush of color bathed cheeks and forehead, and Mrs. Mulford's voice was painfully unsteady as she answered:

"My mother has gone to her rest, Mrs. Tyndall."

Mrs. Tyndall was shocked, and mortified, and apologetic, all in one. She did not know, did not think; it had not suggested itself to her mind as a possibility—and here came a swift glance at the flowered wrapper—it was strange she had not heard of it.

"I am sorry to have troubled you with a formal call at this time," she continued, "but my ignorance of your affliction must be my excuse. I saw you, too, at Mrs. Symonds's the other evening, you remember; and I remarked to Mr. Tyndall on my return that I had neglected to inquire after your mother, but that of course she must be better, since you were out. When did it occur, Mrs. Mulford?"

Mrs. Mulford's voice was perfectly steady after that. Her face had regained its pallor, and she detailed in a calm, almost indifferent, manner various particulars concerning her recent loss, in answer to Mrs. Tyndall's questionings.

Presently Dr. Mulford was inquired for, and it appeared that he was lying down. He was broken of his rest, the pale wife explained, and was not feeling well today; indeed, he had not been well for several days. She hoped he could take a little relaxation soon. Mrs. Tyndall's eyebrows arched.

"Is he going away again?" she queried in a surprised tone. "I thought he only returned three or four weeks ago."

"He went to my mother's funeral."

"Oh; but he was away several Sabbaths, was he not?"

"One."

"Possible! I was thinking that it was two or three. But you know he is away quite frequently, and I confuse the dates. Well—"

And then followed the farewell words, and we were in the street again. We crossed the road and rang at Mrs. Symonds's. We found that lady in her elegant parlor, in elegant leisure, to receive her guests. Mrs. Tyndall gave a well-bred shiver and dropped into the low chair by the register.

"Is it so cold out?" questioned Mrs. Symonds.

Mrs. Tyndall gave one of her little silvery laughs.

"Not so cold out as in," she said. "We have just come from the parsonage, and they are economizing coal, I fancy; at least I felt as if the thermometer must be near zero. What a difference there is in rooms. *Is* the parsonage a particularly cheerless house, Mrs. Symonds? Didn't it feel so to you, Julia?"

"You know they have sickness in the house," I ventured, not prepared to say that the cold and some-what untidy room looked cheerful, and yet feeling quite willing to excuse it all.

"Is there indeed!" Mrs. Symonds said with a show of interest. "Who is ill?"

"Only their little Willie, Mrs. Symonds"; and then she turned to me with a smile.

"By the time you are as well acquainted with the family as we are, my dear, you will discover that Willie's sickness is an everyday affair."

"What is the matter with the poor little fellow?" Mrs. Symonds asked again, still bent on showing a little tenderness of heart; but her guest's answer was not encouraging.

"I'm sure I don't know—the toothache, probably; they *do* make such a sad baby of him. But, Mrs. Symonds, I want to know if you were aware of the death of Mrs. Mulford's mother? I really hadn't been so mortified in years. Why, I actually asked after her. How could I know? She came down to us in a red and green wrapper, and at church she had on that distressing green bonnet. Do you suppose they really cannot afford to wear mourning?"

"I don't know, I am sure. Perhaps she doesn't approve of the custom. You know some people do not."

"Oh, my dear Mrs. Symonds, I *hope* she doesn't belong to that class. One likes to see sincerity, at least, in a clergyman's family; and the sort of people who harp on disapproval are always those who want to economize under a false name."

Mrs. Symonds went promptly over to the enemy's side.

"Oh, it is silly, of course, and shows one to be deficient in common respect, at least so *I* think; but everyone to his taste."

Mrs. Tyndall seemed to be deeply interested in the subject.

"At least," she said, "Mrs. Mulford cannot disapprove of observing the common proprieties of life. Isn't it a very strange proceeding for her to come to your entertainment last week? I never heard of such a thing. She could not have cared for her mother, but one would suppose she would make a pretense of doing so. However, it is not my affair—only I *do* like to see people a little observant of the rules of propriety, enough so, at least, so that they need not be marks of singularity; but then some people enjoy notoriety at whatever expense it is procured. Dr. Mulford is going away again. Don't you wish our husbands could be allowed as many vacations as some pastors have?"

Mrs. Symonds only laughed in response, then asked:

"Who is going to preach for us in his absence?"

"Oh, some old agent or other, I suppose. The doctor produces some very queer people sometimes, you know, to supply his place during his frequent absences. I wish there was a law against allowing agents the use of pulpits; but I suspect that these pastors want to be very careful how they let us hear men of talent—it might affect their own position, you know."

I had never liked Mrs. Tyndall so little as I did at that moment. Her words seemed to be all pins and needles, jammed into the people with whom she talked, which is mean enough certainly, but better than that other and meaner way of pricking and scratching people who are not present to defend themselves. Also I learned afterward that Mrs. Tyndall was aware that she was talking to one of that interesting class of human beings who was such a friend to the minister's family that she would consider it her duty to rush over there at the first opportunity and retell all the items that she had heard or imagined. I joined suddenly in the conversation.

"Is it the custom in Newton for clergymen to supply their own pulpits during vacations? I always supposed that vacations were times that belonged entirely to clergymen, and that the churches had to be looked after by their officers."

Mrs. Tyndall laughed good-humoredly.

"I think you must be at least the grandchild of a clergyman," she said playfully. "It seems to be quite natural for you to battle for their rights; and you are thoroughly posted, apparently, in all their arrangements."

Which was precisely the manner in which Mrs. Tyndall always *did* answer questions that she didn't care to answer directly. She immediately arose and began the preliminary parting compliments. So the only effect of my sharply spoken words was to cut short the conversation.

"So much time saved," she said with a gleeful air as we slipped our cards under Miss Hervey's door and moved on uptown. "Mrs. Hervey is a horrid old poke; it is a perfect bore to call upon her. I'm always heartily relieved when I can make a bit of pasteboard do the disagreeable work for me."

"Why do you call on her at all then?"

"From a sense of duty, my dear. There are hosts of people that one has to call on who are bores, and whom I for one would be thankful never to see again."

I was not by any means in the mood to listen patiently to any of Mrs. Tyndall's peculiar views, so I said curtly:

"Do you imagine that the hosts of people would thank you for your calls if they knew your high opinion of them?"

"Not a bit of it; and it is one of the comforts of my life that people can't know what I'm thinking of them. I'm very careful not to inform them, I assure you."

"I don't believe in that sort of thing," I said stoutly.

"I think it is just hypocrisy. I'm certain I never want people to call on me unless they have a desire to see me; and I mean to treat others as I would have them treat me."

Mrs. Tyndall answered me by that low sweet laugh of unfailing good humor; then she said:

"My dear Julia, do you know you would be a bit of a feminine Don Quixote now and then if I were not here to balance you? Just imagine where your peculiar views would lead me. Suppose, for instance, that I do not return Mrs. Hervey's next call, and the next time I meet her she will exclaim: My dear Mrs. Tyndall, why *haven't* you been to see me this *age?* And I shall respond: The truth is, Mrs. Hervey, it's because I consider you a horrid bore. You know you never talk about anything except your rheumatism and your neuralgia and the damp weather when I do come, and I am perfectly sick of those topics, so I have decided to be sincere and not call on you anymore. Now, Julia, do you really think I should be doing my duty better in that way than in returning the old lady's call and enduring with what patience I can her tiresome tongue?"

Nonplussed again, I knew there was a flaw somewhere, somehow, but I had no words with which to answer. Remember that I was only sixteen; besides, her queer statement of the case made me laugh.

The doctor came late to breakfast the next morning after being out most of the night.

"Have you been to visit a patient so early?" Mrs. Tyndall questioned, and he replied gravely that he had just come from Dr. Mulford's.

"Ah," she said, "they keep you dancing attendance on Willie, I suppose. It is well that you are generous in the matter of clergymen's bills. Is there really much the matter with the boy, Doctor, except overpetting?"

I don't think she ever forgot the look of Dr. Douglass's eyes as he answered her:

"No, madam, there is nothing the matter with him, nor ever will be anymore. God has taken the worn-out little frame into his own peculiar keeping."

Then was Mrs. Tyndall surprised and shocked and grieved. I do not think that anyone in Dr. Mulford's flock excelled her in kind and thoughtful and delicate attentions during the next sad days. Nevertheless as we stood together on the afternoon of the funeral and looked down upon the peaceful face in his coffin, she whispered to me:

"How perfectly singular in her not to wear mourning, and what wretched taste to wear that plaid dress to her own child's funeral!"

11

THE HEAD LEADS THE HEART

IT was about this time that I worked myself into a perfect fever of anxiety over a waterfall. Not the falls of Niagara, nor any of those wondrous lesser glories of that name, but an indescribable *wad* to wear fastened by innumerable pins on the back of my head. My hair was a rich golden brown and was long and plentiful—at least so it had once seemed to me; but do what I would, work and twist until midnight and cry with vexation afterward, I could by no means create the nondescript creature that ladies were at that time in the habit of perching on their heads. My heart had been bitter within me ever since the day in which Mrs. Tyndall had said—

"How very prettily you arrange your hair. I don't see how you manage it yourself; Kate has to do mine. But, my dear, do you know you sadly need a braid of hair to band around the back part? Then you could push the side braids further forward, and you would have an elegantly shaped waterfall. Really, when nature has done so much for you, it is almost wicked not to do the rest."

"But braids of hair are expensive articles," I said, and tried to make my tone an indifferent one.

"Oh, not so very. An elegant short one can be procured for ten dollars; and you know your waterfall really hasn't the right shape without one."

After that, I tried in vain to *make* it the right shape. It is amazing to me, even now, to think what an exceedingly awkward shape it seemed to take after that talk. The subject began to haunt me. It came to me in church, in the midst of Dr. Mulford's sermons. It stared at me from the pages of my Bible. I dreamed of it at night, and thought, and planned, and worried about it by day. How to get a braid of *real* hair to band around my waterfall—that was the momentous question. It must be *real* hair; for Mrs. Tyndall had emphatically declared that she considered all imitations unendurable. There was one way in which to do it. I had been planning certain little gifts for Mother and Sadie and Alfred. I had in mind exactly what each would like. I had packaged them in imagination in a neat little box and written the accompanying letter scores of times; and I had discovered what the whole would cost, and most provokingly the figures stared at my troubled heart during those trying days, for they expressed the exact sum that would also buy that braid of hair. At last the long struggle was concluded. A chance word settled it. When I was dressing for Mrs. Symonds's social Mrs. Tyndall came into my room with a ticket for the Reading-room—a Christmas gift from Mr. Tyndall—and remarked as she watched me braid my hair:

"Your hair is precisely the color that Jerome is always raving over. He says the greatest charm a woman can possess is a great mass of goldy brown hair."

Instead of stopping to moralize over the astonishing amount of mental and moral culture that a woman would have to possess before she could be gifted with this "greatest charm," I hastened my dressing, went out a little ahead of Mrs. Tyndall "to do some errands," and, when I returned, had a braid of "goldy brown" hair tucked guiltily under my shawl.

Poor, silly me! I remember I sat up half the night to fashion a collar for Sadie and to try to construct a cap for Mother that would look as good as new out of a worn-out lace veil; and finally *cried* over the queer shape of the crown and the general air of used-up-ness that the wretched black thing had about it. Oh, the trials of poverty—and waterfalls.

But didn't I blossom out on New Year's morning! Talk of Solomon arrayed in all his glory; it didn't seem to me that he could have compared with me. My black silk had been in the hands of Mrs. Tyndall's favorite dressmaker for three days and returned to me bristling with ruffles and perfect as to pannier—in all respects a wonderful creation. My laces were rich and soft and elegant: befitting the donor. They were Mrs. Tyndall's Christmas gift. I had gathered from the conservatory geranium leaves and a single spray of rare, bright blossoms, which did duty in lieu of a breastpin; and, finally, I was crowned with that magnificent braid of hair, which Mrs. Tyndall pronounced perfect. That lady would have made a study for an artist. She wore her favorite color—a delicate, trying shade of blue—exquisite as to trimming and finish, as faultless in taste as in material. And, arrayed thus, we waited in the handsome parlors for New Year's calls. It was my first experience in that scene of the whisking in and out of half a dozen gentlemen at a time, so constantly followed by half a dozen more that presently one lost one's balance and ceased to remember people as individuals, but as number forty-five or sixty-two, as the case might be, and, as the day whirled on, was dimly conscious of but one idea—an eager desire to reach a higher number than Mrs. Symonds or Miss Hervey, and Mrs. or Miss anybody else. I thought it delightful.

"My patience!" Mrs. Tyndall exclaimed, as, during a momentary lull in which we were alone, something across the street surprised her out of her elegant listlessness, "if there isn't Dr. Mulford making calls! Now, of all the queer things! *Doesn't* that man know that he will not be expected to make calls today? It isn't three weeks since the funeral. Really, Julia, I never saw people in my life so utterly devoid of a sense of propriety as that family seems to be. They are always doing queer things. I do wish there was some way of teaching them how to act. Dear me, he is coming here. I shan't know what to say to him."

Nevertheless, she arose to receive him with the utmost ease and strongly marked expression of gratification.

"This is an *unexpected* pleasure," she said in silvery tones, but with a marked emphasis on the word "unexpected," as, having greeted me with earnestly spoken wishes, he seated himself near her. "I did not suppose we could have you among us today."

Dr. Mulford turned a pair of kindly, but deep-questioning eyes on the speaker's face and smiled quietly as he answered:

"Why was that, Mrs. Tyndall? Am I not supposed to be in a frame of mind to clasp hands with any of my people and wish them Godspeed through the year, because my boy has gone to spend his New Year in heaven?"

I looked to see Mrs. Tyndall confused or silenced. She was neither. Her voice was sweet and prompt:

"If you *can* feel so, Dr. Mulford, I am glad. But it seems to me so sad a thing. It is so recent, you know."

"I know," he said gravely. "It is sad to miss Willie, and I think, if I shall be living until next New Year's Day, it will still be sad to miss him. But you know I shall not then be justified in deserting my social duties because of my sadness; so I cannot see what should justify me today."

Mrs. Tyndall gracefully changed the subject:

"Doctor, I must not offer you wine, I know, but you will not refuse all refreshment?"

But ere she could carry out her designs, he detained her by a gesture and a word of courteous refusal, while his face saddened into a look of absolute pain, and his voice low and full of sorrow as he added:

"Mrs. Tyndall, in addition to my social call, I had an errand here today, a favor to ask."

"Which I shall doubtless be most happy to grant," she said with a deferential bend of her handsome head, and waited with smiling eyes while her pastor hesitated, and his pale face flushed painfully as he spoke:

"You sympathize with my boy in heaven, my friend, and I thank you; but can you understand me if I tell you that I would be thankful today if his brother was as safe as Willie is?"

Mrs. Tyndall's face grew grave, and she waited in respectful silence until he continued:

"I would have been thankful, I think, for almost anything that would have shielded him from the dangers and temptations of the day. You know his besetting sin, Mrs. Tyndall, and my petition is that you will offer no wine to him if he calls on you today."

His hostess looked relieved and even laughed slightly.

"Is that all, Doctor?" she said brightly. "You frightened me. Indeed, I think you are too hard on Norman for a little boyish folly. But you may trust me. I will not offer him a drop of anything dangerous."

"I think it is all absurd," she said to me as the door closed after him. "Perfectly absurd. I wonder if Dr. Mulford is going to march all over town and caution the people against demoralizing that precious son of his? How perfectly shocking in him to say that he would be thankful if Norman were dead! Poor boy, I don't wonder that he drinks, if that is a specimen of his father's regards."

"He didn't say so," I exclaimed, shocked into protest. "He said if Norman were as safe as Willie."

"It amounts to the same thing. According to his delightful theory, people are never safe until they get to heaven."

We were interrupted by more callers; and presently Norman Mulford was announced—a bright, handsome boy of nineteen, fair-faced, except for a slightly unnatural flush. He was fresh from college honors, and seemed almost intoxicated with triumph and wine—just the sort of boy to be led into all sorts of temptation. As I looked at him, there was something about him that reminded me of Alfred, and I felt as though I could understand something of the trembling of the father's heart over his eldest son. He was in an unusually brilliant mood, and flashed quick, witty replies to Mrs. Tyndall's brightnesses; they were pleasant to listen to, or would have been, had not the question of refreshment still worried me dreadfully. Of course his hostess would not offer him wine, for she had promised his father; but with the glittering glasses and sparkling liquid in full view, I did not quite understand how it was to be avoided. Mrs. Tyndall appeared to. She chatted on gracefully, without a shade of embarrassment or indecision and, at last, after other refreshments had been served, said winningly:

"I can't offer you any wine, Norman; for you see, I have promised to be very good today and not tempt you."

A rich, dark flush mounted swiftly over the young man's face, but he answered with apparent indifference:

"Pray, who ought I to thank for being so deeply interested in my welfare?"

"One who, I am sure, is always interested in you and anxious for you, your good father. He has taken pains to come and see me today about this very matter. So you see how anxious he is."

I wondered that she hadn't checked her words by the stormy glare that came into the young man's eyes, and his voice shook with suppressed passion as he spoke:

"I am very grateful to my father, I assure you, Mrs. Tyndall; also to you. I wouldn't have you break your promise; but, I suppose you did not also promise that I should not help myself at your hospitable table?"

Whereupon he walked directly over to the refreshment table, and deliberately poured for himself a goblet of wine, drained the glass, and then immediately made his adieus.

"Mrs. Tyndall, how could you?" I exclaimed, almost before he was out of hearing.

"How could I what, my dear Julia? How flushed your cheeks are. Is it too warm in here?"

"I thought you promised Dr. Mulford not to offer him liquor."

"I'm sure I didn't. He waited on himself," and she laughed good-humoredly. "What could I do? Would you have had me rush after him and frantically demand his glass and dash it to the ground? You might have done it, my dear (only it would have injured my carpet), but I am past the age of heroics. You see," speaking more gravely, "there is nothing left for me to do. I frankly stated the case, and he chose to take the matter into his own hands. I cannot engage to be conscience for him. It serves his father right. If he had taught his son, by precept and example, the impropriety of making calls at all today, all these temptations, as he is pleased to call them, would have been avoided. However, gay young men do not often change their plans for such slight causes. It is all nonsense. I'll risk Norman. What if he does drink a glass of wine now and then? So do all gentlemen."

I here interposed: "Dr. Douglass never does."

There was a very slight curving of Mrs. Tyndall's lips, but her voice was sweet and ladylike.

"Dr. Douglass, my dear, is a saint. He is never at any time to be classed with common, fallible mortals; we must always remember that. As I was saying, all gentlemen take wine, except a few fanatical creatures, capable of but one idea at a time. I think if Norman Mulford becomes a drunkard, it will be his father's foolish interference and mismanagement that will be to blame. Young men do not like to be led around like babies."

12

A SLIPPERY PATH

OUR next caller was Mr. Sayles. His stay was very brief. He looked flushed and tired, yet seemed nervous and unnaturally excited; declined Mrs. Tyndall's tempting cake; begged her not even to mention the name, as he was perfectly surfeited; but he drank a full glass of wine; and, after making arrangements to call and escort me to Mrs. Bacon's New Year's party, he pronounced New Year's calls a bore, gallantly declared this to be the only one that he had enjoyed, and took his leave.

The day was on the wane, and Mrs. Tyndall had gone to her dressing room to rest when Dr. Douglass came in and sat himself down with a weary air. I felt very sorry to see him and earnestly wished I had escaped to my room before he came in. I felt instinctively during these days that Dr. Douglass disapproved of my mode of life. Whenever I was in his presence my conscience became uncomfortable; so, of late, I had compromised matters by avoiding him. I felt a curious sense of restraint, as if I could think of nothing to say, and yet did not feel sufficiently familiar with him to sit in absolute silence—a thing that I would have done unhesitatingly but a few weeks before.

"Have you been making calls?" I asked at last.

"Professional ones," he answered wearily. "I have had time for no others."

Then the silence fell again between us, until at last he broke it again abruptly:

"Julia, are you going out this evening?"

"Yes," I said; "I am going to Mrs. Bacon's for a little while. Are you going?"

"With Mrs. Tyndall?" he asked, ignoring my question.

"Why, no. Mrs. Tyndall is not going. It is for young people, you know."

"May I ask, then, who accompanies you?"

I gave the answer slowly and with an unaccountable reluctance:

"I am going with Mr. Sayles."

Silence again, for a few moments; then he spoke with unusual gravity:

"Julia, may I ask as a special favor that you will not go out with Mr. Sayles this evening?"

"Your favor comes at a late hour," I said with the utmost stiffness. "I have *engaged* to accompany the gentleman."

"Nevertheless, I repeat my petition. Offer some excuse, will you not? I am very anxious that you should, Julia."

"Perhaps you can furnish a reason for so strange a *demand?*" I said with sharp emphasis on the last word.

"I can, certainly," he answered gravely. "Have you seen him today?"

"I have."

"It must have been early, then. He has been making New Year's calls."

This last was spoken in stern tones; but I answered him sharply:

"What of that?"

He waited a moment ere he answered:

"I presume he has been offered wine constantly. It has been a day of sore temptation to many."

His voice had taken a quieter, kinder tone, but mine was as abrupt as ever as I asked haughtily:

"What does all this talk amount to, Dr. Douglass?"

He turned then and looked at me steadily ere he answered:

"Is it possible, Julia, that you do not understand? I mean that I do not think Mr. Sayles will be in a condition to take proper care of any lady this evening; certainly he will not, if he finishes the day as he has commenced it."

There were reasons why this gave me special pain and made me answer in a specially bitter tone:

"I suppose, Dr. Douglass, I can be allowed to be my own judge as to the propriety of the company I choose to keep. I certainly intend to fulfill my engagement this evening. I really do not understand why you have such a hatred of Mr. Sayles, nor how you can find it in harmony with your Christian character to exhibit that hatred on every possible occasion."

To this silly ebullition of wrath the doctor vouchsafed not the slightest response. As may be supposed, I went to my room soon after, not feeling particularly improved in spirits. I could not but be conscious that I was doing wrong. In the first place, there was my mother, who I knew was resting in the happy belief that I was under Dr. Douglass's protecting wing and that therefore no harm could reach me. Also, I felt a little afraid. Could he have meant that Mr. Sayles was intoxicated? I had never in my life been closer to a drunken man than across the road, and even then I had been frightened, and more than once taken shelter in a store or shop until the frightful object had disappeared around some corner. I tried to picture Mr. Sayles—elegant, fastidious gentleman that he was—reeling and staggering through the streets, and shuddering at the frightful picture that I conjured, I took refuge from my thoughts in Mrs. Tyndall's room. That lady had exchanged her elegant attire for a dainty blue flannel wrapper and was lying on the lounge in a state of semiexhaustion.

"I wish I had your spirits," she said languidly. "How fresh and bright you look, while I am nearly dead. My dear, let that blossom droop a little over your left ear—so. Jerome will be charmed with those flowers. He is a great admirer of natural adornments. Your face is a little too much flushed. What is the matter? I heard the doctor come in; has he been quarreling with you?"

"I have been having a curtain lecture," I said, trying to laugh.

"About what, in the name of wonder? Dr. Douglass couldn't be more disagreeable if he were your grandfather. What has offended him now?"

"He thinks Mr. Sayles has been taking wine too freely to be a suitable escort," I said, bent on knowing her opinion of the matter.

"What utter nonsense," she said with spirit. "That is really wicked in Dr. Douglass. Because he is a monomaniac himself on the wine question is no reason why he should insult gentlemen who do not happen to agree with him. But that is too apt to be the way with these extra good people. They wrap themselves up in an I-am-holier-than-thou atmosphere and stalk about the world, hitting against everybody. I hope, my dear, you didn't allow him to prejudice you against poor Jerome?"

"Certainly not," I said loftily. "I can judge for myself with whom to associate without Dr. Douglass's help."

At that moment I received summons to the effect that Mr. Sayles was waiting for me.

The evening at Mrs. Bacon's was a very gay one. With but few exceptions the company were all quite youthful, and the excitement of the day had not tended to foster very quiet spirits within us, so we talked, and laughed, and danced, and performed impromptu tableaux, all with a sort of wild glee that rather heightened than diminished as the hours waned. Occasionally I had an uneasy feeling about my escort; his eyes looked unnaturally bright, and his voice, I imagined, was not quite clear, but he was unusually quiet; and I noticed with a thrill of satisfaction that at the supper table he refused wine, apologizing for doing so by saying that he had a confounded headache and must avoid stimulus, whereupon I moralized upon Dr. Douglass's uncharitableness. When at last it was decided that we *must* go home, and a bevy of us escaped to the cloakroom together, a fearful scene ensued. Very free use had been made of the wraps in the dressing room for our impromptu charades and tableaux, and shawls, cloaks, hoods, and rubbers were in inextricable confusion. One rubber was not. I ransacked everywhere—and when, after what seemed an endless time, I found it rolled in shawls and tossed among the pillows, my hood was missing; then ensued an eager search for that, and I think a full half hour must have elapsed before I emerged from the dressing room properly cloaked, hooded, and rubbered. That fatal half hour!

Half a dozen young ladies were in the same plight as myself, and our escorts, weary of waiting, had resorted with the son of the house to the supper room to beguile the time. I did not know this until afterward; but I knew as soon as we reached the sidewalk, before I had even said good night to the four or five who were departing at the same time, none of whom chanced to be going in my direction, that my hand rested on the arm of a man who did not in the least know what he was about. Shall I ever forget that night? The silent, solemn moonlight, flooding a world that seemed so strangely quiet in contrast with the gay scene I had just left; the white slippery earth, just a deceitful glare of ice; and the silly, unutterably silly face that was bent close to mine, while the sickening odor of liquor breathed on me from every one of the meaningless words that he tried to utter. The walk was long and the streets apparently deserted, and we stumbled and staggered along, once actually fell outright— and then the shame and horror and terror even of the struggle that I had to help him on his feet again—and he laughed and hiccoughed, and called me Julia, and was in every way disgusting. As we turned into Park Street the walk was just a smooth glare of ice.

"We'll have to go in the road," I said breathlessly as I felt my companion's grasp on my arm tightening and his heavy frame swaying to and fro.

"B-b-blamed if I will," he stammered. "L-Let the d-d-darned ole road c-come *here* if it w-wants to be walked on. W-what's the use of going to it? Keep a st-stiff upper lip, Julia. We'll get the b-b-better of the old thing, somehow."

And no arguments nor entreaties of mine could prevail upon him to leave the icy sidewalk, which in his drunken folly he seemed to imagine was somebody trying to conquer him; and he muttered and stuttered something about "Not g-going to be b-beat by any old sidewalk that ever g-g-grew." Oh, the agony of that long walk! I never took it again, even under brighter circumstances, without a shiver of horror over this remembrance. I thought of trying to slip away from him and flying homeward alone, but he held my arm with a viselike grasp and added to my awful disgust. I grew every moment more afraid of him. He seemed to grow more senseless every moment, and began to utter little shrill shrieks occasionally that made my blood run cold. At the corner of Greene and Regent Streets a parley ensued. His home was on Regent Street, a few doors from the corner. He seemed to have sense enough left to know that fact and to be determined to go in that direction, dragging me with him. I pled and entreated; talked to him as I would to a naughty child; begged him to go home, just a few steps more, just around the corner, and let me go down on Greene Street alone. It was of no use. He laughed that disgustingly silly laugh of a drunken man, and declared he wouldn't give up the ship—meant to take me safely home—I needn't be afraid. I was in an agony of shame and terror. Supposing that he knew enough to recognize his own house when he reached it, how was it possible for me to appear there, at the door of my employer's house, long after midnight, with his drunken son grasping my arm like a madman? I pulled desperately in the opposite direction, and he as desperately pulled toward Regent Street, and then lost his balance entirely and fell heavily. I struggled then to free myself, but he grasped my cloak with both hands and uttered a fearful yell. No, I never, never shall forget it all—the terror, the shame, the absolute agony, not the sound of swift-coming feet, nor the voice, startled, stern even in its sound, but steady, and safe, and true. Just one word in which was embodied astonishment and pain.

"Julia!" And then Dr. Douglass stood beside me, seeming in an instant to comprehend the situation. I ceased to struggle the moment I heard his voice. He took my hand and drew it firmly through his arm, that *steady* arm; then fixing stern eyes on my companion, spoke to him:

"Let go of this lady." Which command was, to my surprise, instantly obeyed.

"Now get up." In this, however, he had to give help.

Then he glanced swiftly up and down the street and addressed me.

"Julia, it is very cold; it would be inhuman to leave him here. I think you will have to let me take him home."

I was silent and passive; and presently we commenced our walk down Regent Street, Dr. Douglass supporting my rather trembling steps with his left arm and steadying, indeed it seemed to me almost carrying, my drunken escort with his strong right arm. He meantime tried to give a lucid explanation of our fight, as he called it, and tried to express himself gratified that he had been the victor, but was checked by a stern "Be still, sir." Whereupon his conversation subsided into the silliest of silly whimpers, more degrading, it seemed to me, than his talk had been.

Arrived at his father's door, Dr. Douglass seated him on the steps with no gentle hand, gave a jerk to the bell that sent it pealing through the house, then turned and sped with me, swiftly and silently, through the streets. Only three words were uttered during our rapid walk.

"Are you cold?" he asked, and I shook my head; but

he wrapped his shawl more closely around me, and on we rushed. Reaching the door he applied his night key, turned on a flood of gas in the hall to light me upstairs and said in his usual kind grave tone, "Good night."

13

A FALSE LIGHT

IT was a wretched night to me. After living over all the horrors of that walk with my waking senses, feeling anew the terror, and disgrace, and shame, and pain, I finally slept and went over, in detail, every little incident of the evening; adding to its horrors by every phantasm that my excited, unreasoning brain could conjure. I was thankful for morning; and yet felt ashamed to meet the household. However, that ordeal was safely passed. Dr. Douglass had apparently no remembrance of the frightful scene through which we had so lately passed together. He neither by word, look, nor act alluded to it, except that perhaps he seemed a trifler gentler to me than usual. After scanning Mrs. Tyndall's face as narrowly as I could, I concluded that she was in blissful ignorance of the entire affair, a fact which rather surprised me; for I had come to feel as if she must discover things by a sort of instinct—so prompt and complete was her knowledge of what was transpiring around her. But on this morning she chatted gaily about the party, asking numerous questions about the entertainment, quoted "Jerome" as freely as usual, and seemed entirely at ease and satisfied with everything. At the shop I heard, or rather overheard, that Mr. Sayles had gone somewhere by the early train. Caroline Brighton informed us that she accompanied him to the depot (with a mischievous look divided between Frank Hooper and myself).

"Where is he going?" Frank asked in an indifferent tone; while I felt my face flush to my very temples at the very mention of his name; and I listened nervously for Caroline's answer.

"Couldn't say. I'm in doubt as to whether he knew himself. I asked him; but he answered me very savagely that he was going to the northeast corner of Nowhere, if such a place was to be found. The fact is, he seemed to be in a sad state of mind. I asked him if anybody had refused him, to make him so good-natured?"

This, with a side glance at me; and my cheeks flamed again at the bare thought of what torture such questions must have been to him. Frank seemed entirely unconcerned, and I concluded that at least Mrs. Tyndall must have been mistaken about her.

Meantime, other matters were coming up to claim every leisure moment. The festival that was postponed at Christmastime, because of the illness of some of the prominent workers, was now in full process of preparation—rehearsal for the tableaux and music nearly every evening, and constant planning as to costumes, characters, etc.—in the midst of which I tried to analyze my feelings toward Mr. Sayles. Indignation mixed strongly with the touch of compassion that I had for him; and there had been at first a very decided determination to have nothing more to do with him. But as the days passed, and he seemed willing to take it for granted that all friendship was over between us, a certain sense of pique began to mix with my just indignation; and I said to myself that it would have been more gentlemanly in him to have attempted an apology than to have maintained such a stupid silence. I heard of his return. Our town gossip, Caroline Brighton, announced to us one morning that "Jerome Sayles had just got back from Nowhere, and that his trip did not seem to have improved his temper." But I saw not a glimpse of him and felt guilty and confused when Mrs. Tyndall innocently wondered why Jerome did not call.

It was the fifth day after the party that the doctor came to the shop with my mail. There were long letters from my mother and Sadie, and a drop letter, stylish and graceful in form and penmanship. Frank Hooper passed my desk as I was curiously examining the envelope of my unknown correspondent, and as she glanced down at it I noticed a little pink flush on her cheek. Then I broke the seal with a sudden surmise as to who it was and read:

REGENT STREET, *Friday Evening.*

Miss Ried—

Five days ago, in the event of addressing a note to you, I should have added, My Dear Friend; but tonight I am bitterly conscious of having forfeited all right to call you friend. I have been silent during these fearful days because I could think of no fitting words to couch my—I cannot call it explanation or apology, because such conduct as mine, I am well aware, cannot be explained away; and even to attempt an apology may seem to you insulting. Yet I cannot pass it by longer in silence. I have thought of the matter during these five fearful days and nights in all its phases, and I can but think that if you could imagine one-tenth of the pain that I have experienced during this time, even *you* would feel an emotion of pity for me. I have finally decided to break the silence and—not cast myself on your mercy, for I am conscious that I have no right to claim mercy at your hand, but to beg, implore, your forgiveness. I do not offer it as an explanation, but simply as a fact that I was ill New Year's Day, and that the small amount of wine that I drank had a most unaccountable effect on me— an effect of which I had not dreamed. It was no greater quantity than I have taken many times before with the most perfect ease. I have no memory of what passed that evening; so I do not know what you have to forgive. I only know that it is a great thing to ask; and yet I ask it. I fancy you superior to most young ladies of my acquaintance. I think, when one who has insulted you, though how unintentional only God knows, comes to you frankly, humbly, and says, Forgive me, that your own Christian character will prompt you to listen to his petition. I ask even more than this: that you will not only forgive, but prove your deed by allowing me to call you friend as heretofore. I value your friendship, Julia, enough to sue for it in this lowly manner. More I could not say. I am asking great things; and yet earnestly believe not too great for your large-hearted nobleness of character to grant. I beg that you will answer me by letter; and I pray you, Julia, to grant me an interview. If you will name an hour when you will see me, I shall know then how to thank you.

Yours sadly, but hopefully,
JEROME J. SAYLES

This letter touched me; touched my heart and my vanity. I gave little thought to the vanity then—I gave my heart the credit of all the softened feelings. But I know now that vanity had at least as much to do with it as heart. I was anxious to be "superior to most young ladies." And yet I was very much disgusted with Mr. Sayles. It was curious; but during these intervening days I had not been able to hold the image of Mr. Sayles, the fastidious, courteous, cultured gentleman of my acquaintance, before my eyes. I continually saw that silly-faced creature who floundered on the icy pavement on the never-to-be-forgotten night. I studied over the letter. What should I do—what ought I to do? I earnestly tried to think what would be right. I had seemed to myself to be more under Dr. Douglass's influence during this past week; and I instantly wondered what he would think about it. I remembered penitently that my mother wished me to be guided by him, and I took a sudden resolution to consult him. Chance favored me as I was hurrying homeward at noon. He joined me. I plunged nervously into my subject:

"Doctor, how do you think one ought to treat a person who has injured you, and afterward asks your forgiveness?"

"One ought to follow the Master's own rule—Whatsoever ye would."

"I know—of course that is the guide—and yet—Well, should matters be just the same with such persons as they were before?"

"Ah! that is a question which requires very careful consideration and a definite knowledge of what one is talking about. I can conceive of cases where, with the most complete forgiveness, friendship should by no means be based on the old footing—for instance:

One may have decided that the influence of an acquaintance is injurious. That association is unwise, and in that case, undoubtedly it should be avoided. But I am talking in the dark, Julia. If you feel willing to explain yourself to me, I may be able to help you."

My answer was low and somewhat hesitating:

"I was thinking of Mr. Sayles,"—and I was conscious of receiving a very searching look before he said:

"Has he sued for your forgiveness?"—and when I bowed in reply, he added with emphasis: "He certainly has sufficient reason."

I immediately roused to the defensive:

"He was ill on New Year's evening, and the small amount of wine that he took affected him as it never had before."

The doctor's answer was quick and decisive:

"Don't allow him to impose on you in that absurd way. I have had experience with drunken men and know whereof I speak. The man was simply intoxicated. My only wonder is that he was in a state to come for you at all. I met him three times during that day, and each time saw him swallow liquor enough to intoxicate a habitually sober man. Twice I warned him that he was in a dangerous condition; but he gaily assured me that he was used to it."

This shocked and disgusted me, and I had no disposition to continue my defense, even if I could have found any arguments. So I remained silent, and, after walking the length of a block without speaking, the doctor continued:

"I hope and trust that you may be able to forgive him. But it was a grievous insult. The man must have known that he was in no condition for ladies' society. I told him at five o'clock that he had lost the power of walking straight, and begged him to plead indisposition and send an apology; but he was so far gone that he swore at me for my pains. I am very sorry for poor victims who are led away by the clamor of an awful appetite. But when a man deliberately boasts, as he did twice to me on New Year's Day, the amount of liquor that his brain will endure, I have little charity for him. Aside from this, Julia, the man is not what your mother would like to have an associate of yours be. If you will forgive me for advising you, I would use the opportunity for breaking an acquaintance that can result in nothing but annoyance and discomfort to you."

"But," I said hesitatingly, "suppose I should be the means of discouraging him and helping him downward?"

"Has he begun to help himself upward? Does he promise that similar disgrace shall be spared his friends in the future?"

I was startled by the question, and hastily ran over in my mind the note I had received. There were certainly no promises or resolutions for the future expressed in it. True, they might be inferred from the general tenor of the letter; and yet, if he continued to indulge his taste for liquor, how was he to be certain that no disgraceful consequence would ensue? And I felt certain that Mr. Sayles continued his allowance of wine, even during these days of distress and anxiety. The doctor, finding I made no answer to his question, continued the conversation:

"That idea of discouraging people ought to be sparingly indulged in. In the first place, we ought to be very sure that there is any genuine attempt at reformation; and secondly, that we are strong enough, spiritually, to help tide our friends over the dangerous places."

By this time we had reached the door, and Mrs. Tyndall met us in the hall. So further conversation was impossible. But my resolution was formed, or rather confirmed to have nothing more to do with Mr. Sayles. I was very much puzzled as to how to reply to his letter, and, after thinking about it most of the afternoon, to the great detriment of my account book, I finally decided to make no reply at all; at least for the present. I thought my silence would sufficiently assure him of my desire to drop the friendship; and as for my forgiveness, I concluded that when the next chance threw us together it would be time enough to say a few words on that subject.

We were sitting together the following evening, Mrs. Tyndall and I. There was to be a rehearsal in the hall at seven o'clock, and we had but an hour in which to arrange a toilet for Queen Vashti. Mrs. Tyndall held an exquisite coronal up for my admiration as she questioned:

"Have you seen Jerome today, Julia?"

"No," I answered with deeply flushing cheeks.

"Where can he keep himself? Provoking fellow! I think we shall have to send a note to him. He ought to be present this very evening to practice for that Turkish scene. It is going to need a great deal of practice; and your part is so involved in his that one alone can do almost nothing."

I answered in dire confusion:

"I am not going to take part in the Turkish scene, Mrs. Tyndall. I thought you knew—I mean I thought you had given that up."

"My dear child, I never give anything up—least of all a thing so perfectly beautiful as that Turkish scene is going to be. I expect it to be the crown of all our tableaux."

"Nevertheless," I said steadily, "I cannot take my part. I am very sorry to disappoint you; but it is quite impossible."

Mrs. Tyndall turned her crown thoughtfully around on her hand and said:

"Look here, Julia, don't you think this would be improved if we had one more diamond pin for the left side?" before she made answer to my last remark. It was a way she had, to appear quite interested in her work and but partially attentive to what you were saying—if you chanced to be saying something that you thought would specially move her ire. Then she said:

"I am sorry you did not tell me of your determination before. Explanations are so exceedingly disagreeable; and of course all our party know that you are to be associated with Mr. Sayles in this scene. What am I to say, my dear? That you and he have had a quarrel? It was only last evening we were talking about it—the tableau, not the quarrel—and I explained to Lycia Symonds how it was arranged."

I felt confused and annoyed, but strangely determined not to take Mrs. Tyndall into my confidence. So I answered with what playfulness I could assume:

"You may say that I have done that astonishing thing never done by woman before—changed my mind."

My companion remained silent, and apparently thoughtful, for some moments. When I stole a glance at her face, it had undergone one of the most marked changes of which her face was capable. There was a look of sweet, plaintive sadness about her eyes, and a tremulous tenderness about the mouth, and her voice was low and unutterably sweet and gentle.

"My dear, may I ask you a very solemn question? Are you doing just right in this matter? I have looked on with very deep interest during the past week to see what would be the result of all this. It seems to me that you hold a life in your hands. Poor Jerome! If you would see him, you would understand something of what he has suffered; and if you knew him as well as I do, you would tremble for what might be the consequence of this utter ignoring of his existence. He has had heavy troubles, has been weighed down with disappointment, and yet has contrived not to make shipwreck of himself. I have been so deeply interested in him for so many years, it seems as if he were my brother; and, Julia, I have looked to you to help him. He needs help, needs leading, and I know you can do it; and you can drive him into fury, too, if you choose. Would you rather save him or help push him down?"

I was touched by her words. Yes, and flattered. I see the last plainly, now. *Was* I really such a power in his life as that? I answered in not as decided a voice as I had used before:

"There are circumstances, Mrs. Tyndall, which make it quite impossible for me to continue as a personal friend of Mr. Sayles."

Mrs. Tyndall's eyebrows arched in that peculiar way she had, and her next sentence was full of surprise.

"Julia, I thought you were a temperance woman."

Upon this she knew I prided myself. So I answered with emphasis:

"I am, decidedly."

"I shouldn't have imagined it, my dear, from your present mode of procedure. I assure you, dear child, if you want to make a drunkard of Jerome Sayles, you couldn't take a more certain way than to cut his acquaintance; and how can you do that more thoroughly than to give up this project that has been so publicly planned and discussed? I know Jerome thoroughly, Julia, and I would not assume such a responsibility as you are assuming for *anything*. I presume you think I am talking ignorantly—that I know nothing about the circumstances of which you spoke; but I do. I know every little detail. I knew it at the time it occurred. Mr. Tyndall had to meet the late train that night, and he came uptown just after Dr. Douglass. Then I heard it since from the poor fellow himself. I never saw anyone so completely overcome. It isn't an hour, Julia, since he was here and begged and entreated me to get you to see him. I promised I would try, and told him he might call at half past six to know the result. But, afterward, I determined not to interfere in the matter, but to leave it entirely to your own conscience. Only remember that your responsibility is fearful."

Silence fell between us after that. Presently a little marble clock on the mantle chimed the half hour, and almost immediately a servant appeared with a message—

"Mr. Sayles in the back parlor to see Miss Ried."

And I went down, in a slow and bewildered way, to meet him.

14

STUNG WITH THE TRUTH

AS my hand rested on the knob of the door, I still had in mind the image of Mr. Sayles as he lay floundering about on the ice, but it vanished the moment my eyes glanced on the pale, troubled, cultured face that turned quickly to meet me.

"Oh, Miss Ried!" he said eagerly. "God bless you for this. You have done for me—I cannot tell you what."

He came toward me quickly and grasped my hand as he continued to speak in an eager, excited tone:

"I have suffered—no mortal knows how much— since yesterday evening, when I watched in vain for a line from you. The pain grew insupportable today, and I felt compelled to throw myself on Mrs. Tyndall's mercy. Yet, do you know, I only half trusted your goodness after all? When I told Mrs. Tyndall to tell you from me that unless you came to me willingly to forgive and forget, I could not endure to meet you at all—and to refuse to see me if you could not do this—I was sorry the moment the door closed after her; and in the intervening time I have undergone tortures, lest you should decline to see me at all."

He need not have feared. I had received no such message. I tried to tell him so; but he was in such eager haste to talk, to explain, to palliate, that there seemed no chance for me.

Well, I need not go over in detail the conversation that we had during the next half hour. Indeed, it is not clear to me. It took me at a disadvantage from the first, since my very coming was the sign of peace between us. I remember I felt annoyed and bewildered at first; but as he talked, mingling graceful touches of thanks among his earnest words, I gradually grew to feeling as if some way—by somebody—he had been cruelly abused during the past few days. All my indignation seemed to melt away. I half forgot at what I was supposed to be indignant. The gentleman before me bore no resemblance to my companion during that horrible walk; and it almost seemed to me as if that evening must have been spent in some faraway dream-land—as if the whole scene must have been just a horrid nightmare. I don't know how it happened—I have tried to think, and I can't—but I do know that when I met Dr. Douglass at the foot of the brilliantly lighted stairs that led up to the hall, my hand rested on Mr. Sayles's arm, and his head was bent toward me, while he continued to talk in low, eager tones.

The hall was a perfect babel of tongues. A dozen voices seized upon Mrs. Tyndall. She was the acknowledged leader among the young people. She was one of those fair-faced, youthful-looking, elegant women, with enough of matronly dignity about her to ensure her a hearing and a genuine fondness for all the gaities and frivolities of girlhood. She had few domestic tastes, plenty of leisure, plenty of money, and exquisite skill and tact so that she was equal to any occasion. So it followed that the girls leaned on her, quoted her, followed her lead on all occasions, and allowed themselves to be ordered about in her graceful, good-humored way. As for the gentlemen, the most of them, with the exception of Mr. Sayles, were quite young, and I doubt if there was one among them who had not made the elegant little lady his *confidante*. So the crowd surrounded her the moment we entered the hall—and all talked at once:

"Mrs. Tyndall, Lycia Symonds says that Religion ought to dress in black. Did you ever hear of such a thing?"—"Mrs. Tyndall, Cora Kenyon can't find a costume for the fourth scene in this town. What in the world are we to do?"—"Mrs. Tyndall, have you arranged for Queen Vashti's dress?"—"Mrs. Tyndall, *are* you going to help me this evening? I can't get the curtain the right shape."

"Softly—softly—girls," chimed in Mrs. Tyndall's gentle voice; "you deafen me. One thing at a time, please, and we'll have it all arranged in order."

Meantime Mr. Sayles kept up a running, low-toned commentary:

"Religion dress in black! What does the girl mean? It's appropriate enough, though, for half the religionists in the world—they are walking tombstones. *Do* you imagine that wonderful woman is going to bring order out of all this confusion? She's a remarkable woman, but if this thing doesn't culminate in a grand failure, I shall have an immense increase of respect for her powers. However, we'll help her to the best of our abilities."

Later in the evening I sat busily sewing, just behind Lycia Symonds and Florence Hervey. I was wedged in among bundles and baskets of finery and rolls of curtains. There were a few stitches to be taken on an important ruff for a lady of olden time, and I had dropped down here to attend to it. The two girls were similarly employed over articles wanted at once, and as they worked they gave me the benefit of their conversation. I could not decide then whether they spoke louder than they were aware of, or whether they wished to give me their views on the subjects discussed. I don't know now which it was, and it doesn't matter. I heard them, anyway. Lycia spoke in the decided tone of voice that was natural to her.

"I'll tell you what *I* think about it. I think Mrs. Tyndall hasn't shown her usual good taste in her selection of a character for Religion. My face isn't the right sort at all. I know so little about the genuine article that I can't even simulate it. But I know who could, and that's Frank Hooper."

"Frank Hooper!" and Florence's tone expressed well-bred horror.

"Yes, Frank Hooper. You've heard of her, haven't you? It isn't two years since she was the star at your birthday party; and she still lives, even though she doesn't get invited to our parties. And a capital person she would be to take this part."

Florence's voice was dignity iced as she answered:

"I should think you were decidedly descending in the social scale. I fancy we can find ladies enough in our own circle."

"Social, fiddlestick," Lycia said, waxing warm. *"Don't* talk any more nonsense, Flo, than you can help, because I really haven't much patience left for that sort of thing. However, it's more *funny* than anything else to use such phrases in connection with Frank Hooper. It's a sort of revenge, isn't it, because Frank queened it over you for so long?"

Florence's answer had about as much argument in it as that queenly lady was capable of using:

"I don't associate with shop girls."

And Lycia, in her response, did not lower her voice a note.

"Don't you? I thought you called on Julia Ried."

"So I did; but she is not a shop girl—she is Messrs. Sayles & Getman's bookkeeper."

"Oh! it's the material one works with that makes the lady, is it? I didn't know before. One daubs in ink and the other in paste, and the inky one is a lady and the pasty one not. That distinction is worthy of Mrs. Tyndall herself. My dear, you're a promising pupil. Now, I should prefer the paste myself, because a little clean water will wash that off—and ink sticks."

Florence laughed a good-humored, graceful laugh, as one too assured of her position to make it worth her while to grow indignant over any language that might sound like ridicule, and answered composedly:

"Don't be absurd, Lycia. Of course I know that Julia Ried doesn't belong to our set; but then Mrs. Tyndall chooses to pet her, and she's a bright sort of creature; and now, while we have so much to do about this festival, she is quite a help: so I called one afternoon when I knew she was out. It took very little of my time and probably did her a world of good. I can't imagine, though, why Mrs. Tyndall makes so much of her. Can you?"

It seems to me that today, after the lapse of years, I can feel how hotly my cheeks burned over all this; but I fairly held my breath for Lycia's answer, for I had occasionally pondered over that same question myself. Lycia evidently knew without pondering, for she answered quickly:

"Mrs. Tyndall would make much of a *cat* who would mew and purr when she told it to, and never at any other time. This one looks as though there were

enough in her to scratch and spit occasionally; but
Mrs. Tyndall knows how to stroke her fur and keep her
quiet, I suspect."

And then those two girls laughed, while I, sitting
quietly behind them, felt as though I would like to
choke them both. Lycia continued the subject:

"So far as I am concerned, I rather like the girl. I've
no sort of objection to calling on her, nor on Frank
Hooper, either. I hate all this silly twaddle about social
position. It's real shoddy style to make wealth a mark
of distinction—and that is certainly all that Frank
Hooper has lost."

"Why did she want to go into that shop, do you
suppose? Everybody was ready to befriend her. You
know Mrs. Tyndall offered her a home."

Whereupon Lycia laughed outright.

"I wonder if you are deluded enough to believe all
that?" she said gaily. "You evidently have Mrs. Tyndall's
version of it. The plain English is that she offered her
the position of seamstress in her family. A position
which Frank was much too sensible to accept, for
more than one reason; principally, though, because she
knew Mrs. Tyndall would interfere between Jerome
Sayles and herself. She has succeeded in that, however—and that, by the way, is part of Julia Ried's
mission. If he were not a complete ninny, he would
stand by Frank Hooper through it all. I detest that
fellow. The only sensible thing about him is his admiration for Frank. Now, I'm prepared to startle you in
another way. I know who would make a lovely
Quakeress, and I mean to get her into it—that's little
Ruth Walker; that small, gray mouse who disturbed
you and Mrs. Tyndall so much in class, until you
succeeded in sending her over among the black sheep
in Dr. Douglass's class. She's a shop girl, you know; so

I'm out of my set again—down in the depths this time, for little Ruth was never rich in her life, I think; and I absolutely fear that her mother does fine ironing for a living. She used to sew—which was more respectable, *of course*—until a horrible pain in her side obliged her to disgrace herself still further by taking to ironing."

Miss Florence shrugged her aristocratic shoulders and said simply:

"Suit yourself; so that I don't have to be bored with the white-faced little morsel, I really am indifferent as to whether she plays Quakeress for you or not."

At this moment Mrs. Tyndall came from the staging, where she had been ordering the gentlemen as to the arrangement of curtains, lights, etc., and joined the group of sewers. Both young ladies addressed her at once with—

"Mrs. Tyndall, Lycia has some new and startling plans to offer"—and—"Mrs. Tyndall, I have two new performers for you—excellent ones."

That lady sank gracefully down among the crimson curtains lying in heaps on the floor and answered brightly:

"Enlighten me, then, speedily, for I must return to the platform in a very few minutes. It is going to take us all the evening to get ready to work. Men are so stupid. What is the plan, Lycia?"

"I propose Frank Hooper to take the character of Religion, if we want to make that a success. She is the one that can do it."

"I don't feel at all doubtful about its success with Lycia Symonds as the principal figure; besides, Frank has been invited to join us and has declined: as she does all other civilities. She has chosen her own course. I don't see that we can do anything but quietly let her alone. I know how you feel, dear girls, and I honor your motives; but I think Frank has so entirely separated herself from us by her late conduct that we must leave her to reap what she has sown."

Lycia answered with the utmost composure:

"I have no special motive for you to honor, Mrs. Tyndall. My object in asking Frank to take the character is that I think she will do it justice. As for her late conduct, I think it was a sensible thing to do, and have liked her better ever since."

Mrs. Tyndall laughed and leaned caressingly on Lycia's arm as she said:

"We all know what proportion of your remarks to consider genuine. What of the other project? Consider this one dismissed, will you, please? I cannot possibly spare you from that tableau."

"The other is that I mean to have that little Ruthie Walker for the Quaker scene."

There was a determined glitter in Lycia's eyes. She had evidently yielded the other point, more, I thought, because she knew Frank would have been obstinate; but the tone in which she said, *"I mean to have"* was very decided. I looked to see Mrs. Tyndall as decidedly oppose it, and then I fully expected a disruption; but by this calculation I showed that I did not know Mrs. Tyndall. She instantly and gracefully acquiesced.

"I don't know but that would be a good idea. She has a demure sort of face, and that character is not yet supplied. She would certainly have one immensely convenient qualification: She would do as she was told." With which parting shot she turned to me. "Julia, my dear, is that ruff proving too much for you? You are looking very much flushed."

I expected to see the two young ladies flush guiltily at this reminder of my close proximity; but they did not even glance in my direction. Then they must have desired me to hear them—either that or they had no idea of the loudness of their tones. I have sometimes thought that Lycia at least had a friendly desire to warn me of my nearness to danger and, although she did it in a stinging way, had my good at heart; but I do not know how that may be. I only know that it stung deeply. The rest of the evening was a pain and a bewilderment to me. There were moments in which I fully resolved to have nothing more to do with them, to refuse to take any part in this festival which had suddenly become so disagreeable to me, to leave Mrs. Tyndall, to go away from them all, home to my mother. Oh, Mother, Mother! I remember just how longingly my sick heart cried out after you that night, just as it has cried in vain many, many times since.

I don't know whether Mrs. Tyndall was gifted with a sort of clairvoyant power or not, or at least I mean it used sometimes to seem to me as though she must have been. She came up with me to my room that night. She dropped herself daintily among some red cushions and passed her hand softly over my flushed and heated forehead in a winning way she had, while she talked to me in those cooing tones of hers.

"Poor child! She is very tired and a little bit disgusted with everybody. Don't you find girls very insipid, Julia? Lycia Symonds is, between you and me, the only really brilliant one we have, though it would never do to tell Florence Hervey that; but Lycia is rude and sharp in her language. The child doesn't like me; I thwart her pet schemes too often. I laugh sometimes to think of what stinging things she probably says about me when I am out of hearing. She has one fancy of which I must try to disabuse her. She seems to think that I have dropped Frank Hooper because she has chosen to enter a shop, which, of course, she had the right to do if she pleased, and equally, of course, that can never put her on a level with ignorant, uncultured shop girls. My reasons for declining to continue my friendship with her were based upon her exceedingly improper conduct toward Jerome Sayles. The story is much too long to weary you with it tonight; but sometime I must tell you about it, and you will have more sympathy for poor Jerome when you think of the annoyance to which he has been exposed. Now, my poor tired child, do get to rest as quickly as possible. Do you know that your tableau is going to be perfectly lovely?"

I tossed and tumbled very restlessly instead of sleeping; but I finally concluded that Mrs. Tyndall had been slandered; that whatever her faults she really loved me; that tender, clinging kiss as she said good night was my last pleasant proof; and I dropped asleep very firm in the resolve to show Florence Hervey that in spite of not belonging to her *set* I belonged to Mrs. Tyndall's and Mr. Sayles's, and that I assisted in making a tableau that was "perfectly lovely."

15

WHITE AND BLACK

THE next rehearsal was one continued scene of confusion. Nothing seemed to go quite right—everyone present seemed fully bent on having his or her own way, and no two persons agreed about the fold of a curtain or the position of a table.

I ought to except little Ruth Walker. She was meek and mouselike as usual. Her fair pleasant face had flushed with surprise when Lycia Symonds, in the richest of black silks and resplendent in sable furs, pressed and pushed her way into our shop one afternoon, tipping over several piles of boxes in her transit, and finally reaching Ruth's stand, proferred her request for Ruth's assistance in the tableaux. Flushed with surprise and pleasure—evidently little Ruth liked fun—she gave ready assent; and on this evening of which I write, hovered softly among us the meekest little Quaker one could imagine, and the busiest; her deft fingers made the needle fairly fly, and many were the patient stitches which she took that night in the endless garments which needed a little "fixing." In her way she was the most popular one among us.

Before nine o'clock every girl present had learned who would sew on a string, or pin a bow, or hold "things" while they fixed them, or run to the dressing room for a shawl or a sack, or run into the store below for a paper of pins, or do any of the thousand little things that were constantly pressing forward to be done—doing them, too, with such a pleased and gentle face that Mr. Sayles said to me in undertone:

"I think that Ruth, as you call her, must be a real flesh-and-blood Quakeress, or a niece of Job's."

But there was a great deal of friction. Lycia Symonds, for one, seemed bent on making all the trouble that she could in a gay, good-humored sort of way—bent, first of all, upon coming in contact with Mrs. Tyndall and her schemes. The first general discussion came up toward the close of the evening. We had been rehearsing the most difficult tableau in the list, and had sat down to rest and finish articles for the "grab bag." Then Florence Hervey commenced it.

"Mrs. Tyndall, do you know that Lycia isn't making a *thing* for this bag?"

"Why, isn't that little pink-and-white dolly for the bag? I'm sure I supposed it was."

"She thinks grab bags are coarse and common."

"Ours is an exception," answered Mrs. Tyndall with unfailing good humor. "It is to be made of silk patchwork that is over a hundred years old, and the bag is to be grabbed for afterward at so much a ticket. Lycia, you'll grab for that, won't you?"

"Not I," said Lycia emphatically. "I'm not in sympathy with grab bags. I'm sorry we are obliged to descend to anything of the sort; and, by the way, Mrs. Tyndall, do you know that Dr. Mulford entirely disapproves of ring cakes?"

Mrs. Tyndall sewed on in good-humored indifference as she answered:

"I wasn't aware of that formidable fact, my dear; at least, I do not remember to have heard it. Fanny, a blue sash for that dolly would match her eyes better than the one you have chosen."

Meantime Lycia gave a wicked nod and sparkle of her eyes to her next neighbor and murmured:

"I'm going to transform myself into an angel of light now." Then aloud, "Do you think it is quite proper for us to indulge in speculations of which he disapproves?"

Mrs. Tyndall laughed lightly.

"Why, my dear child, perhaps he disapproves of eating oysters in the evening. Many people do. Shall we, therefore, banish them from our bill of fare?"

It was timid little Ruth, with blushing cheeks, who took up the question.

"But, Mrs. Tyndall, there is no moral question involved in eating oysters."

"I don't know about that," laughed Mr. Sayles. "I ate the articles in question last evening, and my digestive organs have been in a very immoral state ever since."

"And for the matter of that," chimed in Mrs. Tyndall, "I don't see the immorality of a pound cake. I think there is as much of that quality involved in the one article as the other."

"Ruthie," said Lycia in undertone, "when Mrs. Tyndall tries to make you think black is white, don't you believe it." Then she returned to the charge.

"Mrs. Tyndall, if I were a lawyer I should charge you with begging the question. *Isn't* there, after all, a marked difference between ring cakes and oysters? If Dr. Mulford chooses to think that selling slices of cake at so much a slice, so that some ten-cent purchaser will chance to secure a gold ring for a fortieth part of its value, a species of gambling, hasn't he a right to do it?"

"Undoubtedly he has, my dear; but don't put a green ribbon on that cushion, white is better. Suppose *you* choose to think it a perfectly innocent and rather amusing way of making a little money for a good cause, haven't you the same right?"

"The right to think, perhaps, but not to act; for supposing him to be right and myself wrong, which is certainly *possible,* a bad example would be set and much mischief might be done; while on the other hand, no possible harm could ensue from giving up the project."

"That's remarkably well put, Lycia," Mr. Sayles said with a touch of evident admiration in his voice. "I'm not sure but you ought to be a lawyer."

Mrs. Tyndall laughingly agreed and gave her undivided attention to the staring wax doll at her left, while Lycia continued her *aside* comments.

"Do you suppose she will give me a direct answer if I talk from now until day after tomorrow? I mean to try it." "Seriously, Mrs. Tyndall, is it courteous to persist in a matter that the pastor of our church cannot approve, when we call our entertainment a church festival, and the proceeds are for the benefit of the church? Hasn't the pastor a right to dictate in such a matter?"

Mrs. Tyndall hesitated. It was a member of her Bible class who asked the question; it was asked about her pastor, and it became her to hesitate. When she spoke her voice was sweetness itself.

"My dear Lycia, it is a great pleasure to see you so desirous of doing just right and so solicitous for our pastor's honor; it is really very becoming. Now let me explain matters a little. We have to study to please other people as well as ourselves in this world; and Mrs. Chandler, a woman of no religious principle whatever, chooses to interest herself in a ring cake and is thereby drawn in to work very industriously with us. Now Dr. Mulford may not quite approve her manner of work; may say so in a very quiet, confidential way, to your mother, for instance; but he is certainly a man of too correct views of propriety, too much good sense, to interfere openly and thereby cause an unnecessary commotion."

"But suppose, Mrs. Tyndall, that his sense of propriety isn't equal to the occasion and that he does interfere quite openly. What is going to be done about it?"

"In the first place, my dear, we will not insult his good sense by supposing such a foolish thing. Don't you think you are getting that hem a trifle wider than is necessary? There will not be room enough for the fold."

Lycia laughed with the utmost good humor, rather as though she had triumphed instead of being worsted; and, on the whole, I think she did, for I heard her say to Florence Hervey soon after with the utmost glee:

"I told you it would be simply impossible to smuggle her into a corner that she couldn't slip out of."

That was not the only question that came up for discussion during the evening. The next excitement was little Ruthie.

"Put that small Quaker into our Turkish scene," I heard Mr. Sayles say to our commander-in-chief.

"What! Ruth Walker! Do you really mean it? I'm not sure but it would be an excellent idea. Her face would be a capital foil to some of the others."

Ruth, however, on being appealed to, with very downcast eyes and very flushed face, declined being one of the ladies of the harem. Mrs. Tyndall persisted and argued, even descended to coaxing, while Mr. Sayles grew more eager over it every moment. Ruth did not like the tableau, did not think it was pretty or "nice," and *would not* take part in it.

"Sensible girl," Fred Thompson said to Mr. Sayles. "If all the other ladies in the crowd would follow her example it would become them better. I don't like that picture."

But Mr. Sayles shrugged his shoulders and said:

"That is only because you are not the Sultan."

Now all this, in consideration of the fact that I was the chief lady of the harem, was not pleasant to me. I wondered in a bewildered sort of way what they could all mean. When I look back on those days and remember, despite all the careful culture and painstaking education that had been given me, what a poor, silly simpleton I was, I am amazed that I did not get further astray even than I did. Oh, Mother, Mother, how I did dishonor the blessed memory of one who tried so hard to guide me in the right way.

The excitement over the Turkish scene had scarcely subsided when another ensued. We were preparing for our homeward walk when Mrs. Tyndall reiterated her parting injunction.

"Now, girls, do try to be early tomorrow evening. We have very little time and a great deal to do. It will be especially important for *you* to be prompt, Miss Walker, as you have joined us so recently and have a great deal to learn."

Then Ruth's fair, childlike face flushed again as she answered gently:

"I cannot be here tomorrow evening, Mrs. Tyndall."

"You cannot? Why, that is very unfortunate. I wish you had mentioned it before. We supposed, of course, that you would be able to attend the rehearsals when we invited you to join us. I really think you will have to waive your other engagement, whatever it is, and be present tomorrow evening."

"I did not suppose you would have rehearsal tomorrow evening, because of the prayer meeting. That is the reason why I cannot come."

At this earnestly spoken answer I winced a little, for was not tomorrow evening's prayer meeting the one that I was supposed to attend? And yet I had not thought of it and was making eager plans for the evening. Lycia Symonds telegraphed a glance, full of triumphant amusement, to Mr. Sayles and awaited Mrs. Tyndall's reply with evident interest. It was very gentle and courteous.

"Your interest in prayer meeting is certainly commendable; a habit of regular attendance is very desirable, and as you are so young you may readily be pardoned for carrying it to an extreme. But, my dear girl, duty sometimes interferes with our pleasures. Quite a number of us will be obliged to waive our regular custom tomorrow evening and sacrifice ourselves to the work that must be done here. We would willingly postpone it if we could, but the time is very short. So I don't see but you will have to be one of the victims."

There was a peculiar curve to Lycia's lip and an eager interest in her eye as she bent forward for Ruth's answer.

The shy little girl blushed painfully at finding herself the center of observation; but her voice had not lost a shade of its decisive ring as she answered:

"I cannot come, Mrs. Tyndall. I have been taught to consider an attendance at the prayer meeting among my *first* duties, to which all matters of minor importance must yield; and I feel quite sure my mother would not approve."

Just then I envied that quiet, meek-faced little shop girl, whose mother did fine ironing for a living—envied her simple straightforward firmness. I felt that I would give much if I stood just where she did, if I could have consistently stood by her in her decision; but there seemed to be a great mountain of inconsistent acts for me to climb over before I could reach that place, and I had not the moral courage to make a beginning. Ah me! I, too, knew a mother who I was quite sure would not approve of this, nor of a great many other acts of mine.

I have always thought that amid all her faults Mrs. Tyndall had one good quality. She was unfailingly and persistently good-humored. When she absolutely *could not* make things work to suit herself, she gracefully and good-naturedly yielded. She turned from Ruth with a light laugh as she said:

"Oh, well, please yourself. At your age one cannot be expected to be very wise or thoughtful." And to Lycia she added before Ruth was fairly out of hearing: "This comes from your talent for mixing incongruous elements."

"I must say I admired the little thing," Mr. Sayles said as we walked homeward. "She stood up staunchly for what she conceived to be her duty, and it required considerable moral courage." Then, in a kind of muttered undertone: "I wish I had an equal amount."

Mrs. Tyndall laughed.

"Julia," she said, "I am glad that you are a strong-minded and sensible young lady, and will not be likely to rush off to prayer meeting tomorrow evening, leaving us to do all the work, merely for the sake of winning this romantic gentleman's approval."

I had no answer ready, and went to my room grave and somewhat heavy-hearted. Little Ruth had dealt a stab at my inconsistencies that I could not immediately rally from.

We had not heard the last of the ring cake.

Dr. Mulford called on the afternoon before the festival. We were very busy rearranging my costume for one of the tableaux. When the doctor asked for a few moments' conversation I arose to leave them, but Mrs. Tyndall detained me with an appealing hand.

"Pray, Julia, do not desert me. We have not a moment to lose. Doctor, is it something very special and private so that I mustn't keep Julia? You see, we are so exceedingly busy."

It was in regard to the festival that he wished to speak, Dr. Mulford explained.

"Oh, then Julia ought to stay. I assure you she has been quite as wicked as I have during the whole of it."

I sat down again, feeling very much as if I ought to be away. Then the entire question of church gambling came up and was discussed somewhat at length. Mrs. Tyndall tried several different tactics. At first she was gay and playful. The ring, she assured him, should be pure gold of the finest quality, no shamming about it; and the cake should be as white and light as pound cake could be made. The doctor was not to be silenced in that way; he was grave and in earnest. Then she questioned him.

"What possible harm could there be in allowing

young people to extract a little amusement from a ring and a cake?"

He answered her with another question.

"What harm could there be in permitting two gentlemen to play at cards during the evening, for the amusement of the guests at the festival, and at its close present the money thus won to the church?"

"Oh, that was a very different thing," she told him.

"It was money made by chance," he answered, "and by playing upon the passion for trying one's luck—a passion which was found to a greater or less extent in the mind of every young person—the very passion which, if encouraged and cultivated, forms a confirmed gambler. Certainly we did not want to teach any such lesson in a church festival."

Mrs. Tyndall looked laughingly incredulous.

"Now, Doctor," she said with an attempt at gravity, "do you really suppose that there will be a single person at *our* church festival who will be so devoid of brains as to be injured by so trifling a thing?"

Dr. Mulford answered with grave emphasis:

"I don't know anything about that, madam—only God does. There might very possibly be a company gathered together who would none of them become professional pickpockets, even though they were to indulge in that amusement for one evening. Yet I do not think it would be well to set our young people at such work tomorrow evening, even though the proceeds were presented to the church. The simple truth is, Mrs. Tyndall, that we must abstain from all appearance of evil. We must not cover with the guise of charity and religion what the whole world condemns. We must not teach our young people that it is right to gamble for rings and wrong to gamble for farms. If it is right to make ten dollars by chance, it is right to make ten thousand dollars in the same way."

Mrs. Tyndall grew grave and courteous.

"I am sorry," she said gently, "that we did not understand your peculiar views before. It would have been easy enough, in the first place, to have avoided all this; but now—you know Mrs. Chandler, Doctor? She has the matter in hand. You know she is not apt to be interested in religious festivals of any sort—rarely does anything; but she has chosen to do this—seems deeply interested in it. I really think it may be the means of enlisting her assistance in other church matters. You know we must be all things to all men, Doctor. Oh, there will good arise even from this; but I am sorry it has occurred. I would not have you annoyed for the world. It shall not occur again, I assure you."

But she had a man of adamant opinions to deal with; and frankly and kindly, but very plainly, he explained to her that it would be impossible to countenance with his presence at any such proceeding; that if it were carried out he must absent himself.

Mrs. Tyndall had no desire for any such publicity; had not the slightest desire to quarrel with her pastor, and promptly assured him that of course, since he felt so deeply on the whole subject, the whole affair should be suppressed. I think it was at that time, however, that she mentally decided that the First Church of Newton really needed a younger man for their pastor. I have always considered it the very refinement of courteous revenge that Mrs. Tyndall bought the enormous and elaborate pound cake at an exorbitant price and sent it, ring and all, daintily boxed and gracefully addressed:

FOR MRS. MULFORD,
With Mrs. H. F. Tyndall's love.

16

❖

But One Voice

THE festival was a success without either ring cake or grab bag; for the opposition to the latter had proved to be so marked that it, too, was discarded, though the curious silk bag was sold by ticket in a kind of genteel private way.

During the whirl of preparation many of my accustomed duties had been neglected, among others my regular Thursday letter to Mother. For three weeks I had not written a line to her, and I comforted myself with the thought that when this festival was over I should have plenty of time for that, and a great variety of other neglected matters. But no sooner had we calmed down from the excitement of our own festival, when we became eager over one that was to take place in a village a short distance from Newton. Mrs. Tyndall had a niece living there who was deeply interested in the affair; and Mrs. Tyndall's last brilliant idea was that a few of us should go out there and repeat for them our most successful tableaux. I entered into the scheme with great glee—indeed I had reached such a pitch of excitement that I seemed to have lost what little common sense I ever possessed; but some of the girls demurred. Lycia Symonds, when appealed to, answered promptly and with some hauteur that she was "not a professional performer and did not hire out by the night." At which Mrs. Tyndall composedly laughed and remarked as we left the corner where our conference had been held:

"Poor Lycia will never forgive Jerome for not inviting her into the Turkish tableau, nor me for not directing him to do so. She has been spiteful ever since."

"Is that the trouble?" I asked with wide-open eyes; and she laughed as she answered:

"Why, yes, you innocent mouse; you seem to have no idea that you are the envy of most of the young ladies in our set."

Now I had not during all this time remained ignorant of the fact that Mr. Sayles was a general favorite; he was cultured and courteous, and had the air of a finished gentleman; he was reputed wealthy, both in reality and in prospect, being the expected heir of a wealthy uncle. Nor had I been at all unconscious of the fact that while he might apparently have had but to choose his society from any family in town, his preference for me had become so marked and decided that it was a subject of general interest among our mutual acquaintances. I felt immensely flattered and grateful, and those very feelings led me into making some sad blunders.

Well, concerning the festival, there were others who were of the same mind as Lycia Symonds. Among them little Ruth Walker, though her mind was not expressed in the same manner, but simply and gently, that "Mother would rather she did not go"; and Mrs. Tyndall's assurance that it should "not cost her a cent if that were the difficulty in the way" only had the effect of bringing a very becoming pink flush to her pretty face and of giving perhaps a little more decided ring to her voice as she repeated her refusal. But there were others quite as eager for excitement as myself who hailed the proposition with glee, and we made up a company of seven, and planned and rehearsed and frolicked away another week of time.

In the meantime that unwritten letter to my mother lay heavy on my conscience; but my preparations had all to be made after working hours in the shop were over, and they left me very little chance even to think. One thing I carefully did, I avoided all tête-à-têtes with Dr. Douglass, though I could hardly have told why; at least I did not answer the question even to myself. It was the afternoon before the festival. I had been excused from the shop in order to finish my preparations. We were to take the six o'clock train and expected to return on the two o'clock express. Dr. Douglass had hardly been present at table during the week; he was unusually pressed with professional cares. When he was present there seemed to be a tacit understanding that our proposed trip was not to be discussed; at least the subject was not mentioned. As we arose from dinner on this particular day, the doctor turned suddenly to me.

"Julia, can you give me ten minutes of your time? I have a message for you."

And without waiting for my reply he at once led the way to the library and closed the door after us. Then immediately he said:

"Julia, are you going on that singular expedition tonight?"

Dr. Douglass was not wise in his commencement. To address a girl of sixteen, especially one as devoid of sense as I seem at that time to have been, in a kind of horrified tone about something that she had fully made up her mind to do, is nearly certain to exasperate her. Accordingly I was exasperated.

"I expect to go to Westbrook this evening," I said haughtily, "if that is the expedition to which you refer."

He has told me since that he saw his mistake. His tone changed to one of gentle persuasion.

"Julia, I wish you would not; there are many reasons to urge against it. In the first place the evening is fearfully cold and stormy, and you will get no rest tonight; and besides— Have you thought how it will appear to absent yourself during a time of special interest not only from all the meetings of the week, but from this regular Thursday meeting? You have, too, a young lady among your number who last week attended every meeting, and now at the last moment I hear has been persuaded into joining you."

"Who is it?" I interrupted.

"Carrie Seward. Julia, I would not have had her mind led away at this time for anything. It is a very solemn thing to do."

"I didn't ask her to go," I interrupted impatiently. "I didn't even know she was going; and your objections come at a singular time, a few hours before we are ready to start. How could we change our plans now if we wanted to when we are expected and depended upon? You have known for a week that we were going. Why haven't you interfered before if you intended to at all?"

"I did *not* know it, Julia," he said gravely. "I knew that some wild scheme of the kind was projected, but I did not know that Mrs. Tyndall was engaged in it, nor that she had drawn you in. I certainly thought that she had more sense."

"Thank you," I said loftily. "I drew myself into it, and I am not at all disturbed about it. Do you want me anymore? Because I have a great deal to do between this and six o'clock."

"Yes," he said, beginning to walk the floor in the restless way that I remembered so well as a child; "I want you to give up this scheme, Julia. I entreat it of you. It is a momentous time with us; there are solemn interests at stake. Had you been present at the meetings during this week you would understand what a strange thing it will appear to have some of our members absent for such a purpose on such a night as this; besides, there are other reasons. I am sure you have not stopped to think how your mother would look upon your public appearance in such a scene as that in which I saw you the other evening."

"I don't know what you mean," I said, coloring violently and speaking angrily.

"I mean," he said gravely, "that I am sorry to have a friend of mine take for five seconds and in play the degrading and disgraceful position of a miserable heathen woman—a position which Christianity abolishes and which women speak of, when they are obliged to speak of it at all, with blushes of pain and shame. You are young and innocent, Julia, and the blame of bringing you in such a manner before the public rests upon older heads than yours; but, for your sister Ester's sake, I would not have the like occur again."

By this time my cheeks were blazing; and I must say, in extenuation of my own conduct, that I had a very vague idea of what he meant. I was both thoughtless and innocent, and had been led on by another, precisely as I have since seen young misses allowing themselves to be led; and I know just how they will feel about it at twenty, provided they have not by that time decided not to feel or think at all. The doctor checked the indignant answer that rose to my lips.

"There is another point about which I must speak. This morning I received a letter from your mother. She is in a state of terrible anxiety about you. She writes me that she has not heard from you in four weeks, and feels certain that you must be ill. She has spent nights of torture, she says, on your account. I immediately telegraphed her that you were well. I thought we ought not wait to write, for I value a *mother* too highly to keep her long in such suspense as was evidently hers. But since reading her letter I have been led to fear that I was not doing my duty in regard to you. You must let me ask you some very plain questions, Julia. Are you engaged to Mr. Sayles?"

At which question my cheeks, if possible, flamed hotter than before, and I answered with excitement.

"Such a question as that you have no right to ask. No one but my mother has any right to question me in that way."

"I don't feel certain of that," he answered gently. "In this letter which I have received today your mother begs me to remember that she trusts her child to my care, and that she expects me to watch over you as earnestly as I would if I were your brother in name as well as in heart. In view of all the apparent circumstances, if I were your brother I should ask the question which I have just now asked you; and I feel that I must understand this matter before I can reply to your mother's letter."

"I wish my mother *could* remember that I am *not* a ten-year-old *child*," I said angrily. "Well, since you *demand* an answer, I am not engaged to Mr. Sayles and haven't the slightest expectation of being; and you can telegraph that to Mother if you think best. Is that satisfactory?"

"I don't know whether it is or not," he answered with grave sternness, "because I hardly see how I can justify such constant attentions as you have received and accepted from him on any other grounds."

"You are not called upon to justify them," I said pertly; and as I think of it now I am almost surprised that he did not box my ears in reply.

"I cannot, in the first place, see how you can reconcile it with your conscience, or even with your pride, to receive his marked attentions when you think of Frank Hooper."

Curiosity got the better of my pride just then, and I listened eagerly while he continued:

"I don't think you can know quite how base his utter desertion of Frank was. They were to have been married in less than two months' time when the great business crash came that involved Mr. Hooper and ruined his fortune, and then it took this Mr. Sayles but a few days to discover that he and Frank were not suited to each other."

This story was entirely new to me. It made my cheeks glow again; but I answered with an incredulous smile:

"I thought you were proof against gossip, Doctor. If this remarkable history is true, how do you account for the fact that Frank Hooper has twice at least appeared with him in public during the last three months?"

"I can only account for it by the remembrance that she is a loving, forgiving, infatuated girl," he answered gravely. "I believe I had the history on too good authority to discredit it."

"Nevertheless I discredit it," I answered loftily. "And now, if you have nothing further, I really must go. I have a great deal to do before evening."

I moved toward the door as I spoke, but he detained me eagerly.

"Julia, let me beg you to think of this matter. I do earnestly hope that you will decide not to go."

"I shall decide no such thing," I said angrily. "How absurdly you talk. How can I change it all now when I am pledged to go?"

"Very easily. You can have no idea of the severity of the evening. I have heard it suggested several times that the festival would undoubtedly be postponed. Most of their people are from the country, and the country roads will be impassable. You know quite well that if your mother were here, she would not permit you to go; but besides all this, if there are really souls at stake, ought you not to be in your place this evening instead of working against the current?"

I stood silent and thoughtful for a moment, then said quickly:

"There is no use in talking about it any longer. People can't whirl their plans around as quickly as that. I can go to meeting every evening after this one for a month; there will be nothing in the world to hinder."

Then I immediately left the room. Nevertheless, as I closed the door, I was almost decided not to go. I was by no means in so reckless and unconcerned a mood as I had chosen to assume. I crossed the hall, revolving plans in my mind for satisfying Mrs. Tyndall with a change of program. "It would not be such an impossible thing to do," I said. "We are only in two tableaux after all, and the entire festival does not depend upon them; and if the evening is going to be so stormy, it will certainly justify us in not taking a ride of three miles after we leave the station." I was halfway upstairs when Mrs. Tyndall's silvery voice summoned me to the back parlor. She was sunken into the depths of her favorite crimson chair, with an exceedingly listless and inattentive expression on her face; and Dr. Mulford stood near her speaking earnestly.

"My dear," she said as I entered, "you are in demand today; the doctors seem to have you in their keeping. Dr. Mulford wishes to see you."

He came toward me at once, holding out his hand and speaking rapidly.

"My dear young lady, I have come to make a very earnest request that you would reconsider your plan for the evening, even at this late hour. I did not know of it until very recently. Mrs. Tyndall and yourself are the only professing Christians of the party, and you have some among your number, one in particular, who is treading on very dangerous ground. She has simply entered into this scheme for the sake of trying to stifle her conscience. I beg that you will not help her in the effort. Besides, we need your help; your moral support. I am confident that there are many souls among us just trembling in the balance, and such a *very* little thing may turn the scale."

"And what about our pledged word, Doctor, and the expectations that are based upon us? You seem to forget those things."

He turned eagerly toward her.

"I do *not,* madam. Under ordinary circumstances I should counsel you to be exceedingly careful in regard to breaking an engagement; but this is a special matter—it is the Lord's work—it behooves us to lay aside every possible weight and be ready for his appearing. My Brother Reynolds is pastor of that church, and if you will permit me, I will myself explain matters to him. I know him well; and I assure you that he will understand and appreciate the reasons for the change."

Mrs. Tyndall smiled quietly.

"You gentlemen are the most singular creatures," she said quietly. "You think a word of kindly explanation is all that is necessary to justify one in almost anything. Now, *I* am not responsible to Reverend Mr. Reynolds, but to a committee of ladies, and I know them better than to disappoint them.

"My dear, would it not be well for you to commence your preparations? It is growing late. I think the doctor will excuse you." But I lingered for the issue.

"I am sorry, Doctor, that our going makes any difference. I do not quite understand these times of excitement, you know, and fail to be in sympathy with them. To me it seems so much better to live our religion all the time, than to have these periodical and spasmodic fits of it; but then, of course, I have nothing to do with that. As for Carrie Seward, the child came to me last night in the wildest spirits. Your meeting seemed to have afforded her a great fund of amusement; and, by the way, I fear a number of those giddy creatures are deceiving you in the same manner. I should not have asked her to join us had I been aware of your objections; but as it is, you need have no fear; the giddy little thing will be safer with us than she will be frolicking in the prayer meeting."

To all of which Dr. Mulford made no sort of reply; he even bowed his adieus without speaking and immediately went away.

"What an abrupt man he is," was Mrs. Tyndall's comment.

17

TREADING AMONG THE SHADOWS

THE ride from the station was severe enough to justify all that Dr. Douglass had said upon the subject. I thought I should perish. The hall was somewhat dingy and only about half filled. A miserable foreboding of some coming gloom seemed to possess me. I tried in vain to shake it off. Mr. Sayles rallied me upon my low spirits, and Mrs. Tyndall laughingly assured him that two doctors had been too much for me. They had, indeed, succeeded in making me very uncomfortable. I watched Carrie Seward (who was fluttering about in a very unnatural state of excited glee) with a nervous fear of some calamity coming to her because of us—because of me, for I was the important element in our party that evening, and I could have broken it up. Why did I not? How many times after that evening I asked myself the same weary question. And the answer always was that I yielded weakly, wickedly, as usual, to Mrs. Tyndall's stronger will. I, who prided myself, and always had done so, on my firm, strong will, when it came to the test, had no will at all, but allowed myself to listen and be led whither she would.

I have learned, since, a fact that it takes many young people long to learn: that there is a marked difference between firmness and obstinacy.

To add to my discomfiture, the evening had proved so forbidding that we had not been expected, and every individual to whom we were introduced expressed surprise at seeing us. I smiled drearily over Mr. Sayles's wonderment as to what all those people would probably have said if the evening had been clear and quiet, so that they could not have said: "I am surprised to see you here this stormy evening." Then I turned in response to his exclamation. But I do not think I was surprised to see Dr. Douglass standing in the doorway. It seemed to me to be an answer to something for which I had been watching and waiting. I went toward him at once and said in a tone of voice which I remember sounded strange even to me:

"Have you come for *me?*"

"Yes," he said quickly; "your mother is not well, they have telegraphed. If you are very quick, indeed, we may be able to reach the ten o'clock train."

It was like Dr. Douglass, that answer—brief, rapid, to the point, and giving me a strong motive for self-control and haste. I made no outcry of any sort, but went like one suddenly stricken dumb to the dressing room. It was Mrs. Tyndall's quick, deft fingers that robed me for the journey. She was tender and gentle, quiet and rapid, in all her movements; but the face that impressed me, even then, was the white, frightened one of Carrie Seward, and the words that sank like lead into my heart seemed to drop almost unconsciously from her trembling lips:

"We ought not to have come. I knew it; I knew it."

Mrs. Tyndall's last, thoughtful act was to wrap me in her fur-lined traveling cloak, and then I was ready. Dr.

Douglass stood waiting beside the sleigh, and it was but the work of a second of time to seat me therein and give the order, "Drive on." The horses dashed ahead, and the swift, silent drive commenced. The doctor tucked the robes about me, pushed a hot stone to my feet, keeping, meantime, a keen eye on the horses, and saying occasionally: "Go as fast as possible; we haven't a moment to lose." When we were within a quarter of a mile of the station a long, shrill whistle sounded out on the keen air.

"It's of no use, sir," the driver said, slackening his rein for the first time; "that's the whistle. You can't reach the train."

"They will wait, I think. At least we will try. Dash ahead. You shall have ten dollars if we are in time."

Then first I spoke, impelled by a sudden horrible fear:

"Doctor, is she dead?"

"No, oh, no; but quite sick, and delays are trying things at such a time. You shall be with her as soon as it is possible." And then we dashed around the curve and drew up beside the train. The conductor stood on the platform, watch in hand. As he saw us the engine bell began to ring.

"I thought we should have to leave you," he said as we hurried up the steps. "Four minutes behind."

"We are very grateful," answered the doctor. "There is no knowing how much those four minutes may be worth to us."

Oh, no; there was no knowing. I shivered to think of how much they might be worth. I grew every moment more frightened. The doctor must have reason to think her very, very sick, I reasoned, or every nerve would not have been so strained to reach this particular train; for I knew there was another at midnight. When we changed cars at Weymouth I seemed suddenly to arouse to the fact that he was still with me and had not stopped there to wait for a return train, as I had supposed he would.

"Are you going all the way?" I questioned; and he answered me simply and promptly:

"Certainly."

Another proof, then, that the illness was alarming, for I knew he was leaving patients who were very ill. Perhaps they had telegraphed him to come as counsel.

"Did they send for you?" I asked eagerly.

He shook his head.

"No; at least not professionally; but I didn't wish you to go alone."

"Doctor, let me see the telegram."

"I haven't it. I left it in my room when I went there for some articles."

"What did it say exactly?"

"It said: 'Mother is very sick. Bring Julia.' Now you know all that I do, and we will hope for the best and try to be calm and trustful. Can't I arrange those shawls and cloaks into pillows; and will you try to get a little rest?"

I shook my head in horror at the thought, and I remembered just then one of his arguments against my attendance at the festival: "You will get no rest tonight."

It was a night of gloom and foreboding—a long, long night—and when, occasionally, I caught a snatch of sleep, I awoke with hysteric sobbings from dreams of my mother's dying face. It was a clear, still, dazzling midday when we hurried through the streets of New Haven. The mocking sun was lighting the world in splendor, as if it were not a sad, weary, frightful world. I had pictured to myself many a time the pleasure of rolling through the streets of New Haven and stopping at Sadie's door. But I had never pictured it in this way. Oh, never. The sleigh stopped at last, and Dr. Douglass lifted me out. A strange face opened the door and addressed us hurriedly:

"The lady is to come up quick."

"Oh! where?" I asked wildly and struggled to free my arm from Dr. Douglass's grasp; but he held me firmly and spoke with gentle decision:

"Be quiet, Julia. Remember how much may be depending on your self-control."

Then we went up the stairs together, into that pleasant south chamber that had been so accurately described to me as Mother's room. I took in but one object distinctly—that was my mother's form. It was very unnaturally quiet, and the eyes were turned heavenward and had in them a rapt, unearthly gaze.

Dr. Van Anden held up his finger with a hushing gesture, but in almost the same moment said: "She has entered in," and turned pityingly toward me; but there came to me, then, one of those blessed moments of utter and entire unconsciousness. I remember only that when all knowledge of earth went from me, my head was lying where it had so often lain before—on my mother's breast. What a terrible awakening it was! How the dumb, awful sense of my loss and my desolation surged over me! Oh, Mother, Mother! I had neglected her. I had disobeyed her teachings, disregarded her injunctions; but I had loved her! How much I never knew until I knelt there beside a mother from whom the soul had fled. I shall never forget it, that scene, nor the weary hours and days that followed—hours in which I was utterly and sometimes wildly rebellious. Only to have heard her voice once more, to have felt her kind eyes resting on me, to have been able to say to her: "Oh, dear, *dear* Mother, forgive me," and then I thought I could have borne it. I remember how it seemed to me when I heard my brother say in low tones to Dr. Douglass:

"If you could only have reached here on the morning express. I thought you would. I ascertained that my telegram went through. How came you to miss that train? She was conscious for more than an hour, and talked with each one of us. If Julia could have been here then."

I think my voice must have sounded strangely to them. It had a hollow sound to me, and they both started when I spoke.

"Dr. Douglass, is that morning express of which you spoke the one that leaves Newton at eight o'clock?"

The doctor understands my nature very well. He never evades the truth. So he simply bowed his head.

"Did you get the telegram before eight?"

Another silent bow.

"Then, if I had stayed at home that evening, I could have been here in time?"

This time he bent over me and spoke in pitying tones:

"Julia, my poor child, remember the compassionate Savior knows all about it."

But I answered him only by a low murmured:

"Oh, how can I *ever* bear it?"

And truly it seemed to me that I could not. Sadie was all tenderness and thoughtfulness. She talked to me a great deal of Mother, dwelling particularly on the remembrance of how much Mother had talked about me during the last weeks of her life; how great her anxiety was lest I was overworking, lest I was lonely and homesick and grieving for her. Sadie little knew what barbed arrows her words often were. To her these were only little tender memories of Mother's constant, brooding love for her child. To me they were proofs that I had racked her tired heart with unnecessary anxieties and stung her with cruel neglect. During some of these talks Dr. Douglass was present, and he used to stand with averted face—if possible, with his back to us, looking at a book or paper. Once, when Sadie was speaking of my mother's fears when no letter came, he turned suddenly and spoke almost sharply:

"She received my telegram, did she not?"

"Oh yes," Sadie said; "and we were so thankful. She slept well that night; but the night before she said that every time she slept she dreamed that Julia was in great peril, and awoke in fright. We thought seriously of sending for Julia to come and make us a visit and relieve Mother's mind. If we had not received your telegram just when we did, we should have sent for her."

"Then, Dr. Douglass," I said with a burst of uncontrollable tears, "I wish you had never sent it."

He came and sat down by me, speaking gently and tenderly:

"All things work together for good to them that love God."

"I don't love him," I said amid my passionate weeping. "I don't think I ever could have loved him, or I would never have gone on living as I have during this dreadful time. It is all a mistake; everything is a dreadful, *dreadful* mistake."

These times of violent grief were very rare with me; more generally I felt stunned, apathetic, indifferent to everything. I remember what loving care my brother Alfred had over me during those days. I remember principally his earnest, simple, fervent prayers when occasionally he led in family worship. I remember a certain dull sense of comfort I felt in thinking that Alfred was not like me, and Sadie was not like me, and that my mother was with those of her children who must have been a joy to her, and away from the one who would only have given her pain.

It was the morning of the day on which we were to bury our dead that Sadie came to me in my room and, wrapping loving arms about me, said gently:

"Dear Julia, you have said nothing in regard to our dress."

"I do not care anything about dress," I said almost fiercely. "I hate the word."

She looked at me with a sort of pitying surprise. She did not know how persistently this question had robbed me of my peace during the past months; how at times it had seemed a very demon, whose aim was to appear before me whenever there came into my heart a shadow of longing after a different life from the one which I was leading.

"Mother spoke of it," Sadie began again in low tone, after a moment's puzzled pause. "She never approved of the custom of wearing mourning, you know. The feeling grew upon her, and she spoke particularly of her desire that we should make no change. Will that be unpleasant to you, dear?"

"No," I said apathetically. "Nothing is unpleasant or pleasant to me anymore. I don't care about anything.

"Only heaven, and Mother, Father, and Ester, all there, waiting for us," Sadie said tenderly.

But I think the strongest feeling in my mind at that time was a dull sense of satisfaction in the thought that I should go back to Newton and shock Mrs. Tyndall by not wearing mourning. During those days I had a kind of fierce feeling toward Mrs. Tyndall as if she were the author of all my sorrow.

It was a strange time, those two weeks that I spent with Sadie. Dr. Douglass went home the morning after the funeral and left me to rest. I don't think I rested much. I gave entire freedom to the torpor that had come upon me. I did not try to rally from it in the least. My heart felt dead within me, and I let it remain thus, without an attempt or wish to rouse it into action. I told myself there was nothing to live for; Sadie had a husband and a home—I was not necessary to her comfort or happiness. Alfred was intent upon his business, his Sunday school, his little mission class—he had no need of me; and here was Mother lying low under the sod upon which I was sitting, for I went much to my mother's grave, and during this time I do not think I once thought of her as glorified. Heaven seemed nowhere to me. There was nothing anywhere but a grave.

As I look back on those days I wonder that my brain endured the strain that I put upon it. I wonder most of all how those who have no personal acquaintance with a dying, risen Redeemer can ever live through the long weary days that follow the making of a new grave, in which their all seems to be buried. I know now something of what it might have been to have lived so near to Jesus that I could have almost seen him open the gates of the holy city to let my mother in; that I could have almost heard the anthem of the angels as they sang her welcome home. There was no need that I should sit thus drearily upon a grave and look only on crumbling earth when I knew that heaven and Christ and Mother were all realities, and far above and away from *graves*; but yet it was to me as if no Savior of mine had ever lain therein. I was not conscious of feeling it, I was not conscious of a friend. I did not lean my head on his bosom as I might have done. I stood straight and still and sullen; and yet—and yet I know now that all the while he held me by the hand, else I would surely have dropped away into despair.

18

THE BLIND LEAD THE BLIND

THE day on which I journeyed back to Newton was one of those rainy, sleety, unutterably dreary days of late winter. I shuddered as I looked gloomily out on the black and dreary objects past which we whirled. Life seemed to me utterly purposeless and hopeless. I had not rallied from my sorrow as girls of sixteen are wont to do. I think there was too much regret and remorse mingled with my weeping to let my tears be easily stayed. I had steadily resisted Dr. Van Anden's earnest offers of a home, and Sadie's pleading. I was going back to Newton. I had begun to earn my own living. I had meant someday to earn not only mine, but Mother's. All that was past; but I was not in a mood to give up my work. Indeed, I needed it, to keep me from sinking in utter gloom. Those days of idleness and nights of bitter, unavailing weeping, spent alone in Mother's room, well-nigh drove me distracted. I think they all saw this at last and yielded to my fierce wish to get to work.

My employers had been very kind, as kindness goes. The senior partner, Mr. Sayles, had written me a letter

full of well-meaning set phrases. He had reminded me
that sorrow was the "common lot of all"; that I must
expect to be tried in the "furnace of affliction"; that
"in the midst of life we are in death"; and that "I had
one more reminder that time was short"; closing with
the statement that two weeks were the utmost limit
of their indulgence to me. They should like to do
better, especially in this time of trial; but business cares
were very pressing, and they needed all hands at their
posts. I tore the letter into bits and burned it; not that
I considered it a bad letter in its way; not that I was
ungrateful to them for their kindness in sparing me
for two weeks. I knew they were busy and needed me;
but it cut me so to see the cold, hard fact set down in
so many words—that Mother was dead. Everybody
knew it and realized it. I need expect no one to say to
me: "Perhaps you are mistaken; perhaps she is not dead
after all"; or, "Perhaps you will hear from her tomorrow." Never such words anymore. My mother was
dead and buried. Everybody accepted the hard, un-
yielding fact; and yet everybody went on about their
work, and I must go about mine just as usual. The
books must be kept, and everywhere things would be
just as they had been, except that my Saturday evening
letter would never come again. Oh! that awful exception!

I shivered and drew my waterproof closer about me
as I stepped from the cars at Newton. The air seemed
thick and heavy, and yet was keen, and pierced me
through. I expected no one to meet me. I had not
written to announce my arrival. It suited my mood
best to go in sullen loneliness to my boarding place;
but my feet had no sooner touched the ground than
I felt my hand drawn through a firm, strong arm, and
in a moment more I was seated in a close carriage. I

silently gave my check when it was demanded and leaned back in the carriage with a little touch of softened feeling over the fact that I had still a friend.

"How did you know I was coming tonight?" I asked as Dr. Douglass, having attended to my baggage, seated himself beside me.

"Alfred telegraphed me this morning, according to my directions," he said quietly as if it were a matter of course.

Mrs. Tyndall's reception of me was the very perfection of kindness—tender, gentle, sympathetic, and yet not officious. But she jarred upon me. I felt in my heart bitter toward her. I blamed her for all of my shortcomings and heart wanderings. More than all, I blamed her for that last evening of giddy pleasure. *But for her,* I said to myself, in what gloom and desolation only my own heart knew—*But for her, I should have seen my mother again. I should have heard her speak one more word; for I would not have gone that evening if she would have given up.* And then there would come such a rush of hard, rebellious longings into my soul, and I would feel almost as if I hated her. Oh, those heavy days! I began to pray again regularly morning and evening as I had been wont to do; for I did not openly rebel. But there was no comfort in my praying—no sense of nearness to my Savior. A great, gloomy wall seemed built up between Christ and my weary heart, and I could not get to him; at least I thought I couldn't. In the shop I worked steadily and silently. The girls were kind; Frank Hooper spoke to me in softened tones, Caroline Brighton left me entirely out of her practical jokes, and little Ruth Walker kissed me softly and silently, night and morning. And so I dragged my unwilling soul through the dreadful days, and sometimes it seemed to me that I should die.

Sometimes I wished and longed for death. Often and often I fiercely longed for a sharp, protracted, prostrating illness—one that would bring delirium or unconsciousness to me. Many a time since then have I wondered at the goodness of my Father in not answering in all their bitter meaning my wild, unspoken prayers.

It was not a natural condition of mind for one so young as I. It was not a simple, submissive sorrow. But my life for months had not been a healthy life, either spiritually or morally, and the reaction was marked and lasting.

Dr. Douglass pushed open the door that separated the dining room from the library and lingered beside me in the latter place one evening before the others came in.

"Julia," he said gently, "will you not go out with me to the meeting this evening?"

"No," I said with a sudden rush of tears. I recalled vividly how I had said to him that I would go to church every evening after the festival; that there would be nothing in the world to hinder. (And truly there was not; there need be no letters written to Mother now.) "I don't want to go," I continued. "I don't want to do anything, nor see anybody."

"Will she like that, do you think?" he asked me in low, sad tones.

I checked my tears in wonderment and questioned: "Who?"

"Your mother. Do you imagine that she has lost all interest in you because she has gone to another home, especially when she is looking forward to the time when you will come to be with her there? Do you think she is pleased with your utter abandonment of yourself to your sorrow, as if you had lost her forever?"

There seemed a newness and strangeness in these ideas. *"Will* she like that, do you think?" he had said; not that dreadful "Would she have liked it if—" that was always like sharp-pointed needles pushed into me; but this "Will she?"—not as though I had lost my mother—not that she had dropped out of life and left a blank. It flashed across me like a new idea—"My mother is living. She does not live in New Haven now; she has moved, and the City to which she has moved is wonderful and beautiful; and she expects me to come and live with her." The sensation was new, and it thrilled me. She cared for me still. If she was living, she had not ceased to love me. I smiled at the thought. I looked up gratefully at Dr. Douglass.

"I did not think of her as really *living* in heaven," I said. "Indeed, heaven seemed to me to be nowhere. It seemed to me that she *must* be in the grave. I saw her laid there—her very face," and the cloud swept over me again at the remembrance of that open grave, and I finished my sentence with choking tears.

Dr. Douglass's next sentence hushed and awed me, and flushed my face with eager wonder and wild anxiety.

"I have a message for you from her," he said quietly. And he drew from his pocket a small sealed package and gave it to me. "I don't know anything of the contents," he added. "The package was entrusted to me to give to you when I thought you could endure it. I think you need it now."

I seized upon it in nervous haste and hurried away with it to my room. The address was in Sadie's hand-writing, and within, on a slip of paper that was folded carefully around the sheet, she had written a few lines.

My Dear Sister—

Only a few weeks ago I was talking with our mother about Ester's letter to me, read by me long after she was safe in heaven. I told Mother about what an influence I thought it had exerted over my life since then; how much I prized it; then I let her read it. I had never brought myself to do so before, but I thought Mother would like to know about it. She seemed very much interested and deeply moved, and the next evening she entrusted the enclosed note to my keeping. You will see how it is addressed, she said. If I should be called first, you may give it to her. Oh, Julia, I remember with what a great throb of pain I took it from her, hoping and praying in my selfish heart that some other hand than mine might give it to you; that when Mother went away I might be there in heaven to welcome her; not that I wanted to leave my husband and my home, but I wanted to cling to Mother. It was but a few days afterward that God called her; and now, my darling, I send this letter to you. I hope it will not make your pain deeper. I trust that it will come to be a help and comfort to you.

Then I took up with reverent hand the enclosed sheet and read in that dear handwriting that was so familiar to me those loving words: "To be given to my dear daughter Julia when her mother is at rest." That sentence brought a burst of tears, and it was some little time before I was quiet enough to open the letter and read:

My precious child (so it commenced when at last my tear-dimmed eyes could decipher the words), Mother isn't going to make you sad over this letter. I do not want you to be that. I write it rather that it may come to you in your sorrow and help you to be strong and brave. When you read it, darling, think of where I am—in heaven! Your father and Ester and I, waiting there for the rest of the children. It is not to be a long letter—it is only to say God bless you and keep you near to him. Remember, my child, that Mother's great longing, her absorbing desire for you, is that you shall keep close to Jesus. The older I grow and the nearer I come to the end, the more I realize that for us who are his children there should be one absorbing prayer:

> Nearer, my God, to thee, nearer to thee,
> E'en though it be a cross that raiseth me.

Now, my darling child, good-bye. I give you a mother's blessing to follow you all your life. May it be a long, good life, such a one as we, waiting for you up there, will love to look at. I hope it will be a cheerful life, that great trial or pain may not be necessary for you; but remember, above all other things, I hope and pray that it may be a life of single-hearted consecration to Christ.

My darling, good-bye. God bless you and keep you.

MOTHER

I sat still, very still, and held this sacred letter in my hands. My tears were dried; I did not feel like shedding any more. I felt awed and solemnized. It almost seemed to me that I had heard a voice speaking to me from heaven. I had never hoped for another letter from my mother. I had mourned, oh, *so* bitterly, that she could not have said to me "good-bye." Now here it was, the good-bye, the blessing, the earnest parting words. There was no hint as to what my life had been of late. I was thankful that my mother had been spared the grief of knowing. "E'en though it be a cross that raiseth me." I had not prayed that prayer, but perhaps Mother had for me. The cross had fallen upon me bitter and heavy to be borne. Would it raise me to him? "It shall," I said aloud and solemnly. "I will live a different life. Oh, Mother, your prayer shall be answered. I will hide my life in Christ." I prayed that night, prayed long and earnestly, but there was not rest in the prayer, no comfort, no light; the words as I spoke them seemed to sound dully back against my own heart. Still I was in a measure satisfied. I felt that my coldheartedness was the reaction from incessant grief. I made many resolutions. I would begin to live now in earnest. I told myself I would be strong and brave, as Mother had wished. I would make myself what I knew would please her. There was work for me to do in every direction. I would not shrink from or shirk it anymore. As I look back tonight on the resolves and the prayers of that evening, I both smile and sigh—smile at my ignorance and sigh that it was possible to have been so ignorant—I who had been a Christian for more than six years. How wonderful it is that Christ submits to our being named after him, while we are living such miserable, dwarfed, sickly lives! I seemed to imagine that I had but to signify my willingness to retrace my steps and take up my dropped and neglected duties lying about me on every side, when at once the full blaze of light and love and peace would burst upon me. I went to work at once among the girls in the shop; and I worked very much as I prayed, with many laborious, earnest-sounding words that seemed to sound hollow and bound back at me from every point.

"Frank," I said in earnest and disapproving tones when we were alone in the storeroom for a few minutes, "why *don't* you attend the meetings? I should think you might show *so* much interest at least."

Frank bestowed a searching look on me and then answered solemnly:

"Because I am a reprobate. There is no mistaking that fact. I really don't believe there is any hope for me. Suppose you try Carrie Brighton. I shouldn't wonder if you'd find her in a softened state of mind. *I'm* a sad instance of total depravity. There have to be some standing proofs to a doctrine, living witnesses, you know, and I'm one of them."

"I wouldn't trifle about anything so solemn," I said severely.

"Solemn as what? Total depravity? It *is* a solemn truth. I'm convinced of that. *I* don't trifle with it, it trifles with me—lies in wait to deceive me at every point."

She whisked off at the conclusion of this sentence and left me wondering whether indeed her gaily spoken words were not true, and herself a hopeless reprobate; and not a shadow of doubt as to whether I had spoken the right words to her in the right manner for one moment entered my mind. I made one more effort during that day. I asked Caroline Brighton if she didn't think it would be a good idea for her to go to the meeting that evening. She answered me with grave thoughtfulness.

"I don't know. What time do they close? What time was it last night and the night before?"

"I don't know," I answered confusedly. "I wasn't there."

"Oh! well, if I thought it would be out by eight I might go; but you see, I am going to the circus at eight, and if they shouldn't close in time it might be awkward."

There was a chorus of laughter from the girls who had heard her loud replies and guessed at my low-spoken questions.

"How religious that girl is getting," I overheard one of the girls say as I passed out of sight but not out of sound; and Caroline answered:

"It isn't religion, poor child, but she thinks it is. Her mother is dead, and she feels dismal and has mistaken the symptoms. I feel as patient as Job toward her."

And this is all my profession of religion was worth in that shop! Yet I was in earnest. I honestly grieved over my failures—only there was this one difficulty: I never imagined them to be *my* failures. I was being led by my own blind self and mistaking it for the leadings of the Spirit of God.

19

CONFLICTING FORCES

ONE of the marked features of my changed feelings during those days was my aversion for Mrs. Tyndall. It grew upon me, which was no wonder, for I nursed it as a virtuous thing. I could not tolerate the slightest interference from her: indeed, I named her most innocent and kindly words after that title. I really wonder at her patience with my lofty airs and often sharp words. I remember how vexed I was to discover that Dr. Douglass by no means approved of this marked change.

"I don't understand you in the least," I said to him one evening, speaking irritably. "There seems to be no such thing as pleasing you. When I was allowing Mrs. Tyndall to lead me in any direction that she chose, you were always looking grave and disturbed over it; and now that I am trying to break away from her influence and be myself, you seem equally out of sorts about it."

"No, Julia," he answered gravely, "I am not sorry that you do not yield to her influence as you formerly did. I am only sorry for the manner in which you exhibit the change. You seem almost bitter in your

feeling toward Mrs. Tyndall, and unjust in your esti-
mate of her."

"I am bitter," I said fiercely. "I wonder if I haven't
reason? Think what a life she has made me lead. She
has interfered with everything that was ever taught
me. She has warped my judgment and biased my
opinions, and, worse than all, made me neglect my
own mother. I can never forgive her for it."

"But, Julia," he interposed with a puzzled and
troubled air, "was it absolutely necessary to follow in
her footsteps? Had you really no other guide, no other
friend?"

"It makes no difference whether I had or not," I
answered moodily. "I followed her, at any rate."

"But I think it makes a *great* difference; and herein
lies your mistake. You are blaming Mrs. Tyndall instead
of your own heart. You are indulging in bitter, un-
christian feelings toward her instead of going to the
fountainhead of all the trouble and laying bare your
own heart."

"She has been a professor of religion for a good
many years. She ought to have set me a better example."

"Suppose she had done so; is there any certainty
that you would have followed it? Was there no other
example than hers to follow?"

"Oh yes," I said angrily, "I might have followed
yours. I suppose that is what you mean."

To this I received no answer, other than a reproach-
ful look from grave, sad eyes. Then he asked me, in
gentle, tender tones:

"Do you find rest and peace in your religion
nowadays, Julia? Do you find comfort in prayer?"

"No, I do not," I answered with quivering lip. "I try
to pray, and it seems to me that I can't. I am not at rest

at all. I don't know anything about peace. My heart is all wrong, and I can't get it right."

I finished the sentence with a sob. My heart was very sore. All my efforts at reform, either in myself or others, seemed to end in failure, and sometimes I was half angry, and sometimes my heart felt as if it were broken. The doctor answered me gently:

"No, poor child, you can't. If I were you, I would not try any longer. It would do no good if you were to keep trying for a hundred years."

I turned to him, great astonishment in my voice:

"Doctor, what do you mean?"

"Why, my dear child, don't you see, you have reached the very center of all the trouble? Your heart is all wrong; and *you* can't make it right. Why should you try? Why not take it to Jesus, and tell him: Here, Lord, is my heart; it is all wrong. *I* can't do anything with it. Create in me a *clean* heart and renew a *right* spirit within me."

My tone and manner of speech had changed very much during the last few sentences that I had spo-ken—one of those sudden moods to which I was subject during those days had swept over me, and my heart seemed melted. I think I was honestly trying to get into the light and stumbling over my own blind self. I had a letter that evening which had much to do with all the after years of my life. Dr. Douglass sent it up to me when he stopped on his way to prayer meeting—sent that, and a renewed request that I would go out with him to the meeting. But I shrank from that. I distrusted my own nerves and dreaded above all things a show of feeling that would draw me into notice. His request irritated me—perhaps be-cause my conscience desired to avoid the matter—and I gave a very decided refusal and sat down with ruffled feelings to my letter, indifferent as to who had written it, since the penmanship was neither Sadie's nor Alfred's. It ran thus:

Dear Cousin Julia:

Papa and Mamma are going West, for Papa's health. Brother Ralph and his wife are in Europe, you know, and I am still to be disposed of. The question is: Whither shall I go? I want to come to you—share your room, and your bed, and your heart. May I come? Coax your hostess for me. We ought to love each other more, you and I, because of our dear Ester. That is, you ought to love me very much more than you do. I love you enough already. How our friends are gathering home! I want to see you and talk with you about them. How glad Ester must have been to welcome Auntie. I wonder if she is acquainted with Mr. Foster now? I have only one treasure— my very *own,* you know—waiting for me. While you—why you are rich; Uncle, and Auntie, and two sisters, and the little Minie. Isn't it nice to think you will have to leave none of them down here when you go home? I like that thought. I was sorry not to be with you when you laid Auntie's body to rest; that is, somewhat sorry. Not so *very* sorry, you know, because I remember her face as it was when I saw her last; and you know, she will look ever so much more like that when I see her again than she will like the coffined face that, in spite of yourself, comes in between you and your mother in heaven. I know how that is. The veil of the flesh is sometimes heavy, but it lifts; and, my darling, there is glory beyond it.

I want to come to you. I think very likely we need each other. I want to come just as soon as I can. I want you to run down now—this min- ute—just as soon as you finish your letter, and coax your Mrs.—(I've forgotten her name) to take me to board. Tell her you want me, you know. You do, don't you? Write to me this evening, when you have come back to your room, then I shall have your letter on Thursday; and if it is such a letter as I think you will write—such a letter as I want you to write— why, then you will have *me* on the following Tuesday.

Your loving COUSIN ABBIE

It was certainly a very strange letter of condolence; indeed, you see, there was no pity or sympathy ex- pressed, or apparently felt; yet it touched me as none of the good, kind, well-meaning, terrible letters that I had received since my mother's death had begun to do. Yes, I certainly wanted her. I had not realized it before. I had not thought of her at all; but that letter made me feel as though she were just the something for which I had been longing and craving. I went down with the letter in my hand to Mrs. Tyndall. She was lounging on the sofa in the library, and her husband was lounging in an easy chair beside her. They were laughing when I came in, but they checked their mirth as if they must not laugh in my presence. I did not need these constant reminders that my mother was dead. I told my errand briefly and somewhat stiffly—not at all in the coaxing way that Abbie had probably imagined.

Mrs. Tyndall laughingly addressed her husband:

"I declare, Mr. Tyndall, I believe we shall have to open a boardinghouse in self-defense. This is the third application that I have had lately. Julia, I would do almost anything for you, and I feel peculiarly anxious to help you now in your sorrow; but it does not seem quite the thing for me to go to taking boarders. You know I hardly consider Dr. Douglass and yourself in that light. Who is this cousin of yours?"

I had a weapon to make use of that I considered more effective than any coaxings of mine. I briefly produced it now.

"She is the only daughter of Mr. Ralph Ried, of New York City."

Mrs. Tyndall's eyes brightened. She sat up with sudden energy.

"Not Ralph Ried, of the firm of Ried, Wilkison & Co.?"

"Yes, ma'am, that is Uncle Ralph's business address."

"Why! how very singular. Mr. Tyndall has had business dealings with him for years, and I saw him myself once. He is an immensely rich man, even as New York people count riches. And this young lady is his daughter? Why have you never told me before?"

"I do not remember that you ever asked me," I said with exceeding stiffness. Whereat she laughed pleasantly and continued her catechism.

"What is this young lady like? What have I heard about her? Mr. Tyndall, don't you remember the Arlingtons told us of her? She was disappointed matrimonially, or something of that sort, wasn't she?"

"Her intended husband was killed but a few hours before their marriage was to have taken place," I explained.

"Oh yes, I remember. How very sad. Does she wear a widow's dress? No. Well, it wouldn't be wise—might interfere with future marriages. Well, Julia, under the peculiar circumstances I might let her come for a while. I suppose there is really no reason why I shouldn't, only it is rather funny."

I had had not a shadow of doubt as to my success from the moment that she had exclaimed, "Not Ralph Ried, of the firm of Ried, Wilkison & Co." So I went away without exhibiting much elation over my success and wrote my letter to Abbie. Then I waited for her with some impatience and a great deal of curiosity. I had not seen her since my sister Ester's death, six years before. I remembered her very vividly as she was then; but now I reflected she was twenty-four years old. It seemed an age fraught with dignity. I more than half expected to be afraid of her. I made great preparations for meeting her at the depot, enlisting Dr. Douglass in the service, who most unqualifiedly approved of the expected arrival. But she came unexpectedly after all. My cousin Abbie always did and always *will* do unexpected things. I came home from the shop a little earlier than usual on the day in which we were looking for her, and hastened at once to my room, eager to have it properly garnished in her honor. The moment I opened the door two small soft hands were placed over my eyes, and I was kissed, mouth and nose and chin, little gleeful laughs issuing meanwhile from the sweet lips of the kisser. At last she released me and stood back for a more "artistic view," so she said.

"Yes, you look like her. You certainly do," she said at last in a bright, eager voice. "I was afraid you wouldn't, but you do very much."

"Look like whom?" I said at last wonderingly.

"Ester. You see, I wanted you to resemble her, because it would seem so natural. She and I spent so many happy hours together, and now you and I are going to."

This seemed strange to me. I had rarely heard my sister Ester mentioned during these years, and when she had been it was in a solemn tone, as one who was dead, gone out of our life, away from our interests, to be spoken of no more. I remember I thought then that Abbie spoke of her more as we would of one who had gone to Europe to live than as one who had died. When we went down to tea I smiled to think of Mrs. Tyndall's conception of her in widow's weeds, she looked so bright and fresh; her fair hair still clung in rings about her head, and her dress, of soft, clinging material, was as blue as the sky and fitted her fairylike form to perfection. She looked and seemed not a day older than I remembered her as a child. Her reception of Mrs. Tyndall's graceful courtesies was sweet and sunny. I frowned upon them, and inwardly resolved that she should not be deceived as I had been. "I will tell her all about that woman tonight," I said to myself in an emphatic manner. Mr. Sayles was present, and Abbie chatted with him in the free, frank way that it was her nature to assume. While we loitered at the table the church bells rang.

"Do you have meeting this evening?" Abbie asked of me with brightening eyes. "Is it your church bell? Why, wouldn't that be a pleasant omen to attend a prayer meeting on the first evening of my arrival?"

Dr. Douglass explained that they were holding a series of meetings, in which subject she at once became deeply interested.

"Isn't it time to go?" she questioned as we still lingered. "Oh, no, I am not in the least tired. I rested nicely last night; I always do on the cars. I shall like to go very much."

"The little enthusiast!" Mr. Sayles said, laughing.

They were talking about her still when I went back to search for my handkerchief; and as I opened the door I heard him say in an amused tone:

"The little enthusiast. It is really refreshing to hear her talk." Then to me. "Miss Julia, I have promised to conduct your little cousin and yourself to church this evening, if you will allow. Dr. Douglass was obligated to go out professionally, and deputized me."

Mrs. Tyndall laughed.

"You must tell a straighter story than that," she said gaily, "if you want Julia to believe you. Julia, he offered his services to take you to church, and the doctor looked amazed, as well he might. I think the millennium must be coming."

"Or the days of witchcraft returning," Mr. Tyndall said amusedly.

20

SOME SEARCHING QUESTIONS

THE meeting was one of marked interest. I felt thrilled and solemnized; felt also a great longing after that rest, and peace, and joy of which several spoke with great earnestness. I think this was one among the many mistakes of my life at that time. I went about searching for the rest, and peace, and joy, never realizing that to one who was faithfully and patiently lifting her cross, they came without being looked after.

"Was it not a precious meeting?" Abbie said as we walked homeward. "Didn't you enjoy it?"

She asked the question, not of me, but of Mr. Sayles.

He answered in a very amused tone:

"I really cannot say that I did, particularly."

"Oh! didn't you? I am *so* sorry. What was the trouble?"

"The trouble was with me, I suspect—miserable sinner that I am. I failed to get into the spirit of the affair."

Abbie raised her eyes to his face and gave his a surprised, sad look. In the glow of the moonlight her face seemed to me that of an angel.

"Do you mean that you are not a Christian?" she asked after a moment's silence, in low tones.

He seemed excessively amused. It was with difficulty that he restrained an absolute laugh. I felt greatly provoked with him, and a little bit so with Abbie. It seemed to me a decided case of casting pearls before swine.

"It must be the first time that anyone ever imagined for a moment that you had a serious thought on that subject, or any other," I said tartly. "I don't wonder that you are amused."

He laughed with his usual careless good nature, made some light remark about the meeting not having improved my manner of speech, then bent his head toward Abbie and said gently:

"You seem surprised."

"I am," she answered, still sadly. "I surely thought you were a Christian."

"May I ask why?"

"Oh, I hardly know. You seemed such friends, all of you—Mrs. Tyndall, and the doctor, and all. I thought, of course, that bond united you."

He was grave enough now.

"I wish it did," he said earnestly; and then we were at home, and he left me wondering whether he really wished any such thing. It seemed very unlike him; and yet it was the first grave sentence that I had ever heard from his lips on the subject.

Abbie went directly to Mrs. Tyndall's side—nestled, indeed, on the low ottoman in front of her—and said:

"You should have gone tonight. It was a precious meeting. Are you not able to go out in the evenings? What a deprivation it must be to you."

With a person sitting opposite to her who knew that she had been out to a concert, or lecture, or shopping four evenings in succession, it would hardly do to leave this supposition unexplained. So she answered frankly:

"Oh yes, I am able. But the fact is, my dear child, I am older than you, and of course haven't your delightful enthusiasm."

Such a commencement as that had puzzled me once, and it irritated me nowadays. I had been wont to answer it with wondering silence, until of late I was given to turning from her with a disgusted frown.

Abbie asked simply and sweetly:

"What has enthusiasm to do with going to prayer meeting, Mrs. Tyndall?"

"A great deal, my dear. Indeed, I fear that in the minds of many people there is nothing left of the meeting but enthusiasm. The fact is, my dear, I do not believe in religious spasms. I think them very unhealthful. How did you like our church? Don't you think the colors light up well?"

"*Very* well. I thought the church exceedingly pretty. What *are* religious spasms, Mrs. Tyndall?"

Mrs. Tyndall laughed.

"Why, going to meeting every evening," she said at last. "A season of excitement that leaves no one better, but rather worse."

"But, Mrs. Tyndall, what is excitement?"

My cousin Abbie had a most remarkable talent for asking direct close questions and keeping persons to the point, looking at them, meantime, with great, earnest, thoughtful eyes.

Mrs. Tyndall nestled uneasily among the cushions.

"Why, making an unnecessary commotion about a matter."

"Well, but you are talking about something that is not taking place. If commotion means noise, there was none of that this evening. It was very quiet and solemn."

Mrs. Tyndall laid her hand on my cousin's arm and spoke with winning sweetness, but in a tone calculated to check all further discussion:

"My dear, I don't quarrel with other people's fancies in the least. They may go to prayer meeting every night in the three hundred and sixty-five, if they are so disposed; but, personally, I don't like religious fanaticism. Julia, was Mr. Sayles out tonight?"

"Yes, ma'am," I answered briefly; and Abbie asked in her most gentle tone:

"Mrs. Tyndall, won't you please tell me what religious fanaticism is?"

I think it at last became evident to Mrs. Tyndall's mind that she must give a direct and definite answer to Abbie's questionings, or else definitely decline to do so.

"I think," she said, speaking slowly and with dignity—"I think that the getting up of special meetings at a certain season of the year, and insisting that at that particular time people must desert their other employments and duties, and go to church all the time, is fanaticism. I want my religion to be an everyday affair, and not something put on during a few weeks in the winter."

"But, Mrs. Tyndall, do you reason in that way about other matters? Don't we take advantage of the season of comparative leisure to get up lectures, and concerts, and benevolent associations? Why should we not use the same wisdom in trying to reach the religious nature of people?"

"Excitement isn't religion," Mrs. Tyndall said with that delicious disregard for logic that people of that temperament are apt to exhibit. Abbie replied with great calmness:

"No, certainly it isn't; and excitement isn't music either; and yet I never heard people object to a reasonable amount of enthusiasm over some exquisite rendering of a beautiful song, for instance. Don't you think that we are a little bit too much afraid of a *religious* excitement, when we consider excitements over common matters perfectly correct and reasonable? What do you think excitement is, anyway, Mrs. Tyndall?"

Mrs. Tyndall laughed pleasantly.

"How like a moving dictionary you treat me," she said gaily. "Why, I think excitement is—is *excitement*. Don't you?"

And Abbie laid her hand on the lady's arm with a winning, caressing movement, and said gently:

"No—but seriously, please."

"Well, of course, I mean by excitement extreme interest in any matter; interest carried to an improper degree."

"And what degree of interest do you think is proper in regard to religious matters? When does it become extreme?"

The answer was a very cautious one.

"Of course there cannot be too great a degree of interest, but there can be an injudicious expression of it."

"And do you think prayer meetings injudicious?"

"Why, no, of course not. But—"

And then there really seemed to be nothing further to say. Abbie waited a little and then spoke in a very earnest tone:

"Don't you think we sometimes amaze our unconverted friends by no expression at all of, or interest in, religion, or in them, spiritually? How strange it would seem if your husband lay dying in the room above and you sat here chatting with us, and suppressing all unseemly interest in him."

"The cases are not analogous," Mrs. Tyndall said quickly. "If he lay dying, the danger would be immediate and certain."

"How can we ever be sure *how* near and *how* certain it is in regard to the never-dying souls?"

Abbie's voice was very low and tender, but *so* solemnly in earnest, and for the first time since I had known her, Mrs. Tyndall responded only by silence.

The door was no sooner closed upon us, in our room, than I commenced at once:

"I am glad you have learned something already of Mrs. Tyndall's peculiar views. She has a great many of them. I have been dreadfully deceived and misled by her. I'm sure I didn't want you to be. How did she impress you?"

"As a woman for whom we ought to pray," Abbie answered so gently and earnestly that for a moment my volubility was checked. I rallied, however.

"You may well think so. If you knew as much about her as I do!" And immediately I launched forth into the history of my acquaintance with her from the time of my coming to her house to board up to that date. She received the history in absolute silence, and at last, to break it, I had to assail her with a question:

"Did you ever hear of such a woman in your life?"

Her answer was very gentle:

"Dear Julia, I presume the Savior has. He bears with all classes of Christians."

"I don't believe that she is a Christian at all," I said stoutly. "I think she is a hypocrite, if there ever was one."

"I am always so very thankful that we not only have not to judge people's conduct, but are absolutely forbidden to do so. Dear Julia, I think it is harder to pray for anyone toward whom we harbor such thoughts. Don't you?"

"She doesn't think that she has any need for anybody's prayers. She thinks she is perfection."

"Do you pray for her, Julia?"

"No." I frankly admitted that I had never prayed for her in my life. "I can't," I added bitterly. "I know I don't feel right toward her, and I *cannot.* Oh, Abbie, if you only knew what I have to thank her for."

Whereupon I told her with many bitter tears that sad story of the festival, to which I would never have gone but for her, and how I thereby lost that last kiss from my mother, for which my heart would always ache. I told the story truthfully, I thought. I know now that it was strangely colored by my bitter feelings. Indeed, Abbie's first sentence showed it to me in part.

"Poor child, poor darling child, and you could not decide which was right, whether to go or stay? Did no one advise with you? Did you pray about it very earnestly, Julia?"

I was silent and dumbfounded. No one to advise with me! What if she had heard Dr. Douglass's pleading and Dr. Mulford's earnest words? I distinctly remember that I had not at any time felt the least doubt as to which was the strictly right thing to do.

"No," I said at last, speaking more humbly than I had before; "no, I didn't pray about it at all."

"How could you have expected to go right?" she asked me, softening the words with a loving caress and tender kisses.

"Do you pray about every little thing?" I questioned abruptly; and she answered me with brightening eyes and smiling lips as if there was a wellspring of joy in the words.

"For the very hairs of your head are all numbered." She changed the subject after that suddenly and brightly.

"This does so remind me of Ester's and my first evening together. Only we were wicked that night— very wicked. I was, at least. I talked to her until after one o'clock. But, you see, I had so many things to ask her about, Aunt Laura and all of you."

"You will have no mother to ask *me* about," I answered mournfully with the ever-ready rush of tears. She turned toward me with wondering eyes and spoke wonderingly.

"Why not? Don't you like to talk about your mother? You have had no one, though, to talk with; but you will like to tell me all about her, will you not? Because, you know, I love her, too. Oh, I have looked forward to nice talks with you about Aunt Laura."

Again, as I listened to her, there stole over me that strange, sweet feeling that, after all, Mother was *my* mother still, even though God had given her a better home. Abbie said, "I *love* her, too"; not, "I *loved* her," as so many say. Then I need not cease to love my mother. I brought my chair and nestled beside her.

"You talk differently from other people," I said frankly. "Everybody else acts as though Mother was utterly gone out of existence, and when they speak of her, they speak of one who *has* lived but doesn't anymore."

"I know," she said gently; "we all talk like unbelievers in one of the most blessed truths of our religion; but that doesn't make it any less certain that our Christian friends who have gone from us are surely living and loving, and waiting for us in heaven."

"Does it always seem real to you?" I asked wistfully. "I would give anything to realize it as you seem to. Sometimes it seems to me that Mother is in the grave and that heaven is a misty dream. Do you never feel that way?"

She answered me with a bright smile and an emphatic shake of her head.

"No; my heaven seems very near and dear. It is to me as if my friends who are living there had told me good-bye and gone away to Europe to live and were expecting me to come out there to them in a little while."

"But the letters," I said hesitatingly, half feeling as though I ought not to speak of so material a thing in connection with the dead. "If they were in Europe, we should be watching for their letters and expecting them by every steamer; but now it is such a long, long silence; if we could only hear from them."

She answered me in that bright voice of hers that had such a wonderful ring of joy in it.

"And the anxieties and fears lest they may be ill, or in danger, or heavy trouble, what has become of all these? And God himself has written us such wonderful letters about their home."

This was a stretch of faith and love and hope to which I could not reach; but I longed for it, my very soul cried out after it. As I laid my head on my pillow that night I inwardly resolved that I would have it, that I would watch her life and discover if I could from what source she drew her wellspring of joy and hope.

21

CLASS IS NOT CONSIDERED

ABBIE vexed me the very next morning at the breakfast table. I looked to see her assume an air of distant dignity toward Mrs. Tyndall. I considered that I had sufficiently explained that lady's character to make it plain that she was not worthy of the friendship of my cousin. I was therefore much surprised and chagrined to notice the bright, cordial greeting that Abbie bestowed upon her, and their conversation together was frank and cordial. Apparently Abbie was interested in everything that Mrs. Tyndall said and entered with interest, even with eagerness, into the most trivial subjects. I felt very much disgusted with them both. I concluded that my cousin, who the night before had seemed to me almost an angel, was human like the rest of the world; and, of all faults, possessed the one that I detested most—hypocrisy. She could not certainly admire Mrs. Tyndall; indeed, she knew that lady's whole life to be at variance with *her* clearly defined views of right and wrong, and yet she affected to be pleased with her. I contented myself with maintaining a haughty silence, except when I was directly addressed, and even then I made my replies as brief and disagreeable as possible; and I verily thought that I was practicing one of the Christian virtues.

I felt gratified, soon after, when Abbie graciously declined an invitation to ride with Mrs. Tyndall and announced her intention of accompanying me to the shop.

"What in the world are you going to do there?" our hostess questioned with wondering eyes.

"Going to get acquainted," Abbie answered, flashing back a bright, roguish glance at the astonished lady from her blue eyes; and without further explanation she joined me.

I experienced no little satisfaction in walking down Regent Street with my dainty little cousin. She was very simply dressed in a neat-fitting street suit of heavy gray cloth; but everything about her was in such perfect keeping, so faultlessly new and perfect, from the delicately tinted kids that matched her suit to the exquisitely fitted walking boots; and about her entire person was that mysterious, unmistakable air of culture and style that it seemed to me if she had been labeled, "Direct from New York City," it could not have been more evident than it was now.

There was a rustling among the boxes and a general moving of things out of our way when we reached the shop that indicated the sort of impression that my visitor was making. I took her at once to my desk, and she followed my example in laying aside her things, and coolly announced her intention of spending the morning with me. I was puzzled to know what to do to entertain her. I need not have been. She had her own plans of entertainment and carried them out.

"Won't you make the tour of the rooms with me, when you have leisure, and introduce me to the girls?"

she asked me suddenly, after a moment's study of the room and its inmates. I remember with what an air of amused superiority I answered her:

"Why, my dear child, we don't introduce them; they never expect it; would be perfectly amazed if we did. If you want to ask them any questions about their work, you will not be obliged to wait for an introduction. Speak to whoever you please."

Abbie surveyed me thoughtfully with her great blue eyes, but made no answer and presently began to question me closely about the girls.

"Julia, who is the one with hair combed plainly back and with a little narrow collar and no bow?"

"Frank Hooper. She's a character—been spoiled, they say, by a flirtation with Mr. Sayles."

"Did he flirt with her?"

"I presume he did—thoughtlessly, perhaps. Mrs. Tyndall says she flirted with him; but it is too great a stretch of charity to believe much that she says. Dr. Douglass says they were engaged and that he deserted her when her father lost his property. But I don't believe that, either."

I said this with an air that betokened a lofty contempt for gossip of all sorts; but Abbie seemed not to have heard my last sentence. She was looking earnestly at Frank, and, as I finished my sentence, asked:

"Is she a Christian?"

"No, indeed; far enough from it. She is little better than a scoffer. Dr. Douglass has spasms of being deeply interested in her; but his interest doesn't seem to accomplish much."

"Have you done all that you can for her, Julia?"

I answered more faintly, but still steadily:

"Yes, I have. I could do just nothing for her. She repelled every attempt."

I was very sincere. I did not blush then as I do now, in recalling this conversation. I firmly believe that girls of sixteen haven't the slightest conception of what fools they are.

Abbie's attention was by this time turned toward Caroline Brighton. She questioned me as to her name, her character, the influence that surrounded her. I laughed as I answered the questions; it seemed natural for people to laugh when they talked about Caroline.

"She is an embodied spirit of evil, I do believe," I said, still laughing. "She was never known to be interested in anything but mischief of the wildest and most daring nature."

"What has her religious education been?"

"I doubt whether she ever had any. At least there is no present indication of any."

Again my cousin's earnest eyes sought mine, and she spoke slowly and thoughtfully:

"Do you think that is possible, Julia? She must have come in contact with Christian people, and they must have left their impress. For instance: She has come in daily contact with you, and of course you must have influenced her?"

There was a questioning sound to her voice, but I had no reply to make. I think she had given me my first realizing sense of solemn responsibility. It was a new thought that my life, this past winter, must have been contributing to the religious education of Caroline Brighton. It was not a pleasant thought. I shivered under it and spoke suddenly:

"What a fearful thing you would make of life. If we can never come in contact with people without influencing them, I think most of us would pray to be delivered from people."

"Or else, feeling the unmeaningness of that, pray to

be so enveloped with the spirit of Christ that our influence would tell for him."

Mr. Jerome Sayles lounged in at that moment and interrupted further conversation. He brought a bouquet of exquisite hothouse plants in glorious bloom. He made a feint of counting the blossoms and dividing equally between us. Abbie was courteously grateful, but very full of her previous subject, and appealed to him.

"We are talking of influence, Mr. Sayles—Christian influence. Isn't it true that every person with whom we come in contact influences us, more or less, and, if the person be a Christian, educates us in that direction?"

Mr. Sayles was amusedly interested.

"I'm not posted on that subject, you know," he said good-humoredly. "You must constantly remember that my education has been woefully neglected in that quarter. Won't you take me in hand and reform me?"

But Abbie was persistently determined not to trifle with him, least of all on this subject. There was a sweet earnestness in her voice as she asked:

"Is it *really* true that your Christian friends have made no impression on your mind as to their religious character, or that the impression they made has not in the least affected your life?"

He became grave at once; his face even wore a troubled look as he answered:

"They certainly have made marked and lasting impressions. But I have not profited by any of my lessons as I should. Perhaps you will teach me a better way of life?"

If, as I strongly suspected, he was saying this for effect, my cousin was by no means disposed to talk sentiment with him, but turned promptly to another topic.

"Mr. Sayles, are you acquainted with all these girls?"

There was a glance of surprise at the sudden change of subject, a quick glance toward "the girls" whom the question indicated, a curious lifting of the eyebrows, a roguish look at me, all in a second of time, and he replied in his ordinary tone of indolent good humor:

"I have that honor."

"Then will you introduce me to each one of them?"

Mr. Sayles bent an earnest, questioning look on her face; then his manner and tone changed, and he said in a serious, quiet voice:

"Certainly I will, if you wish it."

Abbie immediately arose, shook out the folds of her dress, and prepared to accompany him. They went at once toward Frank Hooper's corner, leaving me meantime in a state of absolute disgust. I was enraged with my cousin, with Mr. Sayles, and, more than all, with myself. It seemed incredible to me that in so short a time I could have sunken so low as to be ashamed of introducing a company of respectable girls to one who asked an introduction, my sole reason for declining being that the said girls worked in a shop. I thoroughly despised myself. I tried to discover how I came to indulge in such miserable pride. It was not difficult to trace the influence directly to Mrs. Tyndall; and as usual I seemed to forget that I could have had any influence over my own life, or could have found help that would have kept me from falling; so I went on cherishing a fierce and bitter feeling in my heart for her. Meantime, I watched my cousin. Mr. Sayles presented her to the girls with all the courteous grace that he would have used in his intercourse with any lady, and Abbie's manner was equally far removed from patronage and hauteur. She was simply her sweet graceful self, as thoroughly composed and at ease as if this were not a novel position to her. Frank Hooper was decidedly the haughtiest and most unbending of the two. Abbie lingered longest beside Caroline Brighton, seeming to find her the most communicative and agreeable. Mr. Sayles left her with Caroline and sauntered back to me.

"She is a very singular little lady," he said, watching her as she leaned against the table, apparently indifferent to paste and brushes, and carried on an animated conversation. "I wonder you didn't give us some idea of the unusual development of character."

"I don't observe anything so very remarkable," I said stiffly, in some doubt as to whether his tone expressed admiration or amusement, and being prepared to resent either with an almost equal degree of earnestness.

"Don't you?" he said, and he gave me the benefit of a very searching look. "That is strange. Now, I consider her the most remarkable young lady I have ever known. She really seems to be in earnest."

My indignant answer was checked by my desire to hear the conversation between Abbie and Caroline.

"Will you go?" Abbie questioned earnestly.

"Really," Caroline answered, assuming most admirably the air of a modest, diffident young lady, "I would go with pleasure, but you see, I am not in the habit of it, and I don't know anyone to go with, and I should feel so queer and strange."

Then Abbie's sweet, gentle voice.

"I think you told me you lived on Jackson Street. Then you have to pass through Clinton Square to reach the church, do you not? My cousin pointed out the church to me at the upper end of the square. Then couldn't you call for me? I board at Mrs. Tyndall's, you know; and I should be so glad to have your company. We might all go together from there. Will you not come?"

"I might do that," Caroline answered meekly, her eyes meantime gleaming with mischief.

"I do so wish you would. It would be very pleasant to us to have you come. May I expect you then?"

"I think so. Shall I ask for you, Miss Ried?"

"Yes, if you please; and if you can come a few minutes before the time we could have a little chance to get acquainted and have a pleasant talk perhaps."

And then Abbie moved away, thanking her meantime as one who had conferred a favor, oblivious, apparently, to the conversation that immediately followed her departure, though I heard it distinctly.

"Aren't you ashamed?" queried Caroline's next neighbor, a blunt-spoken, well-meaning sort of girl. "I wouldn't make game of anyone who treated me as nice as that, I vow."

"Hush!" said Caroline gravely, "I'm to become a means of grace to Mrs. Tyndall. Don't you see? Imagine me seated in her elegant parlor, complacently awaiting the departure of the family for church. Isn't that jolly, though? A shop girl in her parlor! She'll have to clean house for a month after that."

Then in lower tone, but still distinctly, with a glance over her shoulder at Abbie:

"Which is she, Vick, a greeny or a brick?"

What was she indeed? And where was all this to end? How would Mrs. Tyndall tolerate such introductions to her parlor? I felt troubled and provoked.

"I don't know what to do with her," I said aloud

and fretfully; and I couldn't decide whether Mr. Sayles's reply was intended to be soothing or sarcastic.

"I wouldn't try to do anything with her, Julia. I fancy she is a person who will do for herself."

There was certainly sensation enough as we lingered in the dining room that evening, and shortly after a furious ring at the front door a servant announced, "Miss Brighton to see Miss Ried." It is almost a pity that Caroline could not have been present to enjoy the scene.

"Miss Brighton! Who on earth is she?" speculated Mrs. Tyndall. "And which Miss Ried does she want? You, of course, Julia; but I don't recall the name. Have you an idea who it is?"

I was in a blaze of confusion, but Abbie answered promptly and sweetly:

"The message is for me, I presume, Mrs. Tyndall. It is one of the girls whom I met today at the shop. She has come to accompany us to church this evening. I asked her to come in early; I wanted to get a little bit acquainted with her, so I will be excused at once."

As the door closed after her, Mr. Sayles, whose presence was so constant now as to be considered a matter of course, studied for a moment Mrs. Tyndall's face, then burst into an uncontrollable fit of laughter. Peal after peal reechoed through the room; and to the lady's annoyed question: "What on earth are you laughing at?" he only answered by a more hearty outburst than before.

"This is as good as a first-class theater," he said at last, when he could speak again. "Come, Julia, take me to meeting with you this evening; I must see the fun out."

Necessity sent us all shortly after to the parlor to receive other calls, and no greeting could have been more perfect in its way than the one that Mrs. Tyndall gave to the shop girl in answer to Abbie's introduction.

22

✦—✦◈✦—✦

THE COMFORT OF MOURNING

OUR conversation that evening was as far as possible removed from what you would have supposed it would be after a return from a meeting fraught with deep and solemn interests. As usual Mrs. Tyndall was not present and was apparently not in the least interested in that matter. The parlor doors stood invitingly open as we entered the hall, and the lady of the house called to us with a sort of languid mirth to take pity on her, and come and help her entertain her husband, as she was tired to death over the effort to keep him from straying away to the reading room, or some other tiresome place. So we all went in, Mrs. Tyndall giving most cordially the invitation to Mr. Sayles which Abbie and I had intended to withhold, as we wanted to go directly to our room. As it was, Abbie demurred; but I, unable to resist the temptation of the brilliant room and the company of Mr. Sayles, said: "Let us stop a few minutes"; and almost the next sentence that was spoken started our topic of conversation, or rather of debate.

"Julia, that shade of drab is exceedingly unbecoming to you," Mrs. Tyndall said, surveying me critically. "Did you ever see your cousin in pink, Miss Ried? She has a peculiar shade of pink that she wears sometimes which is exceedingly becoming to her. I really wish you could see her in it; but of course she doesn't feel like wearing such bright colors now. Poor child."

This last with a little sigh and a lowering of the voice. The tone and the sigh irritated me strangely. I replied sharply:

"I feel quite as much like wearing pink as ever I did. I'm sure I don't know why I should not." Mrs. Tyndall turned at once to my cousin.

"Do you consider it the unpardonable sin to wear mourning, Miss Ried?"

Abbie lifted very grave, very wondering eyes to Mrs. Tyndall's face, but answered quietly:

"No, ma'am."

"Then this child is not a disciple of yours. She has taken up the most unaccountable hobby of late; really gets quite excited about the matter and, anyone can see, does violence to her own feelings all the time. I really feel that her grief would not seem so heavy to her if she would not fight against nature in this way. Don't you think so?"

Abbie smiled pleasantly and answered promptly:

"If there is a fight at all, Mrs. Tyndall, I should call it a fight against fashion, not against nature."

Mrs. Tyndall emphatically shook her head.

"*I* should not. It is just as natural to wish to wrap ourselves in black when we are in affliction as it is to eat when we are hungry."

"But, Mrs. Tyndall, suppose it was the fashion when our friends went away to attire ourselves in brilliant red; do you imagine that we would follow what was natural to ourselves, or what fashion dictated?"

"It never will be the fashion, Miss Ried. Black always was and always will be the national mourning costume. It would be an offense against nature to have it otherwise; and fashion, after all, must follow nature to be accepted."

"For instance, when she orders waists to become six and a quarter inches in circumference, and monstrosities resembling inverted coal scuttles to be attached to the back of the head, what becomes of nature then?" This from Mr. Sayles in good-humored sarcasm. Mrs. Tyndall promptly hushed him.

"Now, Jerome, don't you interfere. Being a man you must rail against the fashions, of course—all men do; but *I* think there is an immense amount of nonsense talked about these same fashions."

"I heartily subscribe to that sentiment," Mr. Tyndall interposed, rousing up from his half-buried position in the easy chair. "If you want to appreciate the force of it, Sayles, marry a wife, and go with her to all the millinery establishments in town, and wait while she tries rainbow-colored patches on her head and calls them bonnets. That's what I've been about all this mortal day."

"Now, Mr. Tyndall! I wasn't in Madame Darrow's twenty minutes, I *don't* think."

"An hour and three-quarters by my watch." Amid the general laugh that followed Mrs. Tyndall continued:

"That's of no consequence, anyway; has nothing to do with the subject. What I want to know is, why it is such a fearfully wicked thing to wear mourning?"

"It isn't, is it?" queried Abbie in gentle tone.

"Some people seem to think so, and you yourself

don't think it right; at least I don't believe you do. *Honestly* now, *do* you?"

Thus pressed, Abbie answered simply:

"It would not be right for me, because personally I do not approve of it; but I accord to everyone the privilege of deciding the question for himself."

"But, do just tell me what possible harm there can be in it. I really am very curious to know."

There was a little flush on Abbie's cheek, but her tone was as quiet as ever.

"There is the objection that lies directly on the surface, Mrs. Tyndall: the unnecessary and heavy expense, and the heavy drain that it brings on the purses of the poor."

Mrs. Tyndall shook her emphatic head.

"That wouldn't have the least weight in the world with me. I consider the starting point extremely false. There is no necessity for the poor aping us in that matter more than in a hundred others. On the principle I could not have a silk dress because my cook can't afford one."

"Bad illustration, Mrs. Tyndall," interposed Mr. Sayles. "I am witness that only last Sunday your cook flamed out in a red-and-green plaid, and you yourself told me that the material was silk."

Mrs. Tyndall laughed.

"Oh, they will copy us just as far as they are able, there is no question about that," she said pleasantly. "But, Miss Ried, you haven't given me any arguments yet. This one has no weight with me."

"It has with me," Abbie answered with quiet earnestness. "You and I would very possibly not agree on the silk-dress question either; but I don't consider the illustration a fair one. If we accept black clothes as marks of respect for our dead and as tokens of grief, I object to them on the ground that my poorer sister carries just as heavy a heart in her affliction as I do in mine; and in following the prevailing custom I am but giving her one more temptation to do the same. My creed is that we should not even in so small a matter as that of dress lead others astray."

"Miss Ried, you amaze me," interrupted Mr. Tyndall. "You are the very first lady I ever met who considered dress a small matter. The most of them have it in their catechisms that it is the end for which they were created."

Abbie turned toward him with a bright little laugh.

"I am a very small body, you know," she said gaily. But Mrs. Tyndall brought them back sharply to the point at issue.

"Miss Ried," she said, "I hope you will excuse me, but I think that is nonsense, all that about leading people astray. *I* don't profess to lead anybody. I dress as I please, and other people have a perfect right to do the same. But I would like to know, just for curiosity's sake, if that is all the objection you have to black clothes?"

"Whether, therefore, ye eat or drink, or whatsoever ye do, do all to the glory of God," quoted Abbie softly; and then, looking at Mrs. Tyndall: "No, ma'am, I have other objections. To me it doesn't seem a good way in which to cultivate a Christian spirit. It has its rise in heathenism in the first place. Has it not, Mr. Sayles?"

"A Christian spirit!" echoed Mrs. Tyndall in great amazement, ignoring Abbie's question. "What on *earth* has a Christian spirit to do with the color of one's dress? Now, Miss Ried, take yourself for an example. You have lost a friend, I think I have heard. Didn't you truly feel at any time as though you *would not* wear your bright-colored dresses anymore? as though you must wrap yourself in black?"

I turned quickly to see how Abbie bore this cool-blooded reference to her one great sorrow. The red had faded a little from her cheek, but she answered in the same sweet, steady tone:

"Yes, ma'am, I did. There were times when I felt that all the world ought to robe itself in black because of my sorrow. There were times when it seemed to me the sun ought not to shine, nor the birds to sing, and that no one anywhere ought to be glad and happy anymore. Do you think I would have been justified in indulging those thoughts?"

"That, of course, was an exaggeration of grief; but what possible harm could it have done to yield to your very natural desire to dress yourself in nothing but black?"

"Mrs. Tyndall, to me that desire seems a part of the same idea, only not carried to so great a degree. I realized that as a Christian it was my duty to remember constantly that my best and dearest friend, even my Savior, had sent my sorrow to me, and that it was in some way unknown to me the *best* that could come to me. I knew it was my duty to teach my naturally rebellious heart to say, 'Thy will be done,' to check all murmurings, all bitterness; and trying to do this, it seemed to me that it would be not a help but a contradiction, while the spirit was struggling for calmness and peace, to clothe the body in gloom and move about the world a living witness, not to the goodness but to the severity of God."

"Yet people must miss their friends and must grieve over their loss," Mrs. Tyndall said in a subdued, thoughtful tone, such as she rarely used.

Abbie answered very earnestly:

"Indeed it must be so while the body holds us; but the grief is heavy enough without seeking by all possible outward signs to press it more heavily on the weary spirit. I think the whole system of wearing mourning for our dead is productive of two results. To the young and frivolous, when the grief has not been heavy, it affords occupation for the mind and leads their thoughts hopelessly away from what might otherwise have made a solemn and lasting impression, to the business of plunging the body into the outward mockery of deep grief; and to those whose hearts seem almost broken the custom intrudes, obliging them to think of and plan about petty and exasperating details of dress, and affords them merely the poor solace of nursing the heavy gloom that sometimes sweeps over them when they seem given over to wild, rebellious thoughts."

"It's queer business, the whole of it," Mr. Tyndall exclaimed, breaking in upon the little silence that fell between us at the conclusion of Abbie's earnest words. "I don't know another thing in the whole fashionable world so open to criticism and to ridicule as those proprieties that obtain in our set on the subject of mourning. Was it ever your ill luck to meet a grand lady in full array, crape, bombazine, bugles, and whatnot, and all for a rich old aunt or uncle that she hated with all the strength of her civilized Christianized heart? I think that's enough to put the whole thing out of fashion."

"People can counterfeit anything," Mrs. Tyndall said apathetically.

"I don't think I had much temptation to follow the custom," Abbie continued. "It has, as you say, Mr. Tyndall, its ludicrous side, too distinctly marked if one notices and thinks about it much to accord with deep, real sorrow. I have seen it too often, when it seemed to me but a solemn mockery."

"I think it is perfectly natural to desire to wear mourning when one loses a friend."

Mrs. Tyndall said this just as positively and quietly as if she had not said the same thing in substance every five minutes since the conversation commenced. She had a very provoking way of earthing up the old argument that you supposed you had killed and buried, and presenting it as something new and brilliant. I have seen people since who argued in precisely the same way. Abbie answered her as sweetly as if she had never heard that opinion expressed before.

"Do you think it is perfectly natural to continue to wear it, Mrs. Tyndall?"

"I don't understand your question, my dear," Mrs. Tyndall answered with equal gentleness.

"Why, to continue wearing black on and on for years and years, from girlhood until one is an old woman, or until one dies. Would that seem natural?"

"Why, no, of course not. After a proper length of time one ought to lay it aside, of course.

"That brings us to a point that is exceedingly trying to me. Who has given the world a right to say to us, 'There, you have mourned long enough; it is a year now since that grave was closed; yesterday it was perfectly right and proper for you to be wrapped in black, but today get out your blue, and pink, and scarlet, and be gay again'?"

"What a queer way of putting it!" said Mrs. Tyndall, and she laughed her sweet, silvery laugh.

"And yet time *does* heal over heavy wounds." It was Mr. Sayles who said this; but I turned to look at him in order to be certain. The voice was so unlike his, so gentle and tender, almost pleading in its earnest questioning. Abbie answered quickly:

"It does indeed, or how could any of us live; but it would be very hard for me to be dictated to even in this; to be told that such and such things are not in keeping with my *mourning* if they were in keeping with my heart. I like God's way best: that of teaching the Christian heart in its sorrow to rest on him, and go bravely, earnestly, cheerfully about life's duties and cares—yes, and joys, waiting patiently for the rest that such a life will bring, rather than the world's way, which says, Here, today you must wear crape, and you must make no calls—no, even on your best friends, because you are in mourning; but tomorrow you can dress yourself in spangles and go whither you will. It will not be necessary for *you* to show respect to your dead anymore. If it is a mark of respect to *my* dead, who are tonight in heaven, to shut myself in from human sympathies and human pleasures and robe myself in gloom, I for one won't do it forever, not for a year, or two years, or six months, as fashion may dictate. But if, as I believe, it is not only showing more respect to the Christian dead, but more submissive love to the God who called them from us, to go bravely about our usual work, taking what joys we can find, bearing with what lightenings we may our heavy crosses of pain—why, I want to do that."

She rose as she spoke, and having finished her sentence smiled and bowed a gentle good-night.

"Jerome," said Mrs. Tyndall solemnly, "Miss Ried has undoubtedly been very eloquent. I appreciate her efforts in my behalf; but, nevertheless, when I die I want you to wear crape on your hat for me."

"I'll do so with pleasure, Mrs. Tyndall," he answered gravely, with a profound bow. "I assure you there shall not be so much as an inch of the original hat left to view. With this solemn and utterly undeniable proof will I attest my appreciation of your worth."

Then he held open the door for Abbie and myself to pass, giving us only a grave, respectful bow for good-night, while Mr. Tyndall was exploding with laughter over his last remark.

23

---✦✦✦---

THE TRUTH OF AN OLD ADAGE

THE meetings closed, not because the special interest had entirely abated, but because Dr. Mulford was utterly worn out with his long-continued extra labors, and body and brain absolutely demanded rest. Meantime, in a quiet, almost unnoticed way, the work went on. The young people's meeting was largely attended, and Dr. Douglass came home, often with glowing face, to tell of some new trophy. Abbie attended these meetings a great deal. I, only occasionally; for my health during all the wear and pressure of this winter was anything but firm, and I was often obliged to rest quietly at home when I would gladly have gone. Dr. Douglass had also started a young men's prayer meeting in which he was deeply interested. Meantime Abbie was busy; her energy was unflagging; she became a power in our shop, could coax the girls into anything that she wanted done—always excepting Frank Hooper, who held haughtily aloof. The change was more marked in Caroline Brighton than in anyone else. I remember that the morning after Abbie had told me of the decided stand that she took in the young people's meeting I looked upon her with absolute awe. It seemed so wonderful to me that the Spirit of God could descend upon and transform such a one as she.

For myself, I was very far away from happiness or peace. I still industriously read my Bible. I still struggled wearily through my stated seasons of prayer. I still clung to my virtuous indignation over Mrs. Tyndall and still held stated, and solemn, and shocked talks with Frank Hooper, in which she answered me after the old fashion, half haughty, half comic, wholly indifferent. We came home one afternoon, Abbie and I, earlier by an hour than usual. Abbie had called for me, and I got excused to go with her to look after one of her Sunday school scholars. We came down, ready for our walk, and as we reached the hall Abbie said:

"There! I have forgotten the cards that I was going to take the child. Wait here, Julia, and I will run back for them."

I dropped wearily into one of the hall seats and listened to the hum of conversation in the parlor, unconscious that I was listening until I heard my own name, spoken in Mrs. Tyndall's voice.

"Julia Ried, her name is. Her mother was a poor widow, and she—well, the fact is that she is simply a shop girl. We call her a clerk, out of regard to her feelings. She does help about the books, I believe; but then, that is a distinction without a difference, you know. She works all day in the shop, and that is all there is about it."

"And boards with you!" The tone expressed a whole volume of exclamation points.

"And boards with me. That is comical, isn't it?"

"But how in the world did it ever happen?"

"Well, there was a little bit of harmless deception practiced in the first place. Dr. Douglass coaxed me into taking her. He is an old acquaintance of the family, I believe, and looks after this girl a good deal. He is really very kind to her. Well, he led me to think that she was a schoolgirl. I don't remember his precise language now, and it's of no consequence. He was quite sharp about it, anyway. Never gave me an idea as to her position, and of course I thought it was all right; and Mr. Tyndall was obliged to be absent a good deal, so I decided to take her for company."

"How perfectly comical!"

"Isn't it? I felt vexed at first, and disposed to send her away at once; but Mr. Tyndall said, Nonsense, and, What difference did it make?—his way, you know. Nothing ever makes any difference with him. So she just stayed on, and has ever since, owing to my natural indolence and dread of scenes."

"But she goes out a great deal with the family, does she not?"

"Yes, constantly. That's force of circumstances, too. She is Dr. Douglass's friend, you know, and his position is entirely beyond question. Besides, we like her. We do, *really.* I have had a sort of fancy for her all along, and Mr. Tyndall is very much attached to her."

"But who is this cousin of hers? A shop girl, too?"

"Not by any means. She is of a very different grade. Why, *don't* you think she is Ralph Ried's daughter, of New York—the firm of Ried, Wilkison & Co., you know."

"And the other one is her cousin?"

"Her own cousin. She seems very fond of her, too. So you see, I was wise, after all, in not yielding to my first impulses. I think, very likely, it is only a sort of girlish freak, her being a shop girl at all; though she is quite poor. We have given her a number of things."

"What about Mr. Sayles? He seems to be quite attentive."

Mrs. Tyndall laughed her low, silvery laugh and answered:

"Oh, well; *you* know Jerome. He must flirt, and she will do as well as anyone."

Up to this point I had been listening to this interesting conversation in that idiotic way that people sometimes do, without fully taking in the fact that it was not intended for my ears, or even fully comprehending that I was the person who was being discussed. But at the mention of Mr. Sayles's name I roused into eager attention, with a wild desire to hear more; and at the same time there rushed upon me a realization of the fact that I, Julia Ried, my honored mother's daughter, had actually turned eavesdropper! I sprang up and fled away up the stairs. Abbie spoke to me as I opened the door:

"Did you tire of waiting, Julia? I don't wonder. I am sorry to be so tardy. But, do you know, I can't think what *can* have become of those cards. I thought I knew just where they were, and they are perversely *no*where. I think we shall have to go without them." Then she turned toward me and uttered an exclamation of surprise. "Why, Julia! My dear child, what has happened? Your face is perfectly colorless. What is it?"

"It is very little."

I tried to say it coolly, but I was really trembling with indignation; and then I burst forth my torrent of pent-up rage, giving her, with much excitement and many interpolations as to *my* opinion, the entire story. She treated it and me in a very different manner from what I had expected. As soon as she discovered that no one was dead or dying, she turned back to her trunk and continued her search for the missing cards, giving me good attention, however; and, when I made a sort of breathless pause, said coolly:

"My dear Julia, you seem surprised."

"Surprised!" I repeated excitedly. "I should think I might be. It was no agreeable thing to sit in that hall and hear such an exasperating account given of one-self and one's friends."

"Not agreeable, I grant you; but I don't see why it should surprise you."

"Abbie, what do you mean?"

"Why, dear Julia, think a minute. Did you ever, in your life, hear her speak well of an absent person? Don't you know you told me the other day that she had given you a queer opinion of every single person about whom you had heard her talk? Now, why should you have expected to escape this general mael-strom of talk? Don't you know, when a person enter-tains you with the faults and failings and peculiarities of your friends, that your turn for being discussed is sure to come?"

"But she said such mean, untrue things," I an-swered, still speaking in excitement and anger. "If she had only had the decency to tell the truth, I should not have minded what she said."

"Have you reason to think that she has always been strictly truthful in regard to what she has told you of others?"

I reflected. There were Mrs. Mulford, and Dr. Mul-ford, and Frank Hooper, and Mrs. Carson, and, oh! *hosts* of others. What queer things she had told me about them—things that I more than half suspected at the time, and *knew* now, were at least colored.

"Besides," said Abbie, finding that I did not speak,

"let us have a real plain little talk, you and I. You say she did not speak the truth; she said, among other things, that you were a shop girl. Now, please tell me what those two words mean. Don't they mean that a girl is employed in a shop? What is there that is not perfectly right and proper in that? And isn't it just the truth? Haven't you been so employed during the winter?"

I winced a little. *I* had made a distinction. I had not treated the others as though they belonged to my class.

"It means a lower class of persons," I said somewhat sullenly.

"No, it doesn't, dear, not the mere name, any more than music teacher means any particular style of person. If a good many ignorant girls have earned their living in shops, until we have come to associate the name with the ignorant and coarse, that is our blunder, and a very foolish one I think it. Isn't it a strange idea that we cannot tell whether a person is a lady or not until we can discover what she chances to do with her hands and brain?"

"Oh, you don't carry out your own ideas," I said, taking up Mrs. Tyndall's style of reasoning and using one of her old arguments. "You don't associate with Mrs. Tyndall's cook, or go out calling with her."

"Neither is necessary in order to maintain my position. Mrs. Tyndall's cook is not fitted by education and habit to enjoy going out calling with me. She would be neither comfortable nor happy. But suppose she chooses to improve her opportunities and lift herself up to education and refinement; do you suppose I would decline her society because she used to cook my dinners? I should despise such reasoning, and so would anybody!"

I smiled a little in spite of my anger. This sweet, pure cousin of mine did not understand some things so well as I, with my sixteen years of wisdom, if she did not know that half the women in Christendom would do just that thing. Abbie had talked herself into an enthusiasm, and she added:

"I don't like all this talk about class and grade in this country of ours. It is an intensely un-American idea, in a land where the shop girl of today may be the wife of the president tomorrow. But we are running away from the question." She added laughingly: "Dear Julia, don't think I am unsympathetic. Only I wouldn't mind so much. She did not say anything so *very* wicked after all, when one takes into consideration her manner of talking."

"But," I said with hesitation and in a voice that was very near tears, "I thought she liked me. I did, really."

"And you admit that she said she did. No doubt she does. I think she is very fond of you."

"What is such fondness worth?" I said scornfully.

"It is worth quite as much as it receives from you, I think. Don't you see, Julia, what a curious thing you are doing? You are overcome with indignation because of what you have overheard her say. Now, just imagine that she could have repeated to her, accurately and in detail, everything that you have told me about her; what sort of a state of mind do you think she would be in?"

I had no definite answer to make to this. In truth, it startled me a little. I was somewhat surprised to discover that while I had several times frankly stated that I detested her entire character, I meantime expected her to go on liking me just as well as ever.

"She said such mean things about Dr. Douglass," I

exclaimed after a little silence, waxing indignant again.

"Dr. Douglass will not mind it in the least," Abbie answered coolly.

That was true. He certainly would not, and as I thought of the very composed, even amused, air with which he would have listened to the entire story, it served to quiet me more than anything else had done. But I immediately fell into speculation over what had been mysteries to me for several days. I made my thoughts known suddenly:

"I don't in the least understand you, Abbie. Do you admire Mrs. Tyndall's character?"

She answered my question frankly enough.

"No, Julia; I cannot say that I do."

"Well, do you know you act as though you did? You always treat her as if you liked her very much, and I don't understand why it isn't hypocritical."

She answered me with a mischievous glance from her blue eyes as she said:

"Do you think I should exhibit a more consistent Christian character if I said frankly: Mrs. Tyndall, I don't like you in the least. I think you are a very absurd woman, and I can't treat you with any sort of respect?"

"Precisely the style of question that she once asked me, when we were talking about sincerity. But it doesn't help me in the least. Of course we can't talk in that manner to people; and yet that way would be sincere, and the other way is hypocritical. I don't see but it follows that people have *got* to be hypocritical, anyhow."

Abbie was very earnest and gentle now.

"Dear Julia, don't you think the mistake comes in further back? Ought such uncharitable conclusions to be my sincere state of mind toward Mrs. Tyndall?

Ought I not rather to cultivate a tender spirit toward her, a spirit that will lead me, not to dwell upon her faults, but to be on the alert for her virtues? Thoughts about the shortcomings of others are very eager to gain admittance to my heart, but ought I to cherish them, or to turn from them and cultivate a prayerful spirit toward the people who call them forth? If I am striving to do that, is it not a help to me to meet them on common ground whenever I can, to enjoy every bit that is enjoyable about them and love everything that is lovable? Isn't that the better way?"

This was high ground. I could not reach up to it, so I made the defiant and rather irrelevant answer:

"I don't love *her,* anyway."

Abbie had long since ceased fumbling in her trunk and was curled on a soft cushion at my feet while she talked. She laid her head on my lap in a pretty, coaxing way she had, and said softly:

"I wish you did not feel just as you do about Mrs. Tyndall. I don't think it is possible to live close to Jesus and cherish such feelings. Shall not you and I reform in this matter?"

"I can't," I said stoutly. "I *cannot* feel rightly toward her. You may, perhaps; you have never had any provocation for feeling otherwise."

"There is one sure way in which to cultivate right feeling, Julia. Suppose we make her a special, and constant, and earnest subject of prayer, not spasmodically, as we may chance to feel like it, but with all our hearts bent on her attaining a higher life."

"I should *never* feel like it, I am afraid," I said coldly. "I don't think she is a Christian at all."

Abbie slowly raised her head and fixed eyes full of wonder on my face.

"Does that thought preclude the possibility of

praying for her, Julia? First, you know we have nothing to do with that, and in either case, what then? If she is, does she not need a rebaptism? Do you not desire it for her? If she is not, does she not need Jesus? Do you not desire her conversion? In either case, cannot you pray?"

I was entirely silent. There seemed nothing left to say. After a few minutes Abbie added:

"I do not think of Mrs. Tyndall as you do. I think she is a lady very much given to using her tongue. I don't think she means more than half she says, and I don't think she realizes a quarter of the mischief that she does with her tongue."

"I do," I answered briefly and bitterly. Just then the tea bell pealed through the house, and we laid aside hats and sacks and went down to tea.

24

━━━━◆━━━━

A SURPRISE AND A BLESSING

ONE evening we were all in the parlor, Mr. and Mrs. Tyndall, Abbie, and I. Mr. Sayles had been spending the evening with us and had but just left. The spell being broken, I was in haste to get to my room; but Abbie lingered and talked with Mrs. Tyndall about her worsted dog in an exasperatingly interested way. Mr. Tyndall was in a most unusual mood for him—silent and grave. He had not been with us during the evening, but had recently arrived; and since his entrance had spoken very few words; but had kept up a steady monotonous walk up and down the room. The walking seemed to disturb Mrs. Tyndall, for presently she said, half playfully, half in earnest:

"Mr. Tyndall, what in the world has come over you, or overcome you, as our old woman who talked in meeting used to say? I never knew you to pace up and down the room in that solemn fashion before."

At this question he paused half irresolutely for a moment, then went over to her with a determined air and spoke, in tones somewhat husky:

"Fanny, I have something I want to say to you."

228

"Well," she answered, still playfully, but with a sort of wondering tone, "is that a fact so unusual and remarkable that it needs a preface? Don't go, girls"— as Abbie and I arose to depart. "It isn't a private lecture, is it, Mr. Tyndall?" still speaking very merrily.

His face was very pale, but he answered steadily:

"No, it is not private. No, Julia; no, Miss Ried; please remain. I trust I am not ashamed of what I am about to say. Fanny, I ought to have told you of it before, but I did not seem able to. These past weeks have been very eventful ones to me. You remember, perhaps, Miss Ried, that you asked me to go to the young men's prayer meeting two weeks ago last Tuesday night. Did you pray for me that evening?"

"Yes," said Abbie, "all the evening."

He turned to her with a bright smile lighting up his pale face as he said earnestly:

"For which I shall have reason to thank you through all eternity. Well, Fanny, it is a long story, the history of these two weeks. It has been a long two weeks to live—and to fight," he added, drawing a quick, hard breath. "To fight with pride, and unbelief, and temptation in every fiendish form that can be imagined. But there has been a victory. I stood up in the meeting this evening and told the people of my determination to begin *now* to follow Christ; and as they tell me the right way to begin is to do the first duty that offers, I have promised my Savior that I would own him before you as a family tonight. Fanny, I want to have family worship."

Had the marble statue in the niche behind him been suddenly gifted with life and voice, it doesn't seem to me that I could have been more astonished. I looked up at the pale, resolute face with such a new feeling of respect welling up in my heart for him.

What a wonderful thing it was, this new life born into the soul, changing all its springs, quickening all its impulses! Abbie's face was absolutely radiant, but she did not speak. We both waited in silence and no little anxiety for what Mrs. Tyndall might be moved to say. How would she receive this news? Such was my opinion of her that it seemed to me almost impossible that she could care. Indeed, I expected to hear her gaily pronounce him a victim to overwrought nerves and propose a quiet night's rest and the benefit of her society. I had been fascinated with the new look on Mr. Tyndall's face; but now I turned suddenly to watch his wife. There was a little pink flush on either cheek, a strange light in her eyes, and a new tone to her voice, such at least as I had never heard her use before. She laid her hand with a caressing movement on her husband's arm and said in a voice as low and sweet as a silver bell:

"Robert, I am *very* glad"—with a marked, tremulous emphasis on the "very."

Then immediately she became mistress of this new situation. Rising, she moved composedly across the room and wheeled forward the little table on which the elegant Bible always reposed in undisturbed peace, said in her usual tone as she pushed an easy chair toward me: "Take this chair, Julia; you look tired"— then settled back among her cushions with an air of quiet waiting.

Such was the peculiar effect of all this that had a stranger come among us just then I am sure he would have supposed that it was an ordinary everyday custom in this household to gather together for family worship.

Her manner seemed to have a quieting effect on Mr. Tyndall. He took up the Bible with quiet, reverent

hand and read a few verses in a steady voice. Won[
ful verses they were. I wondered if he just chance[
that time to alight on them, or if they had met some
of the great needs which he must have had during the
two weeks of conflict. In any case, I thought they must
be very wonderful verses to him. "The Lord is my
light and my salvation; whom shall I fear? The Lord is
the strength of my life; of whom shall I be afraid?"
Only a few verses, but how full they were of strength,
of help, of promise! Over this one he paused, and
finally read it again, with a ring of solemn triumph in
his voice: "When thou saidst, Seek ye my face; my
heart said unto thee, Thy face, Lord, will I seek."

Then he closed the Bible, and we all knelt to pray.
I am sure we can none of us ever forget that prayer. It
was very brief, very simple, but it had the sound of that
ancient prayer in the Record: "As for me and my
house, we will serve the Lord." It was a plain, solemn,
unreserved consecration of himself, and all that he
called his, to the service of God. There was still an
unusual pallor on his face when we arose from our
knees, but the prayer seemed to have changed him.
There was an added dignity about his manner, as that
of a man who had at last assumed his proper position
in his family—priest of his own household. Mrs.
Tyndall bade us good-night with her usual graceful air
of composure, and I was somewhat divided as to
which ought to astonish me most, Mr. Tyndall or his
wife. Just before he left the parlor he had come over
to Abbie, and holding out his hand said earnestly:

"I owe thanks to you, next to God, for the peace
that I have tonight."

"Isn't it blessed, Julia; isn't it glorious?" Abbie said
with shining eyes and glowing cheeks as the door
closed after us in our own room. "But, oh! Julia, to

think that his *wife* could not have the joy of thinking that she led him to Jesus!"

"I didn't know that you ever had said twenty words to him except at table," I answered, wondering to what he could have referred.

"I am not sure that I did say twenty. I had just a three minutes' talk with him one evening. When Dr. Douglass and I were coming home from prayer meeting he overtook us just at the corner, and Dr. Douglass left me in his care and went to make a professional call. I had been thinking about him all the evening, principally because I knew the doctor had him so constantly on his heart. I had been praying for him, and I simply told him so. He thinks I was the means of helping him, because his heart was just ready to be helped at that time; but I did nothing. It is Dr. Douglass who has just carried him on his heart for months. He is a grand man, Julia. But, oh! do you know, I think I am foolish? I am sure Mrs. Tyndall's heart must be just as full of joy as it can bear; but I cannot help feeling that if I had a husband who was not a Christian it would be such a regret to me that I was not the one chosen to introduce him to Jesus."

"Do you suppose she cares?" I asked incredulously. *"Wasn't"* she equal to the occasion, though? If there should an earthquake swallow us up, house and all, don't you believe she would shake out her robes, after the first surprise was over, and wheel forward an easy chair for somebody? I declare I don't know whether, instead of being sorry that her life has been such that he never could have got into the right road if he had followed her, she is not at this very moment telling him in a private, confidential way that he has made a goose of himself, and that it is nothing but an injudicious excitement."

However, I did not feel all the gaity of manner that I exhibited. In reality, my heart felt very sore. It seemed strange to me that a man like Mr. Tyndall, who a few days before was even almost a scoffer, in a gentlemanly way, could tonight express such a sense of love, and trust, and nearness to his Savior, while I, who for years had professed to love and trust him, felt so far away. It seemed almost unjust. I was glad for Mr. Tyndall, but bitterly sorry for myself. Looking back now on my life at that time, I think one of the marked and never-to-be-forgotten lessons of that period was that a child of God cannot live for weeks and months in a whirl of daily excitement and eager chase after pleasure, neglecting her seasons of communion, or at best giving but a passing moment now and then to her Bible and her prayers, without bringing darkness on her own soul—a darkness that is sometimes long and exceedingly bitter to be borne. I know I shed bitter tears that night. When I knelt to pray, my prayer was only weeping. It seemed to me that I could not long endure this pain; yet I bore it quite alone. I said not a word to Abbie. Beyond the few words wrung from me by Dr. Douglass, I had let no one suppose other than that I was at rest and peace.

On Thursday evening we all went to prayer meeting together. It had been Mrs. Tyndall's custom to attend the Thursday evening meeting when it did not rain and she was not too tired and did not consider it her duty to stay with her husband; but to have him accompany her was an entirely new experience. There was an unusually large attendance, and many glances of surprise were interchanged when Mr. Tyndall followed us down the aisle. The Tyndall pew joined the Symondses' pew on the other side, and Lycia sat in the corner, next to Mrs. Tyndall. She had attended quite regularly for several weeks, but had evinced no other interest. While the first hymn was being sung, Mr. Sayles sauntered in and took the seat back of us. His presence, too, was unusual, although he had been once or twice before. The early part of the meeting was one of great suffering to me. The weight of gloom that had rested on my heart for weeks had grown almost insupportable during the past two days. I had tried, I thought, in every way to lift the burden. I had studied Abbie to see where lay the secret of her peace. I thought one of the marked features of her life was her constant work for the Master. She seemed always to have someone in mind to pray for, to speak a word to as she had opportunity; but I had tried that and failed. I tried again. My desires seemed to cling to Frank Hooper. I spoke with her again and was repulsed more decidedly than before. I know now that I did not talk with her, I preached *at* her. I tried once or twice to pray for Mrs. Tyndall, but *now* I can see very plainly that I prayed for her as a creature immensely below myself in her Christian life, if she had any, and half despised her, even while I prayed. On this particular evening my misery was at its height. I remember I bowed my head on the seat in front of me and struggled to keep my tears under control. There seemed a peculiar solemnity about all the exercises. Those who prayed spoke as if they felt almost the visible presence of the King. I noticed this, and it served to deepen my own sense of something as great as an ocean sweeping between us. Presently Dr. Mulford's voice and question arrested my attention. There was a happy ring to his voice, as of one whose pulses were thrilling with a new joy as he asked,

"Will our Brother Tyndall pray?" There was a sudden rustling of heads, that peculiar murmur of sound that flows over an astonished congregation; and then that equally peculiar silence settling over them as the new voice filled the house with prayer. What Mrs. Tyndall felt during that prayer only God and she know; but it seemed to me that my own heart would break. There was such a sense of security in his words, such a realization of the presence of his Savior. I longed for it so. I cried out after it, but could not find it. What passed after that prayer I do not know; there was some talking and another prayer, but I don't know what was said. I was struggling with my own heart; but I heard Dr. Mulford when he spoke again:

"There may be those present tonight, Christians by profession, who know little in their own hearts of that peace of which our Brother Tyndall spoke, and which God in his mercy has so recently given him; they may be conscious of having lived very far away, unworthy lives; they may be saying at this moment, 'Oh, for a closer walk with God.' Perhaps such a one would like us to pray for him or her—would like to say that our prayers are asked that there may be a renewal of covenant vows, a reconsecration of heart to the Lord. If there be such person or persons present, will they not manifest their desire by rising?"

Could Dr. Mulford have expressed my feelings better if he had known the entire workings of my heart? I did want them to pray for me. I needed their prayers. I felt my own utter sinfulness—felt it that evening as I never had before. And yet it seemed to me as if I could not say so—could not rise up before that assembly and proclaim my sins. I even reasoned

over the evil effect it would have. There were Mr.
Sayles and Lycia Symonds, and I didn't know how
many others, who believed me to be a Christian—
they knew nothing about my miserable backsliding.
What a comment it would be on the professions of
church members if I noised it abroad in this way!
Thus I reasoned, and the opportunity passed. Then
again the bitterness of desolation rolled over me.
While they were singing a hymn, I felt that I would
give anything to have the chance now to rise. No
matter about anything, or what anybody thought, if
only they would pray for me. I was a poor sinful,
unhappy soul, and people must think what they
would so I could but get some help. My sincerity
was to be tested. When the hymn closed, Dr. Mulford
renewed the opportunity, saying he felt impressed
that there were those present who were grieving the
Spirit by going contrary to their convictions of duty.
There was a little rustle beside me. I glanced up, and
Mrs. Tyndall was standing! Now, nothing could
amaze me more than this. It seemed so entirely
unlike Mrs. Tyndall—her elegant, composed way of
doing everything; her utter disgust at anything un-
feminine. Yet there she stood, pale, grave, and with a
sort of beseeching earnestness in her face. It took but
a second of time in which to think all these thoughts.
The next I stood beside her. I don't clearly know
about the rest of this portion of the meeting. There
were others who arose, and then there were prayers
offered—earnest, pleading ones. I recognized Dr.
Douglass's voice, and the prayer he offered was such
a one as I had never heard before. I read when I was
a child the story of Bunyan's Pilgrim. I remember at
the time being greatly impressed with the scene
wherein his pack dropped off and left him free. I

thought of it that evening. I felt that I could realize something of Christian's feeling. The burden was gone. A sinner I felt myself. Oh, I knew that more fully, more plainly than I had ever known it in my life before. But I was a sinner forgiven. My Savior held my hand.

25

❦

MUCH JOY AND SOME WORK

OH, how I enjoyed the remainder of that meeting! My heart felt ready to sing with gladness. Once more I felt the special presence of my Savior; the long, dark night of gloom was gone.

Now, let me not be misunderstood. I do not mean that the mere act of rising in prayer meeting dispelled the cloud that had so long brooded over me. I mean that my life during that time had for weeks been one of rebellion. I was secretly questioning the justice, the goodness of God. I wanted, moreover, to fight my battles alone. I did not want to admit to anyone that I had wandered. I think God called for this act of submission on my part. I mean that I think he chose this particular form of submission for me, and so pressed it upon my conscience that for *me* to have resisted it would have been a sin. Dr. Mulford gave another invitation just before the close of the meeting. I remember how full of feeling his voice was as he said:

"I think there must be at least *one* with us tonight who has decided the solemn question, the language of

whose heart is: I have come over on the Lord's side.
May not our hearts be encouraged by the knowledge
of it? Is there not someone who will, by rising,
indicate to us that the decision is made? We will wait
a moment."

There was a little, almost breathless stillness, then
Abbie touched my arm, drawing at the same moment
a quick little breath of delight. I raised my head and
caught one glance from Lycia Symonds's earnest eyes
as she resumed her seat. "What a *Christian* she will
be!" I said to myself. I knew that she would be a
determined, wholehearted *anything* that she under-
took. I did not seem to be much surprised. My own
heart was so full of peace that the strangeness seemed
to me that anyone could hesitate. Then I heard Dr.
Mulford say in tremulous undertone, "Thank God,"
and the occasion of it was that his only son, who was
alternately his pride and his torture—who was the
child of almost agonizing prayer—had determined
the great question of his life.

There were others. A new impetus seemed to have
been given to the meeting. It seemed a little foretaste
of the joy of heaven. In the hall we lingered. Dr.
Mulford was talking with Mr. and Mrs. Tyndall, and
Dr. Douglass hurried over to speak a word to young
Mulford. Lycia Symonds stood near me. I could not
help saying a word to her, but I couldn't think of much
to say. I held out my hand and said simply:

"I am *so* glad."

"You were the means of my coming to a decision
at last," she said as she gave my hand a hearty clasp. I
felt my face flush with surprised delight as I said
eagerly:

"*I* was! How is that possible? What have I ever said
or done that could have helped you?"

"Nothing," answered straightforward Lycia. "At least nothing until tonight. I never quite believed in you before, but when you arose I felt that there was a hidden power in it all that I didn't understand, and I wanted it."

I could not answer her. My thankful tears kept me silent. God had chosen to use the very means that I had honestly feared would be a stain.

Dr. Douglass and I walked home together, which was a rare thing, as he generally hastened away on professional work the moment the meetings closed.

"It was a wonderful place tonight, was it not?" he said joyously as we left the church.

"Wonderful," I repeated. "And, Dr. Douglass, I don't think you know how much that word means tonight."

"Do I not?" he said, smiling, and added: "I think I know more about it than you imagine, what it means to you. I have not watched your life and prayed for you constantly during these months without knowing more or less of your inner conflict and watching with no little anxiety for the result."

Then we had one of those old, pleasant talks together such as we had not enjoyed in months. Just as we turned the corner of Grove Street the doctor suddenly changed the subject.

"By the way, Julia, what of our other friend," indicating by a backward motion of his head the persons behind us. "Has he any special interest, do you think?"

"Who? Mr. Sayles, do you mean? Oh, no, not the slightest. I don't think he ever had a serious thought in connection with the subject."

"Have you had some serious talks with him?"

"Scarcely ever," I answered humbly, feeling then all

the strangeness of my answer, when I remembered how constant my opportunities had been. "I have not done anything that I ought to have done, Dr. Douglass."

"Come in, Jerome," Mrs. Tyndall said when our party reached the door.

"I don't know about it," he said in undertone to me. "I am afraid I shall be a foreign element."

Nevertheless, he came in. We stopped in the hall to lay aside our things, Abbie and I, and Mrs. Tyndall came out to us just as we were ready to enter the parlor, meeting us in the doorway, with her husband and Mr. Sayles and Dr. Douglass for listeners. She turned to me with that winning air of hers, and touching her lips tenderly to mine, she said gently:

"I have not helped you in any way, Julia. I fear, in every respect, my life has been such as to lead you astray. Shall we begin again and try to help each other?"

I did not answer her in words. I could not. I felt happy and humbled. How I had been despising her in my heart during all these weeks; and yet, in every respect, she had proved the nobler woman of the two. I remember just how my mountain of sin towered high around me that night. Look where I would, I saw only follies and failures.

"And yet you were happy?"

And yet I was happy. In one sense, what matter it? The sins were covered over with the hand of Christ. Very low, very unworthy, very shamefaced for the life I had led, for the ill that I had done, and the good that I had not done, but in spite of all that—forgiven.

"The element that was left out of my composition was moral courage." This is the sentence with which

Mr. Sayles broke the silence that had hovered over us for a little.

"Why, Jerome!" Mrs. Tyndall responded, great surprise in her voice. "I have always thought you a remarkably courageous man."

He smiled faintly, and then immediately growing grave again, said earnestly:

"I presume every one of you think that I have no part nor lot in this matter; that I am perfectly indifferent. I am not certain that I have a part in it, but indifferent I certainly am not. I think I would have given a thousand dollars to have been able to have indicated tonight my desire for your prayers, but it seemed to me that leaden weights were attached to my feet. Julia, when you arose, I thought I certainly should; but you see, I did not. I resolved, however, to speak to you here at home about my hopes, and fears, and resolves. I—"

His voice, that had trembled visibly as he spoke these sentences, now stopped entirely, and the composed, self-controlled man of the world bent forward, his elbow resting on the little table at his side, and shielded his face with his hand to hide the emotion he could not control. No one seemed able to speak. We were all surprised and thrilled. Dr. Douglass broke the silence, speaking in a voice that trembled:

"We had thought our cup of thanksgiving was full tonight, but you have filled it to overflowing."

He raised his head again and smiled in answer to the doctor's words.

"Thank you," he said. "I knew you would be glad. I thank you more than I can express for your faithfulness to me. This is not a suddenly formed purpose. I have been thinking of it for weeks. I have been almost decided a great many times and have been held back with the thought of what my friend Tyndall, here, would think or say; and then the Lord took away that refuge and left me no excuse."

He laid his hand on Mr. Tyndall's arm as he spoke, and that gentleman gave him a glad, bright smile. One could see that those two gentlemen were destined henceforth to be such friends as men rarely are.

"Let us have a little prayer meeting," Dr. Douglass said suddenly, speaking in tones that were throbbing with joy. "I am sure that we must all be in the spirit of prayer, and we have very much to be thankful for."

So we knelt to pray. It was a thankful meeting, to none more so than to me. I remember I wondered if the joy of heaven was not increased to Mother that night, because her wandering child had been called back into the fold.

"The work has commenced anew," Dr. Douglass said, detaining us as we were about to separate for the night. "The Spirit of the Master was never more manifest among us than it was tonight. It is a good time to commence the Christian life, or to gird up our hearts afresh. There is much work to do. I have been thinking what a help it will be to us to select, each, a subject of special prayer and special effort, concentrating our thoughts and our hopes on one soul. I have found it a very great help to me to do so. I think God blesses such special personal efforts. What do you all think? How is it, brother? Are you ready for work?"

This seemed so strange a remark to address to Mr. Sayles. He felt its strangeness and its pleasantness, apparently, for he answered with a bright face:

"Indeed, Doctor, I'm hardly prepared to pledge myself, for I feel that I do not know how to pray for myself; but I know a friend about whom I have already begun to feel anxious."

"Pray for him, then," Dr. Douglass said earnestly. "The Lord will show you how."

We pledged ourselves, and the doctor added:

"One thing more: Let us not forget that the method which God has been pleased to give us by which to show our sincerity is to work for that which we are praying about. I find in my own heart a tendency to forget that part."

My thoughts went swiftly and steadily toward one person. I don't know how I came to have such an intense desire for the conversion of Frank Hooper, but it seemed to burden me. I remembered with a strange feeling of surprise and shame that I had prayed for her heretofore in a very strange and spasmodic manner. Just before or after the times when I had tried to approach her personally on religious topics, I had been in the habit of remembering her in my prayers, and then, perhaps, for weeks I would not think of her again. It was as if I had determined that a prayer now and then was all I had time to bestow on her, and ought to be sufficient. I began to understand something of the folly of my attempts to do good, and to see how very far from real earnestness I must have appeared in the sight of God. I prayed for Frank that evening as I never had prayed for her, or indeed for anybody before.

"Isn't it wonderful about Mr. Sayles?" I asked Abbie. "I was so amazed. I thought he was perfectly indifferent to the whole subject."

Abbie's face had been radiant all the evening, and her voice matched her face as she answered:

"It is blessed, and—yes, it is wonderful; but I do not think I am surprised. I was looking for it. God answers prayer, you know."

"Had you been praying for him specially?" I asked her.

"For weeks and weeks. He seemed to me in such great need and so nearly ready."

I was very much astonished. How different he must have seemed to her from what he did to me! And then I remembered that my life had not been such as to draw from him any secret interest in the subject that he might have felt, and hers had. Perhaps that made all the difference.

I went early to the shop the next morning, very full of the subject that had engrossed my heart the night before, and very eager to find an opportunity to express my desire. I hoped by going early to meet Frank alone. She had of late been working over hours, both morning and evening, plunging into the work with a sort of desperation, it seemed to me; as if she would try to absorb her whole soul in the business before her and leave neither time nor strength for anything else. As I had hoped, she was in her corner, driving her wheel around with nervous haste. No one else was in the room. I went over to her directly. I did not wait for the accustomed "good morning," nor respond to her greeting, "How happens it that you are such an early bird?" but plunged at once into my subject.

"Frank, I have something I want to say to you. I came early on purpose to see you alone. I think my way of talking to you about religion heretofore has been insufferable. I wonder that you endured it at all. I know my life has been such that if you judged from me, you must have thought there was nothing in religion but a name. But there is—there is. Oh, Frank, don't think it is all delusion; don't judge of Christians by me. I have been all wrong—so wrong that I wonder God let me live to do mischief—but I am going to try again. I want to live differently, and, Frank, I want you to love Jesus. I want that more than anything else on earth."

I remember the words I spoke as well as though they had been spoken yesterday. I was all in a tremble of eagerness. When I first began there had been a mocking smile on Frank's face, but it changed, and when I stopped, she had checked her wheel and stood looking at me gravely and thoughtfully. Presently she drew from her pocket a dainty note and said with eyes fixed searchingly on my face:

"Did you know she wrote me this note?"

"She! Who? No, I know nothing about a note. What is it?"

She passed it to me quietly.

"Read it," she said, "and tell me if you know anything about it."

Thus it read:

Dear Frank:

I have ill-treated you. I want you to forgive me. I have been proud and weak and wicked. I have been blind too—but God has opened my eyes. I cannot think how I could have lived as I did. Now, I have begun to pray for you; I know your heart needs Jesus. Don't judge from my life that there is no such person—only try him. I shall pray for you every day, every hour, I think, so great is my desire to have you happy in Christ. I am sorry for all the many ways in which I have hurt your feelings. I think you will forgive me. My Savior has.

Yours truly and earnestly,
MRS. H. F. TYNDALL

My look of utter astonishment during the reading of this letter, and when I handed it back, must have convinced Frank of my ignorance of its contents.

"You knew nothing about it, then?" she said.

"Nothing at all. Isn't it utterly unlike Mrs. Tyndall?"

"It isn't from any Mrs. Tyndall that I ever knew," she answered emphatically. "Then you and she have held no conversation about me?" with another very searching look into my eyes.

"Not a syllable. I haven't mentioned your name to her nor she yours to me in weeks."

Frank turned again to her wheel and began to make it spin again.

"After all," she said with the mocking smile again gathering on her face, "I don't know but there is something in it. Do you suppose if I take to it myself, it will have such a transforming effect on me, as it seems suddenly to have had on Mrs. Tyndall and you?"

I did not answer her. My eyes and my voice were full of tears. It seemed to me that I *could not* let this be the only result of our talk together. A moment after she spoke gravely:

"Julia, I think a good many things that I do not speak. But I may as well tell you—that I respect *your* religion this morning—a thing that I never did before. Perhaps I may do more than that—time will tell."

And then the girls came laughing and chattering in, and I had to go to my desk.

26

DESTINY APPROACHING

"HAVE you ever heard of Mr. Aleck Tyndall, brother to *our* Mr. Tyndall?" This was the question that Mr. Sayles asked me one evening as we were coming home from church. Abbie had been detained at home by a slight illness, and we were alone.

"No—or, yes," I answered. "I have heard of him. Mrs. Tyndall mentions his name occasionally."

"You don't know, I presume, that he is coming home?"

"I don't know where he is, nor where his home is."

"And you are at this moment engaged in wondering why I think you should care to know anything about him," he answered, laughing. "But what if I tell you that his homecoming insures us a wedding in our circle?"

"A wedding!" I repeated in astonishment.

"Yes, and a speedy one I trust. The waiting has been long and weary enough."

"I can't imagine what you are talking about. Where is this gentleman coming from, and when is he coming, and who is going to be married, and how did it all happen?"

"What a rush of questions! Your indifference vanishes the moment a wedding is proposed. Well, this gentleman is coming from California, where he took refuge several years ago after the financial crash. He will be here in perhaps two weeks, possibly sooner: and—now I am going to astonish you—the lady involved in this matter is Frank Hooper."

"Frank Hooper!" I ejaculated in utter amazement. "How can that be possible? Why, when did it come to pass? Is she really engaged to him?"

"She is, and has been for the last four years. There is quite a long story connected with it. Frank's father, you know, was a very wealthy man, but lost everything in the financial panic between two and three years ago—about three it is now. Aleck was wealthy, too, and met with the same fate. He was involved with his brother, and *he* would have crashed, too, if it hadn't been for his wife. She is the wealthy one, you know. Aleck lost everything, and there was no resort but to begin at the foot of the hill. He fled to California, where he has been ever since. He has been successful beyond his wildest hopes, and now I suppose he is speeding toward home and Frank."

"But I don't understand," I said in a greatly perplexed tone. "If they have been engaged all this time, how is it that people know nothing about it? *Nobody* does, do they?"

"Not a soul save myself; that was a freak of theirs. Perhaps you don't need to be told that Mrs. Tyndall hasn't always been absolutely angelic in her dealings with people and didn't love Frank very deeply. Aleck knew her well and had an immense respect for her and her ability to do mischief, so he conceived the brilliant idea of keeping the entire matter a secret. It was a comparatively easy thing to do. You see, he did not live here; he was in business in New York, but he was also connected with his brother's firm, and that of itself brought him here frequently; and so by taking me into complete confidence and letting me engineer the correspondence, we had it all arranged. A tedious time they have had of it, though. I am glad for them that the struggle is over."

"But I thought that you—" Thus much I said, and then I stopped in confusion.

He laughed pleasantly.

"You thought what the rest of the world did, I presume: that I was being attentive to Frank on my own account, and then that I deserted her on the eve of marriage, and still hovered around her much as a moth might be supposed to treat a candle, and no end of nonsense. Frank and I have had merry times over the whole story—only, Julia, I *did* think you would hardly believe it of me; about the base desertion part at least. You know enough evil of me, certainly, but I declare I did not think you would consider me quite so far down as that."

"I only half believed it," I said eagerly. "Some of the time I did not believe it at all. Only I thought there must be some sort of foundation for it. I had the story so very straight."

"Yes, I know; or at least I suppose Dr. Douglass enlightened you. I know he has believed it religiously. It is a wonder that he has succeeded in treating me as well as he has."

"Does he know about it now?"

"Not he. He gives me courteous little hints every day about one of the duties of a new Christian life: to undo the mistakes that have been made so far as it is in one's power; and I know he classes Frank among the mistakes."

"Why don't you tell him?"

"For two reasons: First—Having kept Frank's secret so long, I don't propose to go around enlightening people. I mean to let circumstances do that. It will be vastly more interesting, I think, though I make an exception in your favor, you see. Secondly—I think Dr. Douglass, good, noble man though he is, needs a little bit of a lesson. He is almost as ready as commoner mortals are to deliberately swallow those prodigious lies that go floating around town about people. I'm using very strong language. I beg pardon; but the subject demands some indignation. I'm not offended with the doctor. I used to be. I used to nearly detest him on this very account; and but for interposing circumstances I should almost have merited his contempt by doing the very thing, in a sense, that he believed of me, merely to prove to him that I did not do it. That's talking in riddles to you, isn't it? Never mind. I'm glad you are so pure and openhearted; it is that, in a sense, which has saved me. Well, I am not at all out of sorts with the doctor now. I know him to be thoroughly pure gold; and he certainly had strong provocation for believing the stories about me. You see, Frank and Aleck were to have been married in about six weeks when the crash came; and people *knew* that *she* was, and knowing nothing about Aleck, naturally supposed that *I* was. Only the question is, why should I have been pitched upon as the perpetrator of a great meanness because she packed her marriage robes away in a trunk instead of wearing them, when I was with her just the same, not a break of twenty-four hours in our friendship? Wouldn't that have been a queer way to have managed the other matter? But people were not willing to give me the benefit of the doubt; they were more than ready to pitch into me if there was anything ugly that needed believing. Why, all right. However, the doctor wasn't here during the time that all this occurred, and is more excusable. At the same time it won't hurt him to discover that he made a blunder. Don't imagine that I blame you, Julia, for crediting the story in a measure; it was the most natural thing imaginable under the circumstances."

"I did not credit it," I said earnestly. "At least I mean I thought that it could be explained in a way that would not compromise you; and Mrs. Tyndall, you know, never thought any such thing."

"No," he said, laughing; "she thought something worse. That is, she professed to think that it was a grand flirtation on my part and a grand effort on Frank's part to secure a husband. But I always gave her the credit of thinking that she didn't believe any such thing. She thought I wanted Frank and couldn't get her. I know she did. It was a very reasonable thing to think. It must have looked like that to those who disbelieved the other two stories and must have something to rest their hopes on; besides, Mrs. Tyndall was exceedingly fearful lest that should be the state of things. She didn't like Frank, and she wanted to keep her down, out of her circle. You may imagine I enjoyed her state of mind, knowing all the time that Frank was destined to be her sister-in-law."

"It is all very queer," I said, feeling very lighthearted that all things were just as they were. "When will they be married?"

"Why, very soon, I should think, though I know but little about it. I haven't heard from Tyndall personally for months. I get hosts of envelopes addressed to me in his handwriting, but not a line does he vouchsafe to me beyond the bare announcement that he was to sail in such a steamer and would telegraph me on his arrival in New York. I haven't heard from him directly since December. However, I suffered in a good cause. Frank has had longer letters in consequence, I presume."

"Is this Mr. Tyndall a Christian man?" I asked; and Mr. Sayles's voice saddened at once.

"Oh, dear, no! He is very far removed from that. When I used to be constantly with him, he was nearly, if not quite, an infidel. I don't think he led me as far into the mist as he was himself; but far enough to cause me some miserable days and nights since; and I have no reason to hope that he has changed his views since that time."

"Don't you dread his influence over Frank?"

"Indeed I do. She is so new in the Christian life that she needs much help instead of such powerful hindrance. And I dread his influence over his brother very much, and, I might add, over myself. He is a very fascinating man—has almost a magnetic influence over people; and a very sarcastic man, ready and willing to turn anything into a kind of quiet, gentlemanly ridicule. I don't know how his brother is going to endure it. Aleck will be a member of his family, I presume, for a time. Very likely he will never be in or on hand at the hour of family prayers; but what he will say at the idea of a blessing being asked at his brother's table, or whether Tyndall will have the courage to attempt it or not, *I* don't know. I feel in a good deal of trouble about it all."

"Does Frank feel disturbed?"

"I don't know. I haven't had the heart to ask her. She has had such a stormy life of late years—only so recently settled into calm—that I haven't felt equal to suggesting more breakers ahead, especially as the suggestion could do no sort of good. No, thank you; I cannot go in tonight. I have a little business that must be attended to."

"I am to keep this story quiet, I suppose?"

"Yes, please. They will know in a day or two, if they do not already, that Aleck is coming. Frank says he wrote his brother by the same steamer that her last letters came, but his letter seems to have been delayed. About the rest of it, he must tell his own stories, of course, and I wish him joy of the scene. Mrs. Tyndall is very much changed in many respects, but I fancy she will not like Frank Hooper for a sister. By the way, you can gossip over this matter with your Cousin Abbie, if you choose. I mentioned it to her last evening, but did not tell her particulars. I will not keep you from her longer, for she said she had something special to talk with you about, and I shall have something special to say to you tomorrow evening. Can I see you?"

"Yes," I answered; and then I went in with glowing cheeks and shining eyes.

Just here I have paused, pen in hand, and thought whether or not, since this history of part of my life was destined to be used as a Sabbath school book, it would be well for me to write herein some of the thoughts that filled my heart that night and some of the incidents that followed. It seems to be quite generally believed that a Sabbath school book should utterly ignore two great questions that have to do with human hearts: love and marriage. I never was able to understand why. Certainly young misses of sixteen think of these matters; even those who attend Sabbath school and draw Sabbath school books think of them, I believe, a great deal more than is well for them. I'm sure I did. Why should I, then, in giving to these young ladies the story of a piece of my life in the sincere hope that it may help them to avoid my blunders and causes of failure and unhappiness; why should I be very plain and frank as regards other subjects and quite silent in this, merely in the fear that some critic will criticize my story for having broached in it the awful and forbidden subject? I will tell my story truthfully, without the fear of a critic before my eyes. Plainly, then, I came into the hall in a great flutter. I felt sure that a crisis in my destiny was coming to me on swift wings. Tomorrow evening he would have something special to say to me! Didn't I feel in every throb of my heart what it would be? Didn't I know when he was taking such pains to explain to me that he had never been other than a friend to Frank Hooper, just what he meant me to understand? Life looked very rose colored to me. I remember the feeling well. I went up with swift feet to Abbie. I was eager for sympathy. I pulled down my hair and began in a very nervous way to braid it, while, as Abbie questioned me about the meeting, I tried to determine in my own mind which I should do. Should I tell her first about that last sentence spoken in such a peculiarly meaning tone as he clasped my hand, or should I tell her all about Frank and the wedding in prospect, and the commotion that would probably be awakened in our household; waiting until the glaring gaslight was turned out, and only the soft, quiet moon gave us light, while I told her of the other, and the rush of sweet hopes and plans and possibilities that had been set to throbbing in my heart? I decided on the latter course. She was deeply interested in Frank and questioned eagerly and earnestly, so that it was not until just after I had finished the last braid and said, "Shan't I turn out the gas now, and won't we have a bit of quiet talk in the moonlight?" that she, assenting eagerly and standing there, leaning her head against the window sash and looking out into the glorious beauty of the night, asked:

"Did Mr. Sayles say anything of me?"

"Yes," I answered promptly. "He said I might tell you all about this matter of Frank's, and—oh yes, he said you had something special to tell me about. What is it, Abbie?"

She turned a little then and let me see her face, sweet and pure and smiling, and she said softly:

"I *have*—something VERY special. I wanted to tell you that last evening he asked me to be his wife."

27

A SCENE BEYOND

DEAR girls, you who are sixteen, almost seventeen, if ever you have been, or ever you should be, in just the position that I was that evening, standing there with my Cousin Abbie in the moonlight and listening to that softly whispered sentence, let me commend to you, at least in this particular, my conduct. I did not faint. I did not cry out. I did not push my cousin from me as I would a serpent in heroic novel style. I stood very quietly, and received her sweet kiss at the end of the sentence and returned it; and the thing of which I was dimly conscious was a sense of relief that I had not told her about that last sentence at once, but had waited until circumstances made it unnecessary ever to tell it. I do not remember how I congratulated her, or indeed whether I had brains enough to do it at all. I was very much amazed and a good deal stunned. Of course, I had never dreamed of such a thing. I remember being very glad that the gas was turned out, and only the soft pale moon lighted the room. I know I carried a very heavy heart to bed that night; and I remember that after Abbie was quietly sleeping I shed some bitter tears; but at last I, too, fell asleep, and thus ends the record of the wonderful day in which I felt my destiny coming to me on such swift wings.

"Have you learned anything about the special matter that I had to consult you about?" Mr. Sayles asked me as he came forward on my entrance to the parlor the next evening and held out both hands in greeting.

"I think I have," I answered, promptly and gaily. "But, Mr. Sayles, doesn't the consultation come rather late?"

He laughed merrily.

"Oh, no, indeed; there are a great many things to settle yet, and an obdurate young woman to persuade into anything like reasonable behavior. Julia, were you surprised?"

I suppose my cheeks glowed. I don't see how they could well help it. I know they felt very red; but the room was warm and my cheeks are naturally rosy so, after all, I am not certain that anyone but myself knew about them. I know I answered steadily:

"Yes, I was very much. I don't know when I have been more astonished."

"Why, *were* you?" he said, looking amazed. "I didn't think you would be. I thought you would have seen through it long ago. I have given you credit for more clear-sightedness than you possess, haven't I?"

He had indeed.

"But," he continued eagerly, "this was not the *special* thing after all. I knew Abbie would tell you about it, but I was eager to claim my cousinship and say to you how glad I am that—"

And then followed the usual words on such occasions—very kind and very complimentary—about considering him in the light of a cousin not only, but a brother; he should be so glad to— I interrupted him saucily. "I had a brother of my very own," I told him; "the nicest brother in the world, and I shouldn't accept any platonic brotherhood."

Then followed a great deal of pleasant nonsense, in which Abbie joined merrily, and it was interspersed with some earnest words; but I distinctly remember that the whole talk only served to make me feel sick and miserable and more utterly desolate than I had felt in a long time.

A few days thereafter, as we obeyed the summons to tea, I became conscious soon after I entered the dining room of a strange presence there—a tall, dark, singularly handsome man, and there immediately rushed over me a remembrance of what I had heard about the singular fascination that Mr. Aleck Tyndall's face possessed; so, before Mrs. Tyndall had said, "My brother, Mr. Tyndall, Miss Ried," I knew that it was he. He talked exceedingly well, being one of those talkers whose words flow on smoothly and quietly, without apparently the slightest effort on their part and without seeming to be aware that they are in the least degree remarkable. When we gathered around the table there was one thing that surprised me—it was the instant quiet bending of his head and the shading of his eyes with his hand. This before there had been given him any indication that in his brother's family they had learned to recognize a Heavenly Father's hand in the supply of their daily needs.

Mr. Sayles had misjudged our Mr. Tyndall's strength, or rather, his weakness. His voice was never quieter nor firmer than when he asked a simple blessing on the food. Meantime, I speculated over Mr. Aleck Tyndall's conduct. Had he learned the new order of things, and was this his graceful concession to the ways of the household, or was it his habit, since there was a strange gentleman added to the family, to take all things for granted until proved to the contrary? I inclined to the latter opinion, as that would seem in keeping with his inimitable courtesy, and he did not by word or look express surprise at his brother's new position. During the remainder of the evening part of our household at least were on the *qui vive*.

"I wouldn't be in his shoes," said Mr. Sayles with an expressive shrug of his shoulders, "for an interest in his bank account."

"Why?" I asked curiously. "What do you imagine Mrs. Tyndall will do, or can do? She hasn't them in her power in any way."

"Oh, no; but she has it in her power to make them an immense deal of botheration; and she'll exercise her power, too, or I'm mistaken; and I should hate it so. I do hate scenes and trouble of all sorts."

I remember I wondered whether Abbie would not have been a little, just a little, better pleased with him if he had been a shade more self-sustained and manly. If she would she didn't express it by look or act, but simply questioned in her quiet way:

"Don't you imagine he is equal to the occasion?"

And Mr. Sayles laughed, gave her an admiring glance as if she had said a remarkable thing, and answered:

"Upon my word, I think he is if any mortal ever was."

So on that conviction we rested, waiting for further developments.

Matters were very quiet the next day. Mr. Tyndall was absent most of the day, and Frank was not at the shop. We, Abbie and I, wondered if Mrs. Tyndall knew anything about it yet, and concluded that she did not; and we discovered nothing until the next morning.

Mr. Sayles had come in to get Mr. Aleck Tyndall to accompany him on a drive and found us at breakfast; he drew up his chair, took a cup of coffee with us, and stopped to prayers. The doctor was present and led the service that morning. As we were about to separate, Mrs. Tyndall said in her simplest, most matter-of-course tone:

"By the way, Jerome, you must come in to tea; we are going to have a quiet little family party at teatime, and a few friends in the evening. Aleck is going to bring Frank down to tea. You don't mind these ladies knowing that Frank is one of the family, do you, Aleck?"

"Not in the least," Mr. Aleck Tyndall said with a gracious bow to the ladies; and Mr. Sayles, ere he answered, glanced over at me with such a curious look of delighted astonishment that I disgraced myself by laughing.

I did not expect to meet Frank at the shop, but she was there, and had been apparently for some time, and was working very rapidly. She looked precisely the Frank that she had always been as regarded dress and manner; but there was a radiant look in her eyes that I could account for, though I knew the others could not. In the course of the morning I stood near her; she and I had grown very near to each other in heart during the last few weeks, yet I did not like to speak first of her personal affairs, though I felt very curious and also somewhat anxious to have her understand that I knew of the arrangements. She broke the silence, however.

"You belong to that family party this afternoon, of course?" she said in a low tone, with a vivid blush and a bright smile.

"Yes, I do," I answered eagerly. "Oh, Frank, why didn't you tell me about it?"

"I told nobody," she answered decidedly. "He had been gone a long, long time, and California is very far away, and the world is full of changes; but"—with that brilliant smile of hers—"it doesn't matter who knows it now."

We were hurried in the shop. There was little time for talk. Mr. Jerome Sayles had managed the matter of the afternoon holiday for Frank and myself; the other girls could not imagine with what argument, but of course I surmised. At noon Frank piled up her boxes snugly in a corner.

"There!" she said. "Ruthie, don't let anyone touch my work. I mean to be here bright and early tomorrow morning to finish it. Are you ready, Julia?"

And with a parting bow and smile to the girls, and a gleeful reply that she was going to seek her fortune in answer to their curious questions as to what was going to become of her that afternoon, we left the shop together.

"They are good girls, every one of them," she said earnestly as we went down the familiar street. "I shall never forget how good and kind they have been to me. When I have a house of my own, the first thing I shall do will be to invite them all to spend the day with me. I should have liked Mrs. Tyndall better if she had asked every one of them to meet me tonight. But that would have been too much to expect of flesh and blood."

"And after all," I said, somewhat hesitatingly, "they are not quite your company. I mean, you cannot enjoy their society exactly."

"No," she answered promptly; "we are not congenial perhaps—that is, I have received a good education and enjoy it, and they have not and don't care for it. But they are nice, good girls for all that, and I enjoy their society quite as well as I do Mrs. Shoddy's, for instance, who lives in a palace on Regent Street and uses worse grammar than any of them do. You understand that I think it is not because I work in a shop that I am not fitted to shine in any circle, nor does my working there make me fit; that is merely an accident, force of circumstances, or choice of work, and has nothing whatever to do with position—that's my platform."

And then we parted, to meet again three hours later in Mrs. Tyndall's elegant parlors. Abbie and I were in the room; so also was Mr. Sayles, or Jerome, as we all called him now, when Mr. Aleck Tyndall and Miss Hooper arrived. I think I have spoken before of Frank's severe plainness of dress; she had never varied it in the least. I had never seen her in other than the simplest of material and make, and with her hair stretched plainly back in a net. As she came forward now I could not restrain a start of astonishment, and I saw Jerome's eyes dance. She evidently looked natural to him. She wore a soft, silky, sheeny dress of silvery hue, entirely new, exquisitely made as to trimmings and fit, and it became her as nothing ever had before, and her hair fell loose about her neck in round, puffy, natural curls. It seemed to me that Mrs. Tyndall must have thought the two singularly well mated. She advanced to meet them, held out her hand to Frank as simply and cordially as though she had entertained her but yesterday, kissed her in a familiar, sisterly way, and said:

"You're tired, aren't you, with your long walk? Aleck, you wretch, why didn't you take the carriage? That is a pretty way to take care of her! You think because you are a Hercules in that matter that everyone is. He'll walk you to death, Frank. Take this chair; you get a pleasanter view than in the one you have chosen."

And this was the famous meeting, the wonderful scene that we had planned about, and gossiped over, and been nervous in view of for days.

"Ahem!" said Jerome, by way of attracting my attention; but I persistently talked to Frank and wouldn't look; I knew I should laugh if I did—and he finally contented himself with a walk to the back parlor, where he leaned over the piano and whistled Yankee Doodle in a *very* under tone.

We had an early, quiet tea, with but one surprise. As we settled into that hush which precedes the lifting up of thankful hearts, Mr. Tyndall said in a voice in which there was a great throb of joy, "Aleck, will you ask a blessing?" And the infidel head was bowed, and the strange voice uttered a few reverent, grateful words. Frank's face expressed joy, but not surprise—she had been told of the wonderful change; but Mr. Sayles's face expressed unbounded astonishment. He walked with me back to the parlor—he had lost all desire to laugh—his tone was earnest and solemn.

"The Lord can take care of his own, it seems, without your and my fretting about it," he said emphatically. "But I declare to you I never was more amazed in my life. I could as soon have expected that bit of marble to ask a blessing! But then, when one thinks of it, he might well have been equally surprised at hearing me. The way in which we have all been led is wonderful, perfectly wonderful. How could anyone know of the facts concerning just this small company, without recognizing at once a power above and beyond all human strength."

We had a wonderfully pleasant evening. We had a very choice selection of guests, prominent among whom were Lycia Symonds and Florence Hervey. Dr. and Mrs. Mulford were the latest to arrive. I had to spend nearly half my time in watching Frank. She glided into this new position, or, rather, back into her old position, so smoothly and gracefully, and there was about her a certain quiet dignity, a half nameless deference to those around her, that was new and exceedingly becoming.

"What are they going to do?" I asked Mr. Sayles in the course of the evening.

"Don't know, I'm sure. Tyndall wants to be married at once—I knew he would, and Frank won't. I knew she wouldn't. Women are so confoundedly silly and obstinate, begging your pardon, of course; but they must spend ten thousand years in sewing if anybody is waiting to marry them. They have both wills made of iron. I suppose they will fight it out until one of them yields."

Later in the evening we grew merrier, and some wise brain proposed impromptu charades and tableaux, a suggestion which Mrs. Tyndall caught at eagerly, and Mr. Sayles and I entered into very heartily. We really had some very good ones; I remember them distinctly. Presently Mr. Sayles came over to me with a puzzled look.

"They are going to have a marriage scene, and Aleck and Frank are to be the actors. It isn't in the least like either of them. I wonder that they will enter into it."

"Whose getting up is it?" I asked.

"Mrs. Tyndall's. She seems to be in high glee over that and everything else. What a woman she is!"

"Who will they get to officiate?"

"Don't know. It's a wonder they didn't ask me. I expected it. I always used to be selected for matters of that sort. I wouldn't do it, though. I don't like farces of that kind. The thing has grown too sacred." And he glanced toward Abbie. "Hark!" as the folding doors began to slide. "They are coming. Who *will* they have for a clergyman? I'll be hanged if isn't Dr. Mulford himself!"

And then the hum of voices instantly hushed, for Dr. Mulford commenced the marriage service—the veritable words, without change or omission, pronounced in solemn tone, even to the words, "What God hath joined together, let not man put asunder," and then the prayer! And then we stood petrified until Mr. and Mrs. Tyndall pressed forward, smiling and composed, to greet the bride! It was a bride, then? Yes, indeed—no farce about it! One of the iron wills had broken. Strong as words of man and words of prayer could make it had the service been, and Frank Hooper was Mrs. Aleck Tyndall. I can't describe the commotion that followed. Everybody talked, and wondered, and "oh'd," and "why'd," and laughed, and ate cake, and congratulated the bride, save Mr. Sayles.

"It was rather cruel, Frank," he said when opportunity offered, "to desert and take me so overwhelmingly by surprise at the last moment, when I have been your faithful ally for so long."

"I hadn't an idea of it," she explained eagerly. "I mean, I hadn't the least intention of doing anything so wild. It seemed perfectly absurd."

"How do you happen to be a married woman then?"

"I'm sure I don't know," she answered meekly; and her husband smiled and said, "He did, and it was perfectly satisfactory," and led her away.

"It wasn't a very iron will after all," I said to Jerome.

"Yes, it was," he answered emphatically; "only he has got all of hers and all his mixed up together, somehow."

"It was nice," announced this same gentleman as, every guest having departed, Mrs. Tyndall and I lingered a moment in the back parlor to talk over the strange circumstances with Abbie and Jerome. "It was nice; I liked it. No fuss or getting ready a century beforehand—no gossiping as to when it will be. I wish—" He stopped abruptly and seemed confused.

Mrs. Tyndall laughed mischievously.

"We'll go, Julia," she said gaily. "We are unmistakably too large an audience for the discussion of that subject."

Shall I confess what I did? I went to my room and to bed, and when safe there in the darkness I cried a little. I wasn't exactly unhappy, only miserably lonely, and also somewhat sentimental. But finally I dried my eyes and went to sleep.

28

LED IN UNKNOWN PATHS

"OH, I think I *was* a Christian—a miserable, weak, sick one, not worth the name; yet I know I did have a feeling of trust in my Savior—something that I would not have yielded for anything that I had in the world."

This was what Mrs. Tyndall said in answer to a remark made by Dr. Douglass as we all sat together one evening about two weeks after Frank's marriage. We had been taking a drive together in the large carriage, Abbie and Mr. Sayles, Dr. Douglass, Mr. and Mrs. Tyndall, and myself; and now Mrs. Tyndall was going farther in the little carriage with her husband, and while she waited for him she talked with Dr. Mulford, who had come in to see Dr. Douglass.

"But," continued Mrs. Tyndall, "it was, after all, very unlike the feeling that I have now. I mean to live such a different life. You can't think how many things there are for me to undo. I am so thankful that I have health and leisure; so few people have both. There is no reason why I should not employ all my time in going about at work. I think there is a great deal to do."

"There is indeed," Dr. Mulford answered earnestly.

"People with health and leisure and consecration are very rare, and very greatly needed. Why, Mrs. Tyndall, if you will put yourself subject to my disposal, I can keep you busy every moment of the time."

"I will," she said eagerly. "That is just what I want, someone to direct my energy, for I really have a great deal—it has to be used in some way; but I don't trust my own way of doing things as much as I did."

"Will you tell us," questioned Dr. Douglass, "what was the secret power that wrought upon you this change of which you speak, made you look at Christian life and Christian work in such a different light?"

Mrs. Tyndall turned suddenly toward my Cousin Abbie and gave her a look of loving gratitude as she said:

"It was watching another life, so totally different from my own, and yet professing to be governed by the same springs of action. I have noticed it and watched her, and wondered over her manner of living from my first acquaintance."

"A little leaven leaveneth the whole lump," Dr. Mulford quoted musingly, as if thinking aloud; then he laid his hand on Abbie's shoulder and said tenderly: "God has greatly honored you, my child."

"I!" said bewildered and wondering Abbie. "Why, I haven't *done* anything."

"Only just *lived*," Dr. Douglass said significantly; and Dr. Mulford added:

"It is a great thing for a Christian to *live*."

At this point Mrs. Tyndall left us, looking back to say brightly:

"Remember, Dr. Mulford, I am ready for work and bubbling over with life and energy. I do hope you can give me a right channel to work in at last."

We looked after them as they rode away, remarking

upon how bright and graceful and full of healthful life she was.

"Can the Ethiopian change his skin?" Mr. Sayles said gravely. "It seems he can. Who ever saw a more remarkable change than there is in that woman?"

"She always had energy—plenty of it," Dr. Douglass said. "It is as she says, she was unceasingly at work. The trouble is that Satan pushed himself in as her chief aid sometimes. She was born to be a leader, though, I think. Dr. Mulford, I fancy you will find her very useful."

"I expect to," the doctor said heartily. "I can give her legitimate channels in which to work off her energy. I am glad she is just the woman she is—well and strong, and wealthy and willing."

It wasn't ten minutes after that—no, it could hardly have been five, when a furious ring at the doorbell startled us all.

"That must be a summons for you, Doctor, said Mr. Sayles. "No one else would be wanted in such desperate haste."

And then, listening, we heard the quick, panting voice:

"I want Dr. Douglass. Is he here?"

"Yes," answered the doctor, going quickly forward. "What is wanted, my boy?"

"They want *you* right away, down to the corner, sir; there's been an accident. Mr. Tyndall's horse got frightened at the band, and Mrs. Tyndall, she's thrown and hurt bad. Some think she is dead."

Before this sentence was concluded Dr. Douglass had brushed past him and was halfway to the corner. Consternation prevailed in the house. Abbie still had her wits, and rang bells, and gave orders for Mrs. Tyndall's bed to be thrown open, and hot water to be in readiness, and attended to half a dozen other thoughtful and wise arrangements, while Mr. Sayles and I still stood gazing solemnly at each other and saying: "How very strange!" "How *could* it have happened?" "I thought *that* horse wasn't afraid of the band." "Do you suppose she is much hurt?" and several other of those witless and unanswerable remarks that useless people make to themselves and each other at such times. Dr. Mulford had at once followed Dr. Douglass. Directly there came a trampling of feet and subdued voices; then Dr. Douglass's voice issuing orders right and left. "Stand aside there! Sayles, come and help me here." "No," in answer to my terrified look. "She has only fainted. We decided to bring her home while she was unconscious."

Abbie followed them upstairs. I stayed below, looking after the curious or sympathetic people who immediately began to come on voyages of discovery or with offers of assistance. Mr. Sayles came down presently.

"She *will* do everything!" he said, speaking of Abbie, with a curious mixture of pride and annoyance. "She is hurrying around there as if she had the strength of a Samson."

"Is she much hurt?" I asked, my thoughts still on Mrs. Tyndall.

"No, I guess not. She has revived now and spoken to Abbie. Douglass has sent for Dr. Vincent to consult; but that is more for the sake of pacifying Tyndall, I guess, than because he needs him."

But two hours passed before we knew more. Dr. Vincent came and went up to the room, and Dr. Mulford came down and went out; then presently Mr. Sayles was called for to go to Dr. Vincent's office for a certain case. I meantime was kept very busy below.

People seemed determined to wring from me information that I did not possess, and the servants hung around with scared faces. At last Dr. Vincent went away. Dr. Douglass came downstairs with him, and they stood in the hall, talking in low tones. I waited until the door closed on Dr. Vincent, then I went out. Dr. Douglass turned to me with a sad smile.

"Poor child," he said, "how white it is! Are you very much frightened? How we plan, Julia! Here we were talking about her energy, and health, and strength, and what a work she would do, arranging to give her enough employment for her eager, healthy life; and here, all the time, God had other plans that ran right athwart ours."

"Is she going to die?" I asked in an awed and frightened whisper.

"No, not that," he said sadly. "She may live as long—longer than you or I; but she will never *lift herself* from that bed again."

"Are you *sure?*" I asked him, immeasurably more shocked than I would have been had he told me that God was going to take her right away to himself.

"Most hopelessly sure," he answered. "Both hip and spine are injured."

He had to go back upstairs. I sat down on the lowest step of the long flight of winding stairs and tried in a stunned way to take in the meaning of his words. "Never lift *herself* from that bed again!" Then she would never walk again. Was it *possible* that her graceful form would never flit down those stairs again! I looked around the large elegant hall, arranged with exquisite taste and as well furnished as many parlors. Every article in sight and in memory bore the marks of her graceful, skillful fingers. Only a little, *little* while ago she had set that vase of lilies under the glass and had rearranged their delicate cups, stopping to do it ere she tied the ribbon of her hat, the hat that lay now all battered and mud stained under the table. I went forward and picked it up and tried to bend the torn, limp thing into something like its former grace and beauty. It was of no use; it would never be fit to wear again, and its wearer would never need it anymore. And I sat down with the bright-ribboned, pitiful-looking hat and shed bitter tears.

Mr. Sayles, talking with me about it all the next day, standing before me with folded arms and sad face, said:

"It's hard, Julia, very hard, and the reason of it past finding out. I thought it would be so different. I wanted it to be. I wanted her to be able, as she said, to undo much of her work. I wanted people to see and realize as we do how changed she is. I wanted her to grow into having the influence over people religiously that she has had over them morally and fashionably all her life. And now here she lies, a living, suffering death. It is a hard death, too. No sympathy. People are shocked and sorry, but no one has any tears to shed; they can go right on without her. There is no one to cry out in bitterness of soul, 'I cannot get along without her help.' Oh, my! *I* don't want to die like that. I feel it, you see. That is what my dying now would be. No one to care for me, no one to miss me, because my life had led them nearer to Christ. But I won't die so. If God will give me a *little* more time, I will work for him."

Dr. Mulford had come quietly into the room, and as Mr. Sayles finished his excited sentence, the doctor laid a quiet hand on his shoulder and said, low and gently:

"His ways are not as our ways."

That was all said and done and lived more than three years ago. I am twenty now. It is four years ago today since I first came to Newton. I came back to the place today after a long absence. It was but a little while after Mrs. Tyndall's accident that I went with Abbie to her home to help her make preparations for the wedding. I remembered at the time that my sister Ester went there once for the same purpose. We talked about that time a little while we made preparations. They were married at church one morning and went away together, Mr. Sayles and she. They seemed very happy. I did not go back to Newton. I was tired in body and brain; also I was less wise and self-reliant than when I first went there, and so I yielded to Sadie and Dr. Van Anden's often-repeated urgings and went to New Haven to live. I have heard often from Newton during these intervening years and have constantly meant to visit my friends here, but other plans and cares and duties have intervened. It was finally a telegram that brought me. It read thus: "Mrs. Tyndall died last night. Funeral on Thursday. Will meet the 10:50 train. Douglass."

So at once I started, and today I reached here. Just four years ago today I came here a stranger, and she gave me kindly greeting. Today they led me to look at her white-coffined face. My heart was very sad, and yet when I had taken one long look at the familiar face, lying there so white and still, I turned to Dr. Douglass and smiled. He seemed to understand my meaning.

"Isn't the seal of the Spirit there?" he said. "It is as if one had a glimpse of heaven where she has entered in."

Mrs. Aleck Tyndall was there beside us. She has been the real mistress of that home during these three years, for the nominal one never left the room where they carried her that night until they brought her down today in her coffin. Frank bent over the coffin with fast-dropping tears.

"Yes," she said, "she has entered in; but, oh, Doctor, how *can* we live without her?"

"Does she look natural, Julia?" Mr. Sayles asked me; and I answered quickly:

"No, not at all. She looks angelic."

"Oh, Julia!" a murmur of voices greeted me.

"She looks what she has lived," said Mr. Sayles tremulously. "If ever an angelic spirit lived in a house of clay, we have had one here with us for more than two years."

"Perfect through suffering," Dr. Douglass said softly.

"Did she suffer very much?" I asked him. He bowed his head.

"Fearfully, and with more than human patience."

Dr. Mulford came in, greeted me silently, then went and looked long and earnestly at the face in the coffin.

"It is gain to her," he said at last; "but what a fearful loss to us. The whole church is shaken."

"It may well be," Mr. Sayles said. "What other ten members of our church can begin to do her work?"

I had heard much of all this in letters, but I had not come to realize so as to forget the contrast. Those who had been with her constantly seemed to have forgotten all about any other life that she had lived than that of these last years. I did not refer to the old life, only I said to Mr. Sayles when we were alone together for a moment:

"Don't you remember how past finding out the reason of this living death was to you the day after the accident?" And he, smiling sadly, answered:

"And don't you remember Dr. Mulford quoted to us, 'God's ways are not as our ways.' Truly, they are not, Julia; it has been the most wonderful life. There is not a scholar in our Sunday school, not a child in our streets, but she has managed somehow to reach."

Mr. Sayles is very much changed—very much improved. He is more decided and earnest; but looking at him I realized more fully than I had before how we had probably *all* changed. I had, certainly. I scanned him with a sort of puzzled wonder and tried to decide how it was possible that I could once have fancied that I cared for him! *Could* I be the same person who had so tremblingly awaited my destiny on the night in which it was expected and did not come? Suppose it had? Suppose I had—but I actually turned away from him with a little shiver. He was nice—I realized that, and he was good. I liked him, I thoroughly respected him; but as for anything more than that!—oh, girls, dear girls, we do not see at twenty as we did at sixteen.

An hour ago I stood at the coffin's head, looking down on that spiritual face. Dr. Douglass had come in with me and had been telling much about the beauty of her life and the blessedness of her death. At last he said:

"Once you thought she led you astray. Doubtless she did. It was one of her sorrows; but I comforted her. I told her I thought you had learned to listen first and always to the great Leader's voice and be led *first* by him. Is it not so?"

I answered humbly but decidedly:

"I believe I have."

We were silent for a little, and then he said:

"Julia, cannot we who have adopted the same Leader, and are journeying toward the same home, walk together and help each other?"

The sweet and solemn moonlight stole across the sweet dead face and seemed to make it smile upon us; and I with one hand resting on that coffin and the other laid in his felt that my joy had come to me at an hour when I sought it not. And together we will listen henceforth to the voice of our great Captain and humbly follow where he leads.

Other Living Books Best-sellers

400 CREATIVE WAYS TO SAY I LOVE YOU by Alice Chapin. Perhaps the flame of love has almost died in your marriage, or you have a good marriage that just needs a little spark. Here is a book of creative, practical ideas for the woman who wants to show the man in her life that she cares. 07-0919-5

ANSWERS by Josh McDowell and Don Stewart. In a question-and-answer format, the authors tackle sixty-five of the most-asked questions about the Bible, God, Jesus Christ, miracles, other religions, and Creation. 07-0021-X

BUILDING YOUR SELF-IMAGE by Josh McDowell and Don Stewart. Here are practical answers to help you overcome your fears, anxieties, and lack of self-confidence. Learn how God's higher image of who you are can take root in your heart and mind. 07-1395-8

COME BEFORE WINTER AND SHARE MY HOPE by Charles R. Swindoll. A collection of brief vignettes offering hope and the assurance that adversity and despair are temporary setbacks we can overcome! 07-0477-0

DR. DOBSON ANSWERS YOUR QUESTIONS by Dr. James Dobson. In this convenient reference book, renowned author Dr. James Dobson addresses heartfelt concerns on many topics, including questions on marital relationships, infant care, child discipline, home management, and others. 07-0580-7

THE EFFECTIVE FATHER by Gordon MacDonald. A practical study of effective fatherhood based on biblical principles. 07-0669-2

FOR MEN ONLY edited by J. Allan Petersen. This book deals with topics of concern to every man: the business world, marriage, fathering, spiritual goals, and problems of living as a Christian in a secular world. 07-0892-X

FOR WOMEN ONLY by Evelyn R. and J. Allan Petersen. This balanced, entertaining, and diversified treatment covers all the aspects of womanhood. 07-0897-0

GIVERS, TAKERS, AND OTHER KINDS OF LOVERS by Josh McDowell and Paul Lewis. Bypassing generalities about love and sex, this book answers the basics: Whatever happened to sexual freedom? Do men respond differently than women? Here are straight answers about God's plan for love and sexuality. 07-1031-2

Other Living Books Best-sellers

HINDS' FEET ON HIGH PLACES by Hannah Hurnard. A classic allegory of a journey toward faith that has sold more than a million copies! 07-1429-6 *Also on Tyndale Living Audio 15-7426-4*

HOW TO BE HAPPY THOUGH MARRIED by Tim LaHaye. A valuable resource that tells how to develop physical, mental, and spiritual harmony in marriage. 07-1499-7

JOHN, SON OF THUNDER by Ellen Gunderson Traylor. In this saga of adventure, romance, and discovery, travel with John—the disciple whom Jesus loved—down desert paths, through the courts of the Holy City, and to the foot of the cross as he leaves his luxury as a privileged son of Israel for the bitter hardship of his exile on Patmos. 07-1903-4

LET ME BE A WOMAN by Elisabeth Elliot. This best-selling author shares her observations and experiences of male-female relationships in a collection of insightful essays. 07-2162-4

LIFE IS TREMENDOUS! by Charlie "Tremendous" Jones. Believing that enthusiasm makes the difference, Jones shows how anyone can be happy, involved, relevant, productive, healthy, and secure in the midst of a high-pressure, commercialized society. 07-2184-5

MORE THAN A CARPENTER by Josh McDowell. A hard-hitting book for people who are skeptical about Jesus' deity, his resurrection, and his claim on their lives. 07-4552-3 *Also on Tyndale Living Audio 15-7427-2*

QUICK TO LISTEN, SLOW TO SPEAK by Robert E. Fisher. Families are shown how to express love to one another by developing better listening skills, finding ways to disagree without arguing, and using constructive criticism. 07-5111-6

REASONS by Josh McDowell and Don Stewart. In a convenient question-and-answer format, the authors address many of the commonly asked questions about the Bible and evolution. 07-5287-2

THE SECRET OF LOVING by Josh McDowell. McDowell explores the values and qualities that will help both the single and married reader to be the right person for someone else. He offers a fresh perspective for evaluating and improving the reader's love life. 07-5845-5

Other Living Books Best-sellers

THE STORY FROM THE BOOK. From Adam to Armageddon, this book captures the full sweep of the Bible's content in abridged, chronological form. Based on *The Book,* the best-selling, popular edition of *The Living Bible.* 07-6677-6

STRIKE THE ORIGINAL MATCH by Charles Swindoll. Swindoll draws on the best marriage survival guide–the Bible–and his 35 years of marriage to show couples how to survive, flex, grow, forgive, and keep romance alive in their marriage. 07-6445-5

THE STRONG-WILLED CHILD by Dr. James Dobson. Through these practical solutions and humorous anecdotes, parents will learn to discipline an assertive child without breaking his spirit and to overcome feelings of defeat or frustration. 07-5924-9 *Also on Tyndale Living Audio 15-7431-0*

SUCCESS! THE GLENN BLAND METHOD by Glenn Bland. The author shows how to set goals and make plans that really work. His ingredients of success include spiritual, financial, educational, and recreational balances. 07-6689-X

THROUGH GATES OF SPLENDOR by Elisabeth Elliot. This unforgettable story of five men who braved the Auca Indians has become one of the most famous missionary books of all time. 07-7151-6

TRANSFORMED TEMPERAMENTS by Tim LaHaye. An analysis of Abraham, Moses, Peter, and Paul, whose strengths and weaknesses were made effective when transformed by God. 07-7304-7

WHAT WIVES WISH THEIR HUSBANDS KNEW ABOUT WOMEN by Dr. James Dobson. A best-selling author brings us this vital book that speaks to the unique emotional needs and aspirations of today's woman. An immensely practical, interesting guide. 07-7896-0

WHAT'S IN A NAME? Linda Francis, John Hartzel, and Al Palmquist, Editors. This fascinating name dictionary features the literal meaning of hundreds of first names, character qualities implied by the names, and an applicable Scripture verse for each name. 07-7935-5

WHY YOU ACT THE WAY YOU DO by Tim LaHaye. Discover how your temperament affects your work, emotions, spiritual life, and relationships, and learn how to make improvements. 07-8212-7